Unexpected FATE

A Hope Town novel

HARPER SLOAN

Cover Design by Sommer Stein with Perfect Pear Creative Covers
Cover Photography by Scott Hoover
Editing by Ellie with Lovenbooks.com
Formatting by Champagne Formats

Lyrics for Brett Young's Kiss by Kiss used by permission. Copyright to Brett Young, Jay Ollero and Dylan Chambers.

Unexpected FATE

Playlist

Kiss by Kiss by Brett Young

Got It by Marian Hill

All The Way by Timeflies

I Will Wait by Mumford & Sons

At Last by Etta James

Breathe You In by Dierks Bentley

They Don't Know About Us by One Direction

Trumpets by Jason Derulo

Jealous by Nick Jonas

Thinking Out Loud by Ed Sheeran

Say You Love Me by Jessie Ware

I Want You by Nick Jonas

Waiting Game by Banks

To Contact Harper:

Email: Authorharpersloan@gmail.com
Website: www.authorharpersloan.com
Facebook: www.facebook.com/harpersloanbooks

Other Books by Harper Sloan:

Axel
Cage
Beck
Uncaged
Cooper
Locke

Disclaimer:

This book is not suitable for younger readers. There is strong language, adult situations, and some violence.

Dedication

To PornHub and PornMD.
Seriously.
And all the 'stars' that grace their pages.
For helping making all those kinky moments pop just *a little* more.
I tip my hat to you.
Especially you, bendy girl, **you** are amazing.

Prologue

"AXEL REID, DON'T YOU DARE!" my mom exclaims. Then she yelps when my daddy charges through the front door.

"Don't I dare what, Princess? No way *that* boy is going near my girl. Look at him! He looks like he can't wait to creep on my daughter!"

"Well, there is no need to scare him to death!" she mocks.

My cheeks heat instantly when I see Dane start backing away from the porch. My hopes of being able to actually *go* to my senior prom are starting to go up in flames.

Poof.

Just like that.

Not that I should be surprised about it. Mom did her best to calm Daddy down, but we should have known better. He took one look at me and stormed over, only to return ten minutes later looking like he does now.

So embarrassing.

"You need to stop this nonsense right now, you big lug, or you'll be sleeping on the couch," Mom fumes.

"Like hell I will, woman!" Daddy roars at my mom.

I watch her face get sharp. He stops long enough to sling one of—

1

that's right, ONE of—the rifles he's carrying over his shoulder, where it lands next to the other one he already has over his other shoulder.

Only my mom would be brave enough to deal with him when he's in "Protect Dani from everything with a penis" mode. He looks absolutely ridiculous. He has two hunting rifles now hanging by their leather straps over each shoulder. He has two handguns strapped to each thick thigh, two on each side of his belt, and various knives along the way. His shirt, which he thinks is hilarious to wear when I attempt to go out on a date, says *I kill things . . . and eat them.* I know it's a hunting shirt—for animals, not teenage boys—but Dane doesn't.

Mom moves in front of him, standing in the front doorway and blocking his path, where Dane is still slowly retreating. She's been dealing with this way before they even had me. He's . . . protective. I guess that's the nicest way to put it. Well, she calls him protective. However, I call it possessive, overbearing, controlling, demanding, and jerky.

"This is her senior prom, Ax. You wouldn't let her go last year." She pauses when he grunts. "And I'm sorry, but you won't be stopping her this year. She has a right to experience this. And Dane is a nice boy. Right, Dane?" she yells over her shoulder.

"Uhh . . ." he stammers, causing my daddy to grunt some more.

"The boy doesn't even know how to talk, Izzy. I bet he will be nothing but handsy and think with his little pecker. Nope. No way. Not near my baby girl."

Oh. My. God. I wish I could just fall into a hole right now. I try to see over my parents to find out if Dane heard that, but with Daddy basically being a giant, that's not happening.

"You did not just say that!" I yell at his back.

Daddy turns around, his movements awkward with how many weapons he has strapped to his body. His green eyes, so like my own, slant and harden. He looks down at my dress for the thousandth time

2

since I came downstairs and doesn't even bother hiding his displeasure that it's showing too much of my body. Even if it is about as tasteful as it gets.

My strapless, red dress has a sweetheart neckline, and everything he calls my "girly bits" is covered. There isn't really any cleavage. Well, okay, there is some, but surely with my lack of being busty, you couldn't even call what *is* showing "cleavage." His first problem was with how much of my legs was showing. Then I made the mistake of turning around without my wrap on. That's when he saw that the dress was completely backless to my bra line. Well, what it would be if I had been wearing one. Which is clearly when he lost his mind.

"You look just like your mother did that night twenty years ago when we finally came back to each other. Right down to those strappy shoe things. And I guarantee you, Danielle Reid, any teenage boy who doesn't bat for the other team will be thinking thoughts I'll cut his dick off for. No. You aren't going with that boy, and that's final."

I harden my eyes, and his narrow even further.

I put my hands on my hips, and he squares his shoulders, his rifles clinking together.

I raise one brow, and he mirrors the action.

"Daddy."

"Dani."

"I'll cry."

"No, you won't. You have more balls than that."

"Want to bet?" I attempt to muster up some tears, knowing that he won't be able to handle them, but before I can force the first one out, my brother jumps into my line of sight and blocks our standoff.

"Yo, Dane! You just run along now. Dani is unfortunately feeling a little under the weather. Ebola. Or the flu. I don't know. It's really ugly and you probably don't want to be around this. The boils—they could pop at any moment."

"You did not just do that," I heatedly whisper, fuming at his nerve. Nate turns and smirks at me. "Oh I just did."

"I can't believe you two!" I spin to look at the one person who can help me. "Mom, seriously?"

Her expression softens, and she just shakes her head. "I'm sorry, Dani. I tried."

"You two," I start, pointing between my older brother and father. "You just can't leave it alone? I'll be eighteen in a few months. What are you jerks going to do then?"

"You're not dating, Danielle. Not ever."

"Oh yeah, Daddy? And how realistic is that crap?"

"Watch your mouth, little princess."

"Mom?"

"I'm so sorry, Dani." She walks over and wraps me in her small arms.

I could probably really cry now a lot easier than when I was trying to fake it, but I've never been one of those girls who weep constantly. It would be easier to just go upstairs, take off the dress mom and I spent hours looking for, scrub off the light makeup she helped me apply, and pretend this night didn't happen.

An hour later, I'm sitting in my bedroom, still wearing my perfect dress. My makeup is still done and my hair is still flowing in long waves. And I'm no less mad at the men in my life than I was earlier. I've considered climbing out my window. I've considered asking my best friends, Lyn and Lila, to come help me escape. But what would be the point? Rambo-Dad already scared away my date, the only boy left in school who had been willing to ask me even though his friends had warned him about my father.

I lie down on my bed and stare up at the ceiling. Maybe I should go away for college. I planned on living at home while I attended Georgia Tech, but there is no way I can deal with this stuff any longer. If my father had things his way, I would be shipped off to become a nun. Or he would buy an island and make it an all-girls cult.

"Uhggggg!" I yell to the empty room.

"Seriously, Dani-girl, things can't be that bad."

I jump up when I hear the deep, gravelly, insanely sexy voice coming from my bedroom door. That voice. My lord. The things it alone does to me should be classified as illegal.

My hair slaps me in the face, a good handful landing in my open mouth, and I hastily pull it out before I turn to where *he* is standing.

My lord, he's beautiful. He's always been. My heart speeds up when I take in his smirking face and the mischief dancing in his brown eyes.

"Cat got your tongue?"

I shake my head.

"Speechless?"

I shake it again.

"Do you really have some flesh-eating, boil-slash-Ebola-like sickness?" he laughs.

I narrow my eyes at him, and his rich laughter booms through the room.

"I'm just kidding, Dani-girl. Come on. Get yourself ready and let's go rock this prom."

My jaw drops again. "What?"

For the first time, I notice that he's dressed in a perfectly tailored tux. My eyes travel down his tall form to his shining, black dress shoes. On the way back up, my eyes hit the corsage spinning around his finger before I look back up into those gorgeous eyes.

"Let's go, beautiful."

"Does Daddy know you're here?" I ask, not moving from my spot.

He sighs, steps into my room, and walks over. His cologne, Gucci Black, wraps around me. He's worn the same scent for years. I perversely sniff it every time I hit the mall with Lyn and Lila. That scent—it's my undoing.

He grabs one of my hands and gives my knuckles a kiss before placing the corsage around my wrist. He gives my hand a squeeze before letting go. Placing his strong hands on my shoulders, he presses down until I'm seated on my bed. Kneeling before me, he takes my feet one by one and fastens the straps of my black heels before standing and grabbing my hands, again, to pull me to my feet.

The whole time, I act like a freak and just gape at him.

What in the hell is going on?

"Ready?" he asks.

"Uhhh . . ."

"Right. You're ready," he laughs, grabs my hand, and pulls me through the house, down the stairs, and into the entryway of the house, where my parents are waiting.

Mom has her camera ready, forcing us to take some pictures, for all of which I'm sure I'm just standing there in a daze. I think I smiled in them, but I was too busy trying to figure out what the hell is going on. Daddy smiles big and triumphantly the whole time, like he's won some battle here.

"Oh, good. You got here," Nate mumbles through a sandwich he's stuffing down his throat.

I shake out of my stunned stupor and look over at him. "You did this?" I ask with disbelief.

"Well, duh. Can't have my little sister miss her prom because of some boils. Plus, I knew this guy," he says, pointing at our father, "wouldn't mind *him.*" He takes another bite before he looks over my shoulder. "And I know *he* isn't going to try to pet the cat."

"Nathaniel Gregory!" Mom gasps.

"What? Why do you think Dad acts like he does? Just because I'm willing to say the words doesn't mean you have to freak out."

I look over at my mom, who has turned bright red.

Daddy laughs at her embarrassment and pulls her into his arms. "Are you sure we didn't drop that one a few times as a baby?"

She slaps his hard stomach and shakes her head. "You look beautiful, honey. Have fun, okay?"

I smile at her and move my eyes to Daddy to judge his mood.

He just smiles at me. "I trust *him*. He won't let any of those pimple-faced, prepubescent boys touch a beautiful hair on your head. Have fun, sweetheart."

I walk over and give them both a hug, standing up on my toes as far as a can to whisper my gratitude in his ear. He's annoying, overprotective, and possessive of his girls, but I love him and I know he comes from a good place.

"Uh, excuse me? Do I not get any little-sister love here? I'm the one running this show, you know?"

"You're such a dork, Nate," I laugh and give him a hug before turning back to my date.

He's standing by the door, talking in low tones to my daddy. I can't hear him, but he's still smiling, so I'm guessing there isn't any talk about dismemberment going on. He looks over, his smile deepening and the lines around his eyes crinkling. Something moves behind his eyes that darkens them slightly, but he looks back over at Daddy, finishing up their conversation.

"Ready, Dani-girl?" he asks a few minutes later, making my heart speed up again.

Holy. Crap.

"Yeah. I'm ready." Or at least as ready as I'll ever be.

That night, while dancing to Brett Young's "Kiss by Kiss," I knew I would never be the same. I could feel the jealous waves coming off every female in the room as *he* held me in his arms. Of course, I had a man and not a boy as my date. Five years older than I am and very obviously not a teenager.

Being held in his arms was a dream come true. His scent invaded my lungs with every inhale. His eyes twinkled as his smile held me hostage. I knew I would never love a man as much as I love him.

Yeah. That was the night I confirmed what I had always known. What I had always felt.

Cohen Cage owned my heart and I never wanted it back.

Chapter 1

Dani

Four years later

*U*GH.

I swear to God, if he wakes me up like this one more time, I'll kill him.

Like, really kill him.

Throwing back the covers, I jump out of bed, shivering when my bare feet hit the cold hardwood floor and the cool air hits my fevered skin. Then I march—because really, when you're in a snit, you shouldn't just walk. Full-on toddler-like stomping needs to ensue. The door, yanked open and flung back, bounces off the wall with a loud *thwack.* Then I stomp some more down the hallway until I hit his door. Then, because this is completely normal behavior for a twenty-one-year-old chick, both hands come up and I bang the hell out of his door with both fists.

"You no-good, dirty pervert! I swear to God, Nate., I hope you get a flesh-eating STD and your dick rots off!"

I can hear him laughing at me through the door. The freaking sicko.

"Turn that crap down, Nate!" I yell before a big cough takes over and I have to pause while hacking up a lung . . . or two.

Does he turn it down? Nope, not that low-down, dirty dog. He turns it up and the sounds of female moans, manly grunts, and skin slapping echoes through his doorway and into the hall.

"You're disgusting!" I scream, doubling my efforts to break down his door so I can kill his sick porn-watching ass by kicking my feet between beats of my fist. "When I get in there, I'm going to beat your head in with your porn collection. Go to town on your thick skull with one of those DVDs until it all just explodes! Nasty dirtbag!"

"Little princess, what in the hell are you doing?"

I spin around and march over to where my father is standing. His hair is standing on all ends, his eyes looking tired, and his expression is a mixture of confusion and exhaustion.

"*That* in *there* is exactly why I need my own place. Do you know how disgusting it is waking up to the sounds of your own brother beating his junk? I swear, Daddy, I'm going to kill him!" I end my rant and instantly deflate, coughing a few times. "I just want some sleep. I feel like crap and I literally just fell asleep, and now, the king of pocket play is at it again. Can we just buy him a hooker? Please, Daddy! Let's get him a hooker."

His lips twitch, and his arms unfold from his chest, opening wide for me to fall into them. Which, of course, I do. I'm not ashamed that I'm still very much a daddy's girl.

"We aren't getting your brother a hooker. They're too classy for his ass."

I laugh and hug him tighter when his gruff chuckles vibrate through his chest.

"What's wrong with my girl?" he asks, pulling me back and looking into my eyes.

"Nothing. Just a little cold. I'll be fine . . . *with some sleep!*" I yell towards Nate's bedroom. And, of course, dissolve into a coughing fit that has my overprotective father narrowing his eyes.

"Go on back to bed, little princess. Let me deal with your brother. I'll have Mom come up and check on you." He gives me a strong hug and spins me toward my room. Then, almost like my words just hit him, he says, "And no more talk about moving out. Not happening."

Ugh.

Seriously. He's told me since I was a little girl that I would never leave his house because I was his little princess and, if he couldn't watch out for me, then all the dirty, thieving, no-good men of the world would get their hands on me.

To say that growing up with Axel Reid as a father was a little . . . tough, would be an understatement. Don't get me wrong. I love my daddy. But he is protective with a capitol P. Possessive of "his girls," which is what he calls Mom and me—to the point where he would probably kill a man who looked at us cross.

I love him . . . but sometimes, I want to strangle him.

That being said, I know that, if I ever needed someone in my corner, no questions asked, that person would be my daddy.

I shuffle back down the hall. Now that I know that Nate will be handled and the rush of trying to kill him has started to fade, I realize just how bad I feel. I came home early yesterday from what was supposed to be a girls' weekend at Lyn and Lila's apartment with them and Maddi Locke. We had the best weekend planned of makeovers—and by that, I mean me dying and cutting their hair—junk food, and a Gossip Girl marathon. It wasn't an hour into the night when I felt like I had been hit by a truck.

Maddi made sure I got home okay, and I crashed instantly.

I drop down into bed, pull the covers over my head, and try to ignore how bad my body hurts.

"What's wrong, Dani?" Mom whispers a little while later after walking into my room and closing the door softly behind her.

I can still hear Daddy yelling at Nate from down the hall, but at least the damn porn sounds have finally stopped.

She sits down, and her cold hand presses against my forehead. "Sweetheart, you're burning up. Tell me what's bothering you."

"I'm okay, Mom. I just need to sleep," I mumble and burrow deeper into the pillows.

"What you need is a doctor, little princess," Daddy grumbles from the now open doorway.

"Go away," I groan and try to ignore them so I can go to sleep.

"Go away my ass," he snaps.

I hear him bend down and kiss Mom before whispering to her low enough that I can't understand him. Another kiss—gross—and the sounds of him walking away.

I finally start to drift off with my mom's soothing touch rubbing my back and she begins to hum softly. Of course, that is short-lived, because not even two minutes later, I'm being wrapped up like a burrito cocooned in my blanket and lifted off the bed. I don't have to open my eyes to know that Daddy is getting his way. The scent of leather and cinnamon hits my nose, and I hear his rough complaining.

"Go away, you said? I didn't know you could read my mind, little princess. I'm going to take you away . . . right to the urgent care clinic."

What did I tell you? Protective to the nth degree.

"Whatever," I grouse with a small smile and allow myself to fall back asleep, knowing that he will take care of me.

A few hours later, I'm back in bed with a scowling father standing over me and holding my medication. Scowling because he knows that, if he hadn't pushed the issue, I would have laid my ass in bed all weekend and gotten worse.

The plus side, though, was the promise from the doctor that the cough medicine would have some pain relievers in it and I would be feeling better shortly.

I swallow the pills and then reach out to take my cough syrup from him. His frown deepens when I start coughing instantly. Come on though. You try to take that crap like a champ. It's disgusting.

"Sleep," he shoots out roughly. He sets the empty medicine cup down on my nightstand and proceeds to tuck me in like I'm five again. Every inch of my body up to my neck is covered, and the blanket is pulled tight as he tucks it around me.

"Is this really necessary? I swear I have to move out. Pretty soon, you're going to try to feed me from a spoon again."

His bright-green eyes shoot up from where he's tucking the blanket in around my feet. "Do not tempt me, little girl," he says with all seriousness.

I have to get out of here. Lyn and Lila said that their lease is almost up. We've been toying with the idea of getting a big, old house together. *Their* dad, Greg Cage, is almost as bad as mine, but he still lets them leave the house. They think it's sweet that mine is so protective, but when the role is reversed and it's their dad pulling something crazy, or their brothers—all three of them—they don't find any humor.

"Not moving out, Danielle."

"You can't stop me, you know," I remind him around my yawn, hunkering down into my warm bed.

"Sleep," he demands before he slips out of the room.

So. Annoying.

But do I even give moving out a second thought? Nope. I smile, cough, smile again, and then fall into one hell of a deep sleep.

Chapter 2

Dani

"HEY, DANI-GIRL."

I smile.

"There's that beautiful smile," the voice says, and my smile deepens.

"Jesus Christ. What the hell did they give her? Izzy!" another voice booms. "The fuck did that bottle say? She's out like she's in a goddamn coma!"

I frown when my father's voice enters my heavenly dream.

Good lord, what is he doing in my dream? Daddy shouldn't be here. Not when I finally have Cohen Cage in my bed. Well, besides the fact that that would be sick, he would kill Cohen if he caught him putting a hand on me. Literally. Cohen would be dead.

"I'm sure it's fine, Axel," Cohen says softly. "Mom sent me over with some soup and some show that the girls have been going nuts over. I don't mind sitting with her."

Ha! Yeah right. Sitting with her would mean that Daddy would trust something with a dick near his daughter. Regardless of who it is, that would never happen. Yup—definitely dreaming.

"Yeah, sure, son," he stutters.

I can just picture him rubbing the back of his neck with a helpless look.

"Let me go call that stupid kid doctor and see what the hell he did to my little princess. I knew he didn't look old enough to be out of med school."

"You got it," I hear *him* mumble, and the bed dips.

I listen as my father's footsteps stomp out of the room and the door shuts softly behind him. Ah. Finally. My dreams of *him* never last long enough, and there is no way I want to share good dream time with my father in the picture.

I have a feeling that, even in my dreams, he would be like a giant shield against any man who even breathed in my direction.

"Dani-girl," he whispers in my ear. "I have your favorite soup from my mom here. Why don't you open those beautiful green eyes and take a bite? If you do, I promise I'll even sit here and watch a few episodes of Game of Thrones with you."

"You furrr real?" I slur and open my eyes slightly before quickly closing them when the bright light from the sun hits my tired eyes. "You can't be real. You're in my dream bed, Cohen!" I reach out and pat his stubbled cheek a few times, trying to get my eyes open and focused on his face. "You can't be here. What if Daddy catches you? Wait. Why are you dressed? You're not usually dressed when you're in my dream bed." My hand drops from where I was rubbing all over his face and starts to roam over his cotton-covered chest. "You can take it off. I won't bite." I giggle and start to trail my hand lower to get this stupid shirt off him.

God, he feels like heaven.

A surprised noise somewhere between a choking gasp and a shocked stutter comes from his mouth, which is followed by a groan that rumbles against the palm I have resting against his chest.

I bite my lip, thinking that I can at least try to do something seductive. They're always doing it in the books I love to read. Even if I never understood what's hot about lip nibbling, I might as well give it a go.

"You're so hard," I whisper in awe as my hand continues to palm his pecs, his abs, and everything between. "And warm," I add, nuzzling in close. My head moves to his shoulder, my hand still rubbing his hard stomach, and I pull one leg up to wrap around his hips.

"Jesus Christ," he moans when my leg hits his crotch.

"Are you hard . . . everywhere? My dream is going to stop soon. It always does. You should just tell me now. Then, when I wake up, I won't be disappointed because I once again missed all the good stuff." I sigh deeply. "I bet you're huge," I giggle.

"Fuck. Me," he whispers on a prayer.

"That would be nice too."

"Dani-girl, what in the hell has gotten in to you?" He lifts his body and moves out from under me, lightly swatting my hands when I start to grab after him. "I'm just . . . uh . . . I'm just going to go to the bathroom." He stands from the bed.

I drop back with a pout. "But we were going to fuggle," I complain.

He turns sharply to ask, "The hell is a fuggle?"

"Duh. It's a cuddle fuck," I giggle and reach for him again only to stop when he walks away and starts to pace.

"Jesus fucking Christ."

I was having the most beautiful dream. Well, every dream that involves Cohen Cage is beautiful—overwhelmingly beautiful. And trust me. There have been *a lot* of dreams over the years with him as the sole star. Each and every one of them ends in disappointment, though, when they stop before he can get to the good stuff.

This one, even though it lacked the erotic content that usually partners with a Cohen sex dream, was different—it felt so real. God, what I would give to have him in my arms *that way* for real.

"You coming back to the land of the living now, Dani-girl?"

I still instantly.

Holy shit.

"Uh . . ." I stammer.

"Yeah. There's my girl," he laughs. "Let me go call your dad and let him know you're awake. I thought he was going to lock himself in your room earlier when your mom said they had to go. She tried to tell him you would be fine, but you know how your dad is."

Why can't I clear the cobwebs in my head?

"Anyway," he continues, "they had that charity function for local Wounded Warriors that Maddox runs to go to. If it would have been anything else, I don't think she would have been able to get him out the door. You should have seen it, Dani. I've never seen your dad deflate so quickly." He laughs to himself, and I feel him shift before the bed lets up when his weight is removed.

Oh. My. Gosh!

Cohen's in my bed. Like, really in my bed. I don't think my panic level could get any higher than it is right now. I frantically search the murky depths of my memories to see if I can piece the last few hours together.

All I remember is Nate and his disgusting wake-up call, Daddy dragging me to the doctor, and my Cohen dream. Holy crap. That was a dream, right?

Opening my eyes, I look over to where he's standing with his phone against his ear. He looks up and gives me that panty-melting smile, and I feel myself flush instantly. Blush like an innocent school-girl. How. Embarrassing.

He shakes his head a few times and moves his attention to my dresser full of pictures while waiting for the call to connect. I use this time to study his handsome face.

He's always been an attractive person. When he was a kid, he had that youthful perfection. His skin always looked flawless and he carried a good tan all year long. His brown hair, until he enlisted in the Marines, carried that sexy shaggy look any female worth her salt would get an itchy palm that just begged her to run her fingers through. Now, he keeps it slightly longer than regulation with a buzz on the sides. It brings out the sharp angles of his jaw and cheekbones. Not to sound like a freak—hey, maybe I am—but I've been studying this man for so long that I could probably draw him to exactness from memory alone.

What all his good looks really do is make him look like one deliciously sexy man who puts me in a state of constant arousal when he's around. His dark-brown eyes look over at me again, and he raises a brow when he sees that I'm still looking at him, but he quickly glances away when I'm assuming my dad picks up.

"Axel," he starts only to pause and roll his eyes. "She's fine. Awake, tired, and I'm sure getting more annoyed by the second that I'm reporting to her father . . . Yes, sir . . . I'm positive I'll get an earful as well . . . No, sir . . . I'll get her to eat something as soon as I get off the phone . . . No, she hasn't taken her meds yet. She just woke up, uh . . . She just woke up." He looks over at me almost uncomfortably before looking away.

Weird.

I start to cough, and he rolls his eyes.

"It was just a cough, Axel. She's already back to scowling at me. Yeah, I'll get the soup and her meds and demand she doesn't move a muscle indefinitely. No, sir, I'm not making fun of you."

When I laugh, Cohen shoots me another look. This time, he's warning me to hush before my daddy goes nuts.

"Yes, sir. She's fine. I'm sure she going to listen because she knows that's best too. Okay. Yes, sir. Bye." He shoves his phone back in his pocket and shakes his head. "Your dad. I swear that man still thinks you're six and riding a bike for the first time. Remember when he wouldn't even let you attempt to ride it without training wheels before he had a fully stocked first aid kit attached to his back?"

We both laugh at the memory of just one of his over-the-top parenting moments.

"What are you doing here?" I ask, waving my hand around the general area of my bedroom.

"Nate. Well, Nate indirectly. He called me earlier." He raises one shoulder in a shrug like that should be enough.

"Yeah? And that explains what, exactly?"

"Oh shut up, brat," he teases. "He mentioned, in between his bouts of hilarity over the morning craziness at the Reid house, that you were sick, and I figured I would come bring you Mom's soup and keep you company. You know, like old times."

"Old times?" I question, confused.

"You know. I used to always sit with you when you were sick."

"Cohen, the last time I was sick, I was, like, ten and you had no choice since we were the only two with the flu and our parents didn't want us spreading it to our siblings."

What in the hell is going on here? For a couple of years, he's treated me with a friendly indifference. Not rude, but never . . . this.

"Still, it helped," he smirks.

"Yeah, it did."

Of course, he probably thinks it helps for an entirely different reason than it actually did. I was beside myself the whole week we were basically quarantined together. Not because I was sicker than shit and miserable. I *was* sick as hell, but I was in heaven. Absolute euphoria because I was alone with Cohen—just him and me—for a whole week.

There is seriously something wrong with me. Besides the obvious.

In case you haven't guessed it, I've been madly in love with Cohen Cage since I was a little girl—I think I was six when I realized just how much I loved him and he was ten. That childhood crush has grown over the years into something that is so big—so soul consuming—that even I feel like it will crush me at times.

And the worst part is that he's completely blind to it.

Chapter 3

Cohen

I'M DEFINITELY IN WAY OVER my head here.

I look over at Dani, who is now peacefully—thank God—sleeping again, and drop my head back on the pillows stacked up behind my back. What the hell was I thinking rushing over here? As soon as Nate called, laughing his ass off over how he woke his sister up, and let me know just how sick she was, I couldn't seem to stop myself from getting here as quickly as possible. Mom didn't even bat an eye when I asked her how to make her soup—the same soup she's made for each of my siblings and me every time we were sick. She did ask why I needed it and left it alone when all I said was, "Dani." I didn't miss the look in her eye though.

Curious but hopeful.

It really should have been a concern. How could she possibly be okay with me rushing over to Dani? Someone who is almost five years younger and has never made it a secret, even though she thinks she has, about how she feels about me.

Sure, there was that one time. I think the twins, Lyn and Lila, had just turned sixteen—Dani was around fifteen—when she whispered her feelings towards me with a intensity that no teenager just coming into herself should ever understand.

I'll never forget it. Never. Of course that was a defining moment for our relationship—not that she knows that.

"I'm going to miss you, Cohen. I know you don't look at me like I look at you, but one day, you're going to come back and I'll still be waiting for you. Waiting for you to see me like I see you. Mark my words, Cohen Cage. One of these days, you're going to be mine. And until you're ready . . . I'll be here. I'll be waiting."

Her husky whisper replays in my mind like it just happened moments ago. I haven't forgotten a single word. Not a single one. Over the years, they would come back to me at the worst-possible times. When I would be out on a date—boom, there they were. Instantly, that chick would morph into a vision of Dani so clear that I struggled not to reach out and run my fingertips down her cheek. When I was in the middle of one of the biggest games in my football career, there they were—a hushed whisper that carried over the roaring crowds. And it would never fail—I would look up from a huddle and there she would be standing with my family, screaming louder than any other person in the stadium.

And most recently, when I was in the middle of a warzone, gunfire flying all around us, bombs exploding, and the dust burning our eyes and lungs. Right in the middle of that Hell-on-earth chaos, I would hear her words trail through my thoughts right when I needed an extra push of strength or, God forbid, hope.

I think that was the moment that I realized the enormity of it and that confession whispered all those years ago. Right or wrong, whatever it is between us would always be bigger than I understand. It's something that was so unexpected—that feeling, craving, desire, to make her mine. It's something I've almost felt guilty about over the years. Not only because of how close our families are, but because, until the last few years, it's something that was very inappropriate to feel towards someone that young.

When she woke up earlier—or at least I think she was awake—and started rubbing her body against mine, I thought I was going to come in my pants. That hasn't happened to me since I was a teenager just learning how to control my random pop-up erections.

I have no doubt that it was the pain meds in her cough syrup making her act like that. She's always gotten weird on narcotic pain meds. But when her warm body crushed against my side, I had a hard time telling myself that she wasn't in her right mind. Trying to convince myself not to react was impossibly hard. Then her small but firm tits pressed against my side and it was almost game over.

Her tits had been straining the confines of her small, white tank top since I'd walked in the door. Her nipples were pebbled to firm tips just begging for me to wrap my lips around them. Did she have small nipples that matched her size or would they be large? Are they light pink in color or more tan? Would she taste as good as the promise of her has hinted at when I finally pull them deep into my mouth and tease her with my tongue and teeth?

Yeah. Ever since *that* moment, I've been as hard as steel and ready to pound into her small body.

Yup. I'm in way over my head here—so far over that I'm shocked I haven't drowned yet.

"Fuck me," I groan, pressing my palm against my cock, willing it to calm the fuck down.

If her brother—or, worse, her father—were to come in here right now, I have no doubt that I would be put in the hospital with the force of their beatdown.

She shifts, and I look away from Game of Thrones, where the little dude—or "imp," as she and the girls call him—she is always raving about, is playing with his whore.

Jesus, is everyone getting some action?

After making sure she got her meds, I heated up Mom's soup and called her brother to see if he would be home soon. Of course he said that he was too busy on his date with the Carver twins to come home and take care of his sick sister. One thing about Nate—he loved his sister, but he loved pussy more.

Axel and Izzy had left for their night for the charity event, the same one my parents and all the other parents from our group would be at. Axel had already planned on being out all night with Izzy, something about a bed and breakfast, so I told him that I would stay here with Dani and make sure she was okay. There is no telling Axel Reid that his adult daughter can take care of herself.

If he had any idea about the thoughts I've had about his daughter, there is no fucking way he would have left me alone with her. No. Way.

"Coh," she moans and moves in her sleep. Her legs shift, and she moans again.

Fuck! How the hell am I supposed to not get messed up over this? I jump off the bed and pace around her room. Looking around, I try to find something to focus on that will help me move past the fact that she is clearly having some heated dream.

Cuddle fuck. What did she call it? A fuggle? I shake my head and wince when my cock swells even further. Fuggle. What in the hell is that supposed to mean, anyway?

Focus, Cohen. Focus on something other than your desire to bury yourself balls-deep in sweet Dani pussy.

I look around her room for anything to form some sort of distraction. Her dresser is full of pictures. There are some of her and my sisters. Some pictures of Maddi and Dani alone. Some of Maddi, the twins, and Dani together. More pictures of her and Liam Beckett—her best friend other than my sisters. My eyes go past the pictures to the canvas paintings she has hanging up around the pale-blue room, and I know without checking that they're some of Ember's, Maddi's little sister. She has a huge chaise lounge-type sofa thing in the corner by her floor-to-ceiling windows that overlook their backyard and lake. It has a worn throw tossed carelessly over the back, and a book has been thrown on the ottoman.

That chair would be the perfect chair to take her on, I muse. *I would put her on her knees, facing the back, her elbows bracing her body against it, and take her hard. Goddamn, I could sink myself so deep into her tiny body.*

Okay . . . Quickly moving my eyes past the chair, I look back at her sleeping form. Her tan skin looks flushed, her full lips are parted slightly, and her chest is rising slowly. Just like an angel, my Dani-girl.

An angel sent from Heaven who is without a doubt always going to be my greatest temptation.

Chapter 4

Dani

COHEN WOKE ME UP TWICE while I slept to have me take more medicine. I don't remember much from that night, just that he never was far from my side when I woke on my own and he played with my hair until I was able to fall back to sleep after a good coughing spell. Well, that's a lie. I remember dreams so vivid that I'm still getting hot and bothered over them.

He was gone when I woke up the morning after, and for once, I didn't have to wake up to Nate beating his junk with porn on surround sound. It's been four days of sleeping off and on. Every time I close my eyes, though, it's all about Cohen.

Sluggishly, I pull myself from bed and make quick work of showering and getting ready for the day. I've missed way too much work, and even though I have the coolest boss in the world, I can't afford to miss much more. Especially now that, after all of this, I'm even more convinced that I have to get the hell out of my parents' house.

Grabbing my phone, I press the screen and wait for Lyn to pick up. One half of my best-friend duo since birth, Lyndsie Cage has been my go-to for everything—and I mean *everything*. She loves the fact that I have a ridiculous crush on her unattainable brother. She encourages my love for him. God, I love the little head-in-the-clouds dreamer.

"Yo, bitch!" she laughs, and I smile.

"What's up, hooker?" I throw back.

"Nothing much. Lila just left to head off to school. I swear she is never going to graduate," she jokes.

"Yeah, well, that's what happens when you're going after your doctorate, Lyn. I think she has to sign her soul away for the next twenty years or something," I snicker.

I couldn't be prouder of Lila though. She has always told us that she is going to be a doctor; I guess we all just assumed she meant the medical kind. It wasn't until the summer of our junior year in high school, when we were all working at a local day care, that she decided she had found her calling. She didn't just want to work with kids. Nope. Not our Lila. She wanted to own, operate, and specialize in a day care for handicapped and special-needs children. Ever since then, she's had one goal in mind. Her dual degree in special education and business management have had her eating, sleeping, and breathing school since graduation.

"You aren't far off, I'm sure. Anyway, what's up?"

I hear her fiddling with stuff in the background and visualize her puttering around her bathroom, getting ready for work as well. She probably has her thick, black hair up rolled in a bun on the top of her head while she makes sure her makeup is two hundred percent perfect.

"Nothing much. Just getting ready for work. I feel like I've been off forever. Has the place gone up in flames since last week?" I ask, only half joking.

"Not really," she giggles.

Oh shit.

"Lyn," I warn. "What did he do now?" I probe, dreading her answer. The last time I took a week-long vacation, I came back to work to a nut house.

"Well, where do you want me to start? You should know by now that, just because he has calmed down some over the years, when he gets some wild hair, there is no stopping him."

"Start from the beginning," I spit out through my teeth.

Using my shoulder to hold the phone, I pull my black pants over my hips, step into my favorite four-inch, black-suede heels with the gold-studded bowtie adorning the top. They're freaking fabulous, and with the "must wear at least one item that is gold" requirement at work, they work perfectly. Of course, my feet will be screaming before the day is over, but at least they're going to be screaming while looking badass.

I've worked for Dilbert Harrison for the last two years. Dilbert Harrison also lovingly known as Uncle Sway. He's the most over-the-top, not-a-care-in-the-world, fun-loving, and flamboyant man I know. I've heard stories about how, when we were younger, before he and his partner adopted their daughter Stella, he would prance around with a long, blond wig and heels taller than any of our mothers would brave wearing. Even Aunt Dee, who always has the coolest heels, wouldn't even touch them.

But his fun-loving, not-a-care-in-the-world personality can also be a little larger than life at times. I mean, hello. Because of him, the whole sidewalk outside the salon and a few other local businesses, including Corps Security, is painted gold with flecks of glitter.

"Well, first he decided that we needed to touch up the flooring. Since we had to close down because the paint fumes were a little much for the clientele trying to relax the last time he touched it up, he was doing it in sections with a huge box fan bungee-corded to the rolling front desk chair. Then Samantha almost broke her neck when she tripped over the extension cord, so I talked him into waiting until we closed and stayed until four in the morning helping him touch up the damn floor. I told him he needed to consider having a laminate company custom make him some gold glittered flooring and maybe it wouldn't need touching up. I believe he might be considering it." She stops, and I hear her moving around her house.

"Is that it?" I ask, knowing that there is no way that's all.

"Nope," she states but doesn't elaborate.

"Okay?"

"Then he decided we needed to have theme Fridays. Dani, theme fucking Fridays. You are going to shit yourself. This week, he wants a burlesque-type theme. He actually wants all of us girls, plus Jonathan—the new guy that started while you were out—to dress up in complete burlesque gear. If he could get away with it, I think he would even incorporate some sort of dance number into the end of every hour."

"You're joking?" Son of a bitch. I knew better than to leave Sway unattended for too long. I've always been able to keep a leash on his wilder-than-normal ideas.

"Not at all. He even mentioned something about a pole-dancing class to teach us how to move before we had a stripper-slash-Vegas-showgirl day. Dani, he mentioned headdresses. Head. Dresses!" she yells in my ear.

"I'll talk to him when I get in. Maybe I can talk him out of this."

"I wouldn't put any money on it. He's already taken an ad out in the local paper. He's gone off the deep end ever since they wrapped filming of the reality show for *last season* and started their pre-filming for the next season. Sway All the Way is definitely making him battier than normal, and you know, once the show airs it's only going to get worse."

"God, Lyn. Can you freaking believe that is actually happening? I'm going to die when the first show airs." I slap my palm against my forehead when I remember what happened during the first episode's filming.

"Well, that's your own fault for not rescheduling my brother's haircut for a non-filming day," she laughs.

"Jesus, he's going to see it, isn't he? Do you think we can break all the televisions he could possibly be around before it airs? Luckily, Daddy already said he wasn't watching that 'chick shit,' so he will remain blissfully unaware."

"You can only hope, Dani. I don't know what the big deal is though. It isn't that bad."

"Uh. I basically have 'I'm daydreaming about running my hands through your hair while you fuck me' written all over my face and then I stupidly admitted my feelings to the producers during our camera interview!" I shriek.

"Ew. Don't be so dramatic, loser. You didn't look that obvious, and I'm sure they won't even show that part of the interview. It was the first show. They have to . . . I don't know . . . introduce the place and all that is Sway first. They wouldn't start off with your crazy ass lusting after my brother."

"You don't know that," I challenge.

"Yeah, and you don't know they will do anything different. Calm your tits. Look, I have to go and finish up my makeup. I've got a wedding party of five coming in today, and if I want to grab up all those hopeful bridesmaids' business, I have to look like hot shit so they know I'm capable when the time comes for them to not be the poorly dressed extras in the wedding. Marketing is such a bitch sometimes."

She doesn't even give me a chance to say bye. She just clicks off the phone. I can imagine she is going all out on her makeup—not that she needs it. Lyn is stunning. But she always gets a little eccentric when it comes to wedding makeup. She's convinced that the bridesmaids are living in some jealous fog and, when they get makeup done by her, meet their Prince Charming, and then in turn have their wedding in the plans, they're going to somehow remember the girl who made them stunning and created that snowball effect.

Yeah, Lyn is also the most confident person I've ever met, and she's convinced she can do anything. Since she's booked for more weddings of repeat bridesmaids, I have to kind of agree with her logic here.

Burlesque- and showgirl-themed days? Good lord, it's going to be a long day.

Chapter 5

Dani

*A*S PREDICTED, IT IS INSANE the second I step foot inside of Sway's. The madness starts with Sway and ends with Sway. Madness and insane being the key-words.

"Sweet heavens you, my little belle! Sway was imagining you on your deathbed! When that hunky father of yours—stop looking at me like that, you would have to be blind not to see how hunky he is! Anyway, when he told me that my Danielle-Bell was sick, I was so worried. Darling, you look like you've lost weight. Weight, I will remind you, that you did not have to lose. Such a tiny little tinker." He spins me with two hands on my shoulders, and I have to work hard not to bust my ass when my heels struggle to keep up with the rapid movement. "It's a good thing you have your mother's lush bottom or you would look like a stick. As it is, you look like a stick with a great ass."

He spins me back around and looks down at my chest. Oh here we go. Reaching up to my black blouse, he unsnaps the two buttons that kept me decent and nods to himself when my red bra is peeking through the opening.

"Perfect. Now give the girls a little tuggero and we're done. I'll make sure to put some more weight on you, Belle."

"You do realize that this would be considered sexual harassment in most work environments," I remind him. Again.

"It would. But lucky for you, I haven't swung for the kitty cats once in my life. I think, for the harassment to be sexual, I would have to actual want to get in those pants, darling. The only pants I ever want to get into happen to be carrying far different equipment than you, sweet girl." He laughs and smacks my rear when I turn to walk to my station.

"Good God, Pops! Do not talk like that!" I hear Stella yell as she walks in from the back room, where we do all of our color mixing. "That's just . . . No, that's just too much, even for you. I don't ever want to think about my dad's junk or my pops lusting after it." She rolls her eyes and walks over to give me a hug. "Hey, you. I missed you around this circus."

"I heard that, Stella!" Sway laughs and struts to the front of the studio in his glittery, gold heels—heels that, as predicted, are taller than mine.

"I wasn't trying to hide it, Pops!" she yells at his back.

Ah. Never a dull moment at Sway's.

I was busy doing Karen Oglethorpe's hair for about twenty minutes before the cameras walked in. Of course. Film day. I must be completely off my game if I had already forgotten the filming rotation.

I loathe film day.

Not only are the cameras always in my way when I'm trying to do hair, mix color, and move between the washing station or the blower station, but the producer and his people are freaking annoying. Devon Westerfield. He's been a constant presence around the salon since this time last year, and I think I might actually hate him more now than I did then. Not because he's a bad person. He really isn't. He's doing his job just the same as I am. But it's because of him that I might publicly, in front of millions, make a fool of myself when the reality series goes live.

"Ah! Danielle Reid. Aren't you a sight for sore eyes," he says and leans in to give me a light hug. "You know Don and Mark?"

"Hey, Dev. Nope, I don't think I've had the pleasure," I respond with fake enthusiasm.

"Hmm. Oh that's right. You weren't here the other day when I brought them by to meet everyone. They're my assistants this go-around. Here to help with the crew and also with anything small to large that I might just be too stretched thin for." He starts looking around, and I can tell he has already forgotten about me.

"Okie dokie, Devy boy."

Returning my attention back to Karen is effective enough in getting him off my back, but the two shadows-to-be stick around. I pause in my brushing of her color and look up.

"Is there something you two need?" I ask in annoyance.

"Well, Devon said you were the go-to person here. Manager and head stylist of Sway's. We just thought—" the short one—Don, I think—starts, but I interrupt him before he can get started on his crusade to get me to tell him how to do his job. They're all the same. Devon has been through more assistants than I can count in the year and a half I've known him.

"One thing to know and remember, boys: I don't have time for you to act like you don't know your head from your ass. Nice to meet you and all that, but please don't act like the last few idiots who all but licked the ground Dev over there, walked on. It won't earn you points with him. In case you haven't noticed, he's a little tunnel-vision prone, and I assure you that it won't do you any good to try and fuse yourself to me." Dismissing their shocked faces, I look in the mirror and give Karen a wink, earning a giggle from her in return. She loves it when the girls around here are sassy.

They mumble something under their breaths, and I turn to give them a sharp glare, which of course they miss because they've tucked their tails again to run after an order-barking Devon.

Two hours later, I finally have a chance to go grab a quick bite to eat. Well, I would have if Sway hadn't yelled from the front that I had a call-in that would be here in fifteen.

I hate call-ins. Since I'm one of the best stylists in the local area, my appointments are booked weeks out. But there are a handful of people I always allow to call in, and Sway wouldn't have said yes to them had it not been one of those select few.

Mentally, while shoving as much of the sandwich Stella grabbed me when she did a lunch run down my throat, I try to figure out who could be coming in. I know it's not Nate or Liam; I cut their hair last week. Daddy doesn't need a cut since I did his the other day. I've seen the others it might be recently enough. I pause with my last bite to my mouth when I realize who it will be—the only person who I haven't cut in a while.

Cohen. Freaking. Cage.

Son of a bitch. I know I told Sway no more scheduling or allowing him to come in on a film day.

"Breathe, fancy pants," Lyn whispers in my ear on her way towards the back breakroom. "He hasn't been a biter since he was a kid." She continues walking with her laughter trailing behind her.

I'm going to kill Sway, I think to myself before going to wash up so I can prep my station.

I have just put down my trimmers when I feel it.

That magnetic charge that floats over my skin, heating every inch and leaving a trail of awareness in its wake. That pull that has always been connected to one man. I shiver and give myself a pep talk about how to treat him with friendly indifference while there are cameras around. Of course they have been filming a few things that the cameras mounted all over the room can't capture perfectly. I have already tripped over one of the assistant asshats twice today.

"Dani-girl." His voice, that rich rumble of masculine excellence, washes over me and I shiver again before cursing under my breath. The rumble of his low laughter tells me that he definitely didn't miss that little move.

Kill me now.

"Hey, Coh," I say with a smile. "What brings you in? Last minute, I might add." I pat the chair before walking around and holding the back while he sits down.

When his scent hits my nose, I almost come on the spot. Lord, he smells good. I wonder what he would smell like while his body covered mine, all sweaty from hours of good lovemaking. I run my fingers through the longer lengths on the top and feel my cheeks heat slightly, thinking about doing the same when his face is buried between my legs.

" . . . needed a trim."

Shit. I missed what he said because, naturally, I was thinking about him naked. Naked and thrusting into my body. Naked and feasting between my spread thighs.

"You feeling okay? I thought Nate said you were better?"

"Uh, I'm fine. Just—is it hot in here?" I fan my face and avoid his eyes.

He's silent, so I take that as a sign that it's safe to bring my attention back to him.

Big mistake there. His knowing eyes are boring right into mine. The chocolate depths sparkling in a way that makes it clear he has a good idea about where my mind was going.

"Did you hear what I said, Dani-girl?"

"Of course I did, Cohen. What, did you think I was standing here daydreaming?" I joke.

"Well, yeah, that's exactly what I think." His eyes darken and he smirks a devilish grin. "Did you know you talk in your sleep, Dani?" he asks, and I drop my comb.

Oh, God. Shut up, shut up, shut up. This is not happening. No way.

"No, I don't," I childishly snap.

"Dani, you do. So, yeah, I do think you were standing there day-dreaming. Want to know why?" He uses his booted foot to move his chair so that he's facing me, and then he leans in so that his face is dangerously close to mine. Even when he's seated, his head is almost level with my own. Curse my horizontally challenged self. "While you were zoning off into space with your fingers running through my hair, you had this smile on your lips. The same smile you had the other day when you were dreaming. About me, Dani. And don't deny it, because you don't moan my name if you're dreaming about another man. Yes, Dani, you very much do talk in your sleep." He smiles again before leaning back and looking down to his phone. "Clean up my neck please, cut the length off the top, and give me a buzz on the sides. Other than that, you're clear to continue with your thoughts."

I must have been standing there like an idiot because he looks up from his phone, laughs to himself, and, with one tan hand, reaches out and pushes my mouth closed.

"You're going to catch flies that way, Dani-girl. One day, maybe you can clue me in on what those dreams are about."

Drives me insane, the control he has over me. There isn't a single person in the world, other than Cohen, who can turn me into a ridiculously stupid, sputtering fool. My normal confidence disappears. And clearly, he isn't as oblivious to my feelings as I originally thought.

How in the hell am I supposed to handle this?

Wait a minute. Cohen or not, I'm not going to let him pull my strings when I know he is just doing this to make me feel uncomfortable.

So, time to call his bluff.

"Why? You planning on doing something about it?"

He looks up sharply, clearly not having expected me to actually say something in return since he was going for shock value.

"Try me," he demands, his voice thick and even deeper than normal.

I throw my head back and reach out to run my fingers thought his hair again, just barely suppressing the shivers. Curling my fingers slightly so that I can grab a good hold, I lean in and pull his head back at the same time. With my nose just a hair away from his and our breaths mingling together, I say, "Cohen, you couldn't handle the truth of my thoughts when it comes to you and we both know it. So how about *you* let *me* know when you're ready for me to *clue you in*." I give his hair a light tug and smile when he swallows loudly and shifts in his seat. "Ready for that trim?" I ask with a wink, and I'm rewarded with his groan.

I have no idea how I do it, but I manage to get through his cut without coming unglued. I can see Lyn trying to get my attention from across the room. Stella had to leave after she overheard my words to Cohen because her giggles were getting the best of her. Cohen has remained silent the whole time. His eyes though . . . They're speaking louder than his words ever could.

They haven't left my reflection in the mirror since I started. I can feel them every time I shift. When I stopped to go grab another comb after I dropped my fourth one, I felt his gaze follow me across the room to Stella's station. The few times I stopped cutting to meet his eyes, the heated promise written all over his face almost did me in. I almost just said 'fuck it' and climbed on his lap to have a go regardless of the people watching our every move.

I finish the last buzz of my clippers around his right ear and move to brush all the stray hair off. "All done," I say softly and unclip his cape.

He stands, shoving his phone in the back pocket of his jeans, and walks over to stand in front of me. I continue to pretend I'm busy with the cape I just removed, brushing stray hairs off here and there, when his hand comes up, his finger and thumb hitting my chin, and my face is lifted until I have no choice but to look in his eyes.

"Do not tease me, Dani. It's not a game you want to play if you don't intend to follow through."

"I-I wasn't . . . I wouldn't," I stammer.

"You did, and I have no doubt you'll have the brilliant idea to do it again. The next time you allude to those dirty thoughts I know you have about me, don't think for a second that I won't drag you to the closest bed to show you just how fucking dirty they'll get." He leans close, his scent hitting my nostrils, and I involuntarily inhale deeply, earning me a rumbled chuckle. "What you don't know, Dani—because contrary to what you think, you don't know me well enough to assume what having me would really be like. But I promise you this: every little thought that you have had that causes you to moan my name while scissoring those perfect legs back and forth, praying for completion—it would be so much hotter than you could ever imagine." He gives me a soft, sweet kiss against my temple that has fire racing from that spot all over my body until it ends in the awareness that I'm pretty sure I just came in my pants.

Chapter 6

Dani

"YOU WOULDN'T EVEN BELIEVE IT if you had seen it with your own eyes." Lyn laughs and points across her living room at me. "I'm not joking at all, Lila. It was ridiculous. It was even making me hot and he's my damn brother. Of course it wasn't *him,* but the whole sexual chemistry taking over every ounce of space in the whole room. It could have turned on a monk." She laughs again and takes a big pull of her wine.

"I knew you two would be explosive," Lila jokes.

"You have no idea, sister. It was out-of-this-world insane. The whole time she was cutting his hair—and ignoring him, I should add—he just kept glaring at her like he wanted to throw her over his shoulder and drag her out of the salon."

"Cohen did that?" Maddi asks in shock.

"Yup. Swear it. But don't worry. If you don't believe me, just wait until *that* episode airs. I shit you not, Devon was about to have a heart attack. He hit television gold with that right there." Lyn takes another swallow and giggles to herself.

"Ohmigod. Ohmigod! Shit. Lyn! How could you let me act like

that when they were filming? How could I forget that? Oh no, oh no. This isn't good at all." I jump off the couch, knocking Maddi's legs off from where she had them resting on the coffee table, and start to pace the room. "Lyn! He's going to have to see that again. People we know are going to see me saying that to him."

"So?" she says with confusion.

"What's the big deal, Dani? So what? You finally opened your mouth and gave him a little something to think about. You shouldn't be ashamed about that," Lila, ever the voice of reason, argues.

"I shouldn't be ashamed?! This is Cohen. Your brother, my brother's best friend, the same Cohen that I've been hopelessly in a state of lust over for *my whole life!*" I scream.

"Someone is a little dramatic today," Maddi says with a sigh.

"I'm not being dramatic! I'm being realistic. What if things get weird?" Things are so going to get weird. The next time I see him, I'm just going to run the other way. It will be safer than trying to act like I'm not completely humiliated. Or that I have completely humiliated him.

"Realistic would be you shutting the hell up and realizing that maybe, just maybe, my big brother finally has his eyes wide open when it comes to you," Lila adds.

I look over at her, catching Lyn nodding emphatically out of the corner of my eye. Maddi sighs again and voices her agreement.

"You all think this way?" I ask the room and get three yeses. "Okay. Say I believe you. Now what?"

"Easy!" Lyn yells, almost falling out of her seat with her excitement. "Now we make *him* the one that is craving *you*." She nods to herself like this is the best advice in the world.

"And how am I supposed to do that?" I ask the know-it-all currently sloshed off Asti.

"Just leave that to me, Dani. Just leave it all to me."

If I were in my right mind, maybe I would be alarmed here, but because we are on our third bottle of Asti, I have to agree with her and let myself believe this is a brilliant plan.

Ready or not, Cohen. Ready. Or. Not.

"This is a stupid idea," I complain under my breath and look over at Lyn.

"This isn't a stupid idea. This is an awesome idea. As sexy as you are, you've always been clueless to your own sexuality. You dress the part, look the part, but the second *the part* is shoved in your face, you start doubting yourself. I get it. Years of trying to get someone's attention makes you feel like you're lacking something, but I assure you that isn't the case. So . . . this will help to bring out some of that confidence. Would I lead you the wrong way here, Dani?" She ends her speech and puts both of her hands on her hips with a huff.

"Pole dancing, Lyn?"

"What? It's technically a gym activity. I did tell you we were coming to the gym. I just didn't tell you what for. Doesn't matter. Sway brought it up, and after doing a little research, I found out you get the workout of your life during these classes, so just think about it as a positive-type thing. Even if you can't open that brilliant mind of yours up and see that I'm right."

"Let's get this over with."

She gives me a bright smile and pushes herself out of the car. I give myself another pep talk and try to convince myself that this isn't going to be a mistake. She's right about one thing: I could always use some more gym time. Tiny or not, I won't stay firm with all the sweets I eat.

"Is this even something I'll be able to do, Lyn? I mean, we all can't be tall warrior princesses like you and your amazon sister." I laugh, but I'm dead serious. I'm five foot two on a good day. The twins tower over me. Always have. They have upper-body strength that could rival a grown man, and mine is more like that of a small child. "I'll never be able to get off the ground," I mutter to myself as we walk through the door to the studio.

The first thing I notice is that it's really cool in the room. Like, instant nip boner. I bring my arms up to cross around my body and pray that no one sees my headlights beaming. Lyn confidently marches ahead of me and waves to Lila, Maddi, and Stella. I give them a wave of my own and quickly cover myself up. How am I the only one freezing my ass off here?

"You girls ready to learn some moves?" Lyn asks the group with a huge smile.

"I'm just here for the workout. Mom says this is an amazing way to keep your body toned in a fun way," Maddi says with a smile. "Of course she would think that since she used to strip herself." She laughs when all three of us look at her in shock.

"Emmy? Aunt Emmy? Sweet little Emmy who has a husband so protective and possessive of her that he makes my dad look like a choirboy? That Emmy?" I ask, causing her to laugh even harder.

"Yup. Hard to believe, right? She doesn't talk much about it, but they have never kept secrets from us. They told us a few years ago when we were getting a lecture about what life choices can do to people. Or better yet, how some choices can lead to bad shit and even worse shit. Whatever. I forget the whole point of it, and when you think about it, it's what brought Mom and Dad back together, so it's kind of romantic." She waves her hands and turns to walk into the room I'm assuming class will be in.

"Did you just call stripping . . . romantic?" Lila giggles after Maddi.

"Oh shut it, Doc. It really is. I'll tell you the whole story later, but basically, some stuff went down and Mom got all weird and ran away.

Dad found her at a strip club of all places, and when she went to, you know, strip, he jumped on the stage and carried her out of the place over his shoulder. See? It's romantic."

"Uh, Maddi . . . if you think that's romantic, I would hate to see what happens when you have someone send you roses." Lyn snickers.

"Roses are boring. And overrated," Maddi snaps back.

God, I love my weird friends.

Twenty minutes later, I hate my weird friends.

We, of course, were the first to arrive. The room—a long, white rectangle—has ten poles going down a line and all facing the huge, daunting, floor-to-ceiling mirror. After the five of us filed in and were introduced to the instructors, Sarah and Felicia, they asked us to sit tight for a second while they waited for the other ladies who had signed up for the class. Who, of course, were late.

And now, here we are. After stretching every possible muscle in our bodies, the music still low, Sarah and Felicia got to work on some basic instructions. Instructions my short-as-hell ass was just struggling with.

"You want me to do what?" I ask Sarah again.

"Sweetheart, get it out of your head that you can't do this. It isn't about upper-body strength so much as it is about core strength. You're using your arms to pull, but you are pushing off with your feet, all the while using your core to hold. Don't focus so much on the mechanical stuff. Let your body do the work, and shortly, your mind will follow."

"How is my body supposed to climb this thing again?" I ask, watching Lyn, Lila, and Stella slowly worm their way halfway up their poles. Maddi—the little slut—is already practically hanging from the ceiling. Of course she would be a natural.

"Watch," Sarah says and grabs the pole with one hand. Then she reaches up and grabs the pole right above her other hand. She continues to alternate hands until she's standing on her toes. Then she mimics the movements with her feet. And just like that, the monkey-slash-instructor is in the air. She elegantly lands back on her feet and, with a wave, says, "Now you try."

It takes me a few times, but the next thing I know, I'm halfway up. "Woohoo!" I yell and stupidly remove my hands from the pole. My eyes widen about two seconds before I'm ass to the ground and once again cursing the pole.

"Next time, don't get so ballsy," Maddi laughs from the other side of the room, still twirling and swirling like she was made to be attached to a metal pole.

Okay, once I am out of my head, it really isn't so bad. It only takes me a few more times before I feel confident to try something new.

"Well done, ladies! Now it's time for the good stuff."

Oh, hell.

Another ten minutes and I'm having more fun than I ever thought was possible. I'm covered in sweat, but the moves we've learned against the pole—and some off the pole—have my body humming with confidence. Okay, Lyn was right. Not that I'll admit that to her.

I laugh when I see Lyn twist her body and almost fall off the heels on her feet. After about thirty minutes, we are told to shed the gym shoes for the heels we were asked to bring. Looking straight ahead to the mirror, I have to say that I look hot as hell.

My body looks tall with my five-inch heels, my legs long, tan, and toned. My gym shorts are looking more like sexy boy shorts at this point since they've all but ridden into my vagina. I'm normally not proud of my less-than-spectacular tits, but my small boobs are pushed up with my sports bra, and with the way I'm breathing, those barely-a-B cuppers are heaving like a busty pro. (Okay, so a B cup might be pushing it.) My cheeks are bright with all the exertion I've been putting out, my light-green eyes bright and shining with excitement, and my hair, which was in a long, perfectly stylized ponytail, is now looking more like a messy but sexy up do.

"All right, ladies. Class is almost over, so now it's time for the fun part. Each of you, grab a chair off the far wall. I want you to use that chair and pretend that it's whoever you need it to be. Work it like you mean it. Roll your hips, pop that ass, and make it mean something. Pole dancing isn't just a dance of seduction. It's an art form in how to get a man to crave you like you're the air he needs to breathe. Like, if he can't have his hands on you right that second, he is going to die. Make that chair crave you, ladies."

When she turns and changes the music, I look over and read the name off the iPad screen—Marian Hill's "Got It." The music starts off with the perfect beat to warm my body with. Her sultry and seductive voice feeds my newfound confidence. It isn't long before I'm lost in the sounds pulsing through the room. I move with ease and ignore the burn in my muscles when I bend over and grab my ankles with my hands, shaking my ass in the air . . . right where the object of my desire's face would be if he were sitting there.

With that image fresh in my brain, I end the dance giving it all I have. My hips are rolling and undulating in a feverish nature, so when I catch my refection in the mirror, even I have to admit that it's hot. Standing up, I run my hands from my neck, over the sides of my tits, and down to my inner thighs.

The music owns me.

It isn't until the song ends and the girls around me start to clap that I remember where I am and stand up quickly.

"Well done, Dani! I knew you had a little slut in you yet!" Maddi whoops from the corner where she is standing with Stella and Lila, who are giggling.

"Very good, Dani. If I didn't know better, I would have thought you weren't even seeing that chair, right?" Lyn knowingly jokes and throws her arm over my sweaty shoulder.

I don't say anything. Not even when Maddi keeps cracking jokes. Stella laughs a few times, but her focus is quickly lost when we walk out of the room and she sees that the gym filled up with hot guys since we went into the class almost two hours ago.

"Oh my God," Lila laughs.

"Uh oh," Maddi giggles.

"This is going to be so freaking good," Lyn chuckles just seconds before my elbow is grabbed and I'm spun around before looking at a very angry Cohen Cage.

"Shit," I mutter.

Chapter 7

Cohen

*I*T SHOULD HAVE BEEN AN easy workout. Chance, my roommate and ex-Marine brother, said that I needed to get my shit in gear and get off the couch since I would be shipping off in two weeks.

The plus side of being in a unit that was as dark as it gets is that we aren't reporting to a base every day and dealing with shit day in and day out. We report, but it isn't to a base in the middle of the public eye. No, our shit is buried deep. We have once-a-month training missions that can last up to two weeks. Those keep our skills sharp and our bodies ready.

We were lucky this time. Normally when we're needed overseas, things have gotten worse than they can control. Then we come in and clean house.

This time, we're being sent in with notice, which always means we're going to be gone for a long period of time with no set end date. We could be over there for a few months or over a year. Mom is her normal freaking-out-but-staying-strong-and-supportive self. Dad, I know, is worried, but he won't speak a word of it. He's been there.

The Special Forces unit I'm in is almost a carbon copy of the one he served on almost thirty years ago. He is more aware of the reality that I might not come home than anyone else is. But he also knows that this is very much a part of me and wouldn't dream of being anything less than supportive.

Chance served with me during our last deployment, but when we were ambushed and, in turn, he was injured, he was discharged honorably and has been heading up the personal security end of Corps Security ever since. We've been roommates on the home front ever since boot camp, and I wouldn't have it differently. He's just as much of a brother to me as Cam and Colt. He's been so busy in the two years since moving to town, often out of town for long periods, that he has rarely gone out with all of the crew.

"Yo, Cohen. Isn't that Maddox's daughter?" Pause. "Uh . . . and your sisters? And Axel's kid?"

My head was already turning when he mentioned one of Maddox's girls, then a little quicker when he mentioned the twins, but the second he mentioned Dani, my head snapped so rapidly that it's a shock I didn't break my own neck.

"What in the hell?" I ask, not expecting an answer.

"Damn, you didn't tell me the girls were looking like that these days," he grumbles and lets out a deep, "Umphh," when I elbow him in the gut.

"Shut the fuck up," I snap. "Is that the fucking pole dance room they just went in?"

"One in the same, brother," he laughs on a sharp exhale. "Did you have to give me all your strength, fucker?"

"Don't be such a baby. I hardly touched you."

"Hardly touched me. Well, Superman, you don't know your own strength."

I spend the next hour and then some fuming, imagining what is going on behind those doors. The more I think about it, the more I fume. I take it out on every piece of equipment I hit. I push my body to the edge just to get some of the anger out before the girls get out.

To make matters worse, what I thought would be a good idea to get my curiosity out of the way backfired in a big way. Ten minutes ago, I thought it was brilliant to just peek. Just a little peek to make sure there wasn't anything crazy going on. But that peek will forever be branded in my memory as one of the hottest things I've ever witnessed.

Dani coming unhinged and all but fucking the air between her and one black, metal chair.

I've been fighting a raging boner ever since one of the facility's staff members came and shut the door, giving me a warning about dis-enrollment if I am caught again.

Ever since then, her body and the way it looked, moved . . . Fuck me. I've been picturing every way I would take her when I finally hear Chance's voice break through my fantasy.

"Don't look now, Iron Man, but the girls have emerged, and now, they're all hot, flushed, and sweaty," he whispers down at me from where he's spotting my lifting.

I slam the bar home and leap off the bench, pausing to punch him in the gut again before I stomp through the gym.

"Oh my God," my sister, Lila, laughs.

"Uh oh," I hear Maddi giggle.

I don't even look at them.

"This is going to be so freaking good," Lyn chuckles right as my hand snags Dani around her tiny elbow and forces her to turn until her startled eyes are looking up into my own.

"Shit," she mumbles.

"What. The fuck. Was that?" I seethe.

"What was what?" she hedges.

"Do not fucking play games with me. You went into there to do what? Knit a sweater?"

She narrows her eyes but doesn't speak. I can hear my sisters laughing and look over to give them a hard stab of my eyes. I would never talk down to my girls, but right now, they're pushing the limits of my patience.

"I know what goes on in there, Dani-girl," I say and point behind her in the direction of the pole dancing room. Every man in this building knows what goes on in that room. We've been watching fine-as-hell chicks go in and out of there for years. The instructors alone are enough to keep some of these douchebags going for years in jack-off fantasies. "What I want to know is what in the *fuck* you think you're going to do with what you learned in there, Dani? Hm? Who in the hell is he?"

I can't stop the shit coming out of my mouth now. Ever since that night in her bed when I watched her sick with a fever dream all night with my name escaping her lips, all I've been able to think about is Dani. The only thing I've wanted is to throw her over my shoulder and take what my body keeps screaming is mine.

But it isn't mine.

Not yet. If I weren't about to ship off for a future unknown, I would throw her down and take her right fucking now. The only problem is, as much as I want her, I won't take something when I can't give her anything in return. And unfortunately, right now, I can't give her anything but the next two weeks. For a woman like Dani, that would never be enough. However, that doesn't mean I'm going to sit on my thumbs and let her show that sweet body off, work herself in preparation for someone else.

I do *not* think so.

"That isn't any of your business," she huffs and pulls her arm out of my hold.

"You don't think?" I ask, narrowing my eyes to slits.

"I don't think. I know."

"That's where you're wrong, baby." I step into her space and wait for her to make the next move.

"I'm not wrong, Cohen. Realistic. I'm not the one who's afraid. I haven't been afraid to admit how I feel for a long time. You, on the other hand, well . . . I'm sick of waiting for you to come to terms with it. Time to move on." She crosses her arms, and I want to groan when it brings attention to her tits. I've always been a breast man, but even though she isn't huge, there is more than enough to fit perfectly in my palms and I've been thinking about it for way too long.

"I'm not afraid of you," I scoff.

"You're terrified," she challenges.

"You're delusional."

"Ha! As if. Have a good workout, Cohen." She reaches up and pats my cheek, still trying to play off this indifference. If her palm didn't linger a little too long on my stubble, then I would possibly believe her.

What happened to my sweet Dani-girl?

I watch with a slack jaw as she turns, her long ponytail slapping me in the face, and struts out of the gym. My sisters, Maddi, and Stella all trail behind her, laughing.

Chapter 8

Dani

MY BODY IS SHAKING SO badly that, once we clear the gym's front doors and get out of sight of the windows, I almost collapse.

"I am so proud of you," Lyn says, reaching out to take my black heels out of my hand so I don't drop them. You do not drop Louboutins on the ground. Ever.

"Holy crap, that felt . . . amazing! I mean, I kind of feel like I'm going to puke, but holy crap!"

"Told you. Confidence. It means everything when dealing with men."

"When did you get so smart?" I ask her, trying to calm my heart down after that showdown with Cohen.

"When you started letting your hormones take over your common sense."

"Bitch," I laugh.

"Slut," she smiles.

That night, I'm pretty sure I am still feeling the adrenaline of my

Cohen showdown. He sent me a text shortly after that simply read, "We need to talk," to which I responded with a very mature, "No we do not." He didn't reply, but then again, that isn't Cohen's style. When he wants something, he just takes it. I have a feeling that, the next time I run into him, there will be a whole lot of taking.

Daddy was up when I came home, but I'd left the heels in the car and pulled on some sweatpants and a hoodie over my normal workout gear. He narrowed his eyes, but didn't say anything. I swear that man knows everything.

It is most definitely time to move the hell out.

"Dani?" I hear Mom yell from the kitchen.

"Hey, Mom. What's up?"

"Nothing much, sweetheart. I just wanted to let you know your father and I are going up to the mountains next weekend." She looks up from her dinner prep and gives me a smile.

My mom, even at her age, with some gray hair mixed into her dark-red locks, is beautiful. You would never guess that she has two children. She's just a little taller than I am, but where I got all slim and small, she has the curves. I'm pretty much an exact replica of my mom—which is why Daddy has called me his little princess since the day I was born. Mom is his princess, so it makes sense.

"And you're letting me know this because you're worried Nate will starve?"

She gives me another smile. "No, my smartass daughter. I'm letting you know this and telling you that there are some boxes in the attic that you can use and giving you a heads-up that I'll have your very loving but overprotective father hours away and unknowing for four days. Plenty of time for you and the girls to get you packed up and moved into their new townhouse. Melissa and I checked it out this afternoon, and it's in a gated community, so when your father does become aware that you moved out on a sneak attack, he will only be upset for a little while."

I look up at my mom and have to fight back the emotion. Not because she is basically kicking me out—lovingly, of course—but because she is giving me the one thing I have been basically begging for.

"You're helping me escape?" I whisper.

"I'm not helping you escape, sweetheart. That would imply that we've been holding you hostage," she laughs. "I would keep you home for as long as I could, but I know you need to fly. And if I don't help make sure it's at least done in a way that your father can't argue about when he does find out, then you're never going to convince him that you aren't his little toddler just learning how to walk. He was made to protect you, baby. He loves you and it comes from a good place, but even I can admit it's time."

"What about Nate?" I ask.

"What about him? That big old baby wouldn't know what to do without me to wash his clothes and feed him."

I laugh because she is not wrong.

She turns and walks over to the sink to wash her hands. After drying them off, she walks over to me and gives me a big hug. I soak up the strength of her love and pull back to look into her eyes.

"You're okay with this? He's going to be so mad," I laugh.

"I'm okay with it. And your father mad isn't a bad thing if you know how to calm him down," she jokes with a wink.

"God, Mom! That is so gross."

We both laugh, and I thank my lucky stars that I lucked out with such amazing parents.

"Why don't you go change out of your gym clothes and those sweats you think fool anyone with. Then you can come down here and tell me what's going on with you and Cohen."

I gasp and look at her in shock. "What? How?"

"Oh you silly girl," she says and tucks a piece of hair that fell from my ponytail behind my ear. "Not only have I been watching this unfold for years, but I watched him all but fly out of here the morning after he stayed with you. Not only that, but the twins are chatty with their mom, and their mom is chatty with me."

"Oh, God. This is so embarrassing."

"I don't see why. Just because I haven't been screaming it doesn't mean that I haven't been your biggest cheerleader when it comes to you ending up with Cohen. Go get changed and come fill your mom in. I think we have about an hour before the men come looking for food."

I make my way up to my room and think about everything she just said. Obviously, the girls didn't know or they would have said something today. I can't believe she and Melissa went through all of this trouble. Especially knowing that Daddy is going to hit the fucking roof when he comes home to find I've moved out.

This should be fun. Maybe I can talk the camera crew from work into following me home. You know, for video evidence if he snaps and starts to go all Hulk-raging mad.

"Start from the beginning, Dani. I'm having a hard time following here. Lyn said what now?" Mom asks and hands me the spoon to stir the sauce.

"Okay, so we might have had too much wine, but she had some brilliant idea that all I need to do is work on my confidence when it comes to my . . . sexual side, and then the rest of it will fall into place with Cohen."

"And she said this because why? Because you've been a little shy with him lately?"

"Mom! Yes. It's been terrible. Ever since he was here with me when I was sick, things have just been weird. It's like my body is hyperaware of him when he comes around. Then boom, I turn into a mute freak."

She laughs, stirs the noodles and moves over to work on the salad.

"Sweetheart, that—everything you're feeling—is completely normal. You and Cohen have been traveling two different roads on the way to this point for so long that it only makes sense that there will be a head-on crash when you finally connect. You should listen to her. She's right."

"I am listening to her. That's why we went to the pole dancing class," I mumble.

"You did what?" she asks, shocked.

"We went to a pole dancing and sensual empowerment class at the gym. It was a lot of fun, but it really worked. And . . . uh, Cohen was there when we left."

"Oh wow. And how did that go?"

"I think my heart is still about to beat out of my chest."

She laughs and reaches over to pull me toward her body. "That, my sweet girl, is the calm before the storm. If you think that is powerful, just wait until you're hit with it full force."

I shiver and she laughs.

"What are my girls in here gossiping about?" Daddy says, coming into the room and around the island to give me a kiss on the forehead and one to Mom that has me looking away.

"You two really need to remember that some things can't be unseen," I gripe.

"Little princess, just how do you think you got into this world?" he asks and then booms out a laugh when I cringe.

I look over at Mom, who gives me a wink, and shake my head when Daddy continues to laugh.

I watch them both for a little while and pray, not for the first time, that one day I'll have what they have.

Hopefully one day soon.

Chapter 9

Dani

"**D**AD IS GOING TO KICK your ass," Nate grumbles under the weight of my favorite reading chair that he and Liam are carrying up to my new bedroom.

The townhouse that Mom and Melissa picked out for the twins, Maddi, and me is a lot more than just that. It's a freaking townhouse on crack. It's a five-bedroom, three-story, huge-ass house located in one of the best gated communities around. She clearly downplayed it. I expected them to have put the house in their name, which I would have had a huge problem with, but Thursday morning, I had a call from the realtor asking me to meet him in his office on my lunch break. Seems my mom and Melissa had gone above and beyond. They had put first and last months' rent as a down payment and wouldn't even entertain the arguing. Emmy had been there with them. Three against four should have given us good odds—but then they brought out the big guns and started to talk about 'the dads' finding out and what would they say if we weren't in the best of the best.

Whatever.

We signed the lease, all four of us, and in less than thirty minutes, we were handed the keys.

It was amazing!

It's been two days since Mom took Dad up to the mountains, and I've enlisted Nate and Liam to help me get the heavy stuff out of my room. Mom told me to take all the furniture, but I felt too bad about it knowing that, if Daddy came home to an empty room, he very well might have heart failure. My new bedroom suite is being delivered tomorrow. Maddi and I went in on the living room stuff and entertainment systems. Lyn and Lila picked up the kitchen and patio furniture.

"If he kicks my ass, what's going to happen to you? You're the one who helped me move out!" I laugh when his face pales.

"Don't be such a baby, Nate," Liam says, continuing to lift the chair up the stairs.

I give him a smile. Liam Beckett, Aunt Dee and Uncle Beck's son, has been my best friend for so long that I couldn't imagine moving out and not having him here to witness this moment. I've been begging for him to come help hold my dad back so I could make my escape for years. I've always been close with Liam. Our mothers have been friends forever, and since we're close in age, we just kind of became buds. We were born close together, so we were lucky to grow up together and hit each grade in the same class. There was one year—third, I think—that we weren't in the same class. Mom and Aunt Dee say all the time that I cried for weeks until they realized I wouldn't stop until the school moved Liam into my class.

I don't believe it for a second. Even if there is home video footage of it somewhere.

"Lee, where did you put the keys to my car?" I call up the stairs, where he and Nate climbed with my reading chair.

"I don't know, Dani. Look by the front door table thingie!" he yells down.

"It's an accent table, doofus!" I yell back.

"What the hell ever that is," I hear him grumble.

I spend the next few minutes looking all over for my car keys. I need to get the last of my clothes and shoes out so I can start organizing my closet. My purses and the first, second, and third waves of my clothes and shoes came over early this morning. The girls left to get dinner a little while ago, so I knew they wouldn't be any help.

"Where the hell are they?" I grumble, looking in the coat closet before moving into the living room, which is just off the entryway, and bending over to look under the couch.

"Looking for these?"

I jump when I hear Cohen speak in a gruff tone just behind me. Coming off the floor with a squeal, I land right in his arms, my back pressed firmly against his chest and his arms clasping my arms to keep my steady.

"You jerk! Are you trying to give me a heart attack!?" I yell as I push back against him and try to move away. I realize my mistake instantly when I feel him go statue still and his harsh intake of breath against my ear. Then I feel him, really feel him, hard and hot against my back, and it's my turn to groan.

"I wasn't trying to sneak up on you." His hips move almost as if they have a mind of their own. "You just didn't hear me call your name."

"Can you let me go?" I ask.

"Why, Dani-girl? Scared?" He hums when I push back lightly and roll my hips.

"Hardly. Just depends on if you want Nate and Lee to see you manhandling me when they come down here." I'm only half joking. I wouldn't call what I'm feeling scared. Well, not scared of him. Scared of the enormity of these feelings? Absolutely.

"I'll hear them coming," he responds.

His hands shift, and then he spins me so that we're facing. I look up until our eyes meet, and my breath comes out in a whoosh.

"You're so beautiful," he mumbles.

"Thanks," I reply lamely. Thanks?

He laughs and drops his head some, his brown eyes becoming so dark that they're almost black.

And that's when I hear dumb and dumber with the worst-possible timing in the world arguing about real tits versus fake tits, stomping down the stairs. Cohen drops his forehead against mine, gives my arms a squeeze, and then steps back. I watch, baffled, as he reaches out and holds my car keys up. Mutely, I take them from his hooked finger and watch as he walks away, over to my brother and Lee and starts to weigh in on their conversation.

Humiliatingly enough, he sides with the fake tit side.

Cohen

I could be agreeing that the sky is green and the grass is blue. I have no fucking clue what these two are talking about. I enter in and pretend I have a care about the topic, grunting when I feel would be appropriate, and steal glances over at Dani as she drops her shoulders, her head dropping and her eyes focused on the floor in front of her. She looks so deflated. I just want to pull her back in my arms and take that kiss that was just seconds away from finally happening. Take her in my arms and promise her the world.

But then I remember why I've been holding back and realize I made the right move. She gives me a sad glance before squaring her shoulders and walking out the front door.

I finally tune in to the conversation around me and shake my head when I realize what they're talking about.

"If you prefer fake tits, then something is wrong with you, Nate,"

I say and sigh. "There is something to be said about feeling a woman, all woman, in your palms and you just can't get the same feelings when you can feel a bag of fluid rolling around under your fingertips."

They both look at me like I'm a fool, and I look between the two of them while playing my words back in my head, trying to figure out what the hell their issue is.

"Dude, two seconds ago, you agreed with me when I said big, huge, fake tits is the way to go." Nate reaches out and puts his hand against my forehead before continuing. "Are you feeling okay there, big guy?"

Belatedly, it hits me that Dani might have heard me, and I groan. Shit.

"I'm fine, asshole. I just have a lot on my mind." Which isn't a lie. I have a shitload of things I need to do before I leave, and on top of all that, this thing, whatever it is, between Dani and me has me running in circles around myself.

"Sure you do, Coh. Do you need anything?" Nate asks, no trace of humor left in his tone.

"Nah. Just need to work on things myself. I've got some loose ends I need to tie up before I leave. Mom and the girls are having a hard time with it. Cam and Colt haven't said as much, but I know they're worried, and Dad is being Dad." All true. I leave out that I also need to figure out what the hell I'm going to do with Dani too before I leave. If I leave things how they are, knowing I'll be gone for a while, I'll constantly be thinking about it. If anything, I need to sit her down and at least explain why I'm holding back when it's clear we both want this.

Well, it's clear to me that I want her and she wants me. I'm guessing she has no clue the depth of my desire for her.

"Makes sense. Don't worry though. We'll watch out for the girls," Lee, ever the peacekeeper and do-gooder, says.

If Dani were best friends with any other guy, I would probably shit a green brick of jealousy, but not with Liam. He's helped me chase off more guys than I can remember, and I have no doubt he will continue when I leave.

"Thanks, Lee." I slap him on the shoulder and give him a nod before I head to the door in search of Dani. I almost run into her when she comes back in with a stack of shoeboxes taller than she is. "Whoa, Dani!" Reaching up, I snag a few boxes and smile when her flushed face comes into view. "Show me to your room?"

She nods, walks around me, and moves up the stairs. I watch her firm ass with rapture with each step I climb behind her.

Yeah . . . we definitely need to have a talk.

Chapter 10

Dani

*I*CAN'T DO THIS ANYMORE. I just can't. This hot-and-cold shit with him. Me suddenly forgetting how to act like a normal adult around him. All of it. I'm just so tired of it all.

I've always known he would be stupid to love. I've known it since before I made that last tumble ass over elbows and landed in a mass of limbs. I knew before the fall that it would be a painful tumble, but I still jumped and fell in love with him regardless.

"Dani, look at me," he implores when we step in to my room and place the boxes on the floor of my walk-in closet. "Please," he adds.

With a deep breath, I turn and look him in the eye. Gone is the boiling lust, and what's taken its place is acceptance that we won't ever be.

"Talk to me," he pleads.

"What do you want me to say? You know how I feel, Cohen. I've told you before. I know you heard me in my sleep when I was sick. Plus, there is this . . . thing between us. Bottom line—you know how I feel and it isn't your fault that you don't return those feelings." I sigh and sit down on my chaise lounge, which Nate and Lee just placed in the middle of my room. "I'm tired of feeling like I need to run or act a certain way around you. It used to be easier to hide the way I feel."

"I don't want you to hide. Not from me."

I feel my brows pull in at his words, confused by the mixed signal.

"I don't want you to be anything but yourself around me," he continues. "I just don't know what to do about this, Dani. I know what's right here. I know what I should and shouldn't do when it comes to you. It's just getting harder to keep those lines from blurring."

"What are you saying, Cohen? Spit it out in plain terms so I don't get your words mixed up and seek hope when there isn't any to be found."

His face hardens, and he takes a step towards me, leaning down, placing his hands on either side of my hips, and not stopping his body until his face is level with mine. His harsh breaths hit my lips, and I lean back, only to stop when his body follows the movement.

"When you were fifteen and you sat in my parents' basement, you told me that, one day, I would see you the way you see me. You told me that you would be waiting, Dani. Waiting for me to become yours and you mine. I wasn't ready, but that doesn't mean that I didn't see you and haven't seen you every day since and thought about what it would be to have you. You told me you would be waiting. You sat there with all the courage in the world and laid it out there, Dani. Are you telling me now that you take it back?"

"You remember that?" I gasp.

When he starts talking next, I swear that my heart stops. Shock. But complete wonderment. His voice, a pitch higher, whispers the words I said to him almost eight years ago verbatim. I should know—I practiced them for weeks in the mirror before I worked up the courage to actually say them to him. They were words I would never forget. Especially since he treated me with the indifference of a good friend after—until recently.

"I'm going to miss you, Cohen. I know you don't look at me like I look at you, but one day, you're going to come back and I'll still be waiting for you. Waiting for you to see me like I see you. Mark my words, Cohen Cage. One of these days, you're going to be mine. And until you're ready . . . I'll be here. I'll be waiting."

Holy shit.

"Holy shit," I repeat out loud when he stops talking. "I can't believe you remember that."

"I will never forget it," he vows.

"What does that even mean?" I throw back. Once again, here he goes with his hot-and-cold shit.

"That means exactly that. I won't ever forget it. Just because I haven't acted on this chemistry between us doesn't mean I don't want to. Back then, I couldn't. You know that it wouldn't have been appropriate with our ages. And now . . . Now, I don't even know what it is because my head is in a million different places right now. But one thing I know is that I'm getting ready to leave. I'm getting ready to leave and, Dani, I just can't put you in the position of being in limbo for months, years, who knows, just so that I can feel what *you* feel like." He drops his head against mine and sighs. "I've never wanted someone as fiercely as I want you, Dani-girl."

The tone of his voice is so heartbreaking that my chest clenches.

"I wish it were a different world. One where I wasn't leaving and our future wasn't unknown. If it were, you would have been mine already." He gives me a sad, small kiss against my forehead—not pulling back for a few beats. He looks me in the eyes again before pulling himself up and walking out the door.

Well, if that doesn't suck, I don't know what does.

I might be grasping at straws here . . . but what he didn't say was that we didn't have a future at all. Just that he wasn't sure what it was.

It's not much hope—but it's something. And that was more than I had an hour ago.

Chapter 11

Dani

Two weeks later

"DANI!" NATE YELLS UP THE stairs, his impatience clear as day. He just got here two minutes ago to pick me up and he's already reached his patience level.

"What?"

"You need to stop putting all that shit on your face so we can get going."

"I'm not 'putting that shit' on my face, Nate!" I yell back as I recap my mascara and go over my lips again with bright-red lipstick, giving myself one more look to make sure everything is perfect. I have to look perfect today.

Summer has come to stay in Georgia. If my daddy saw me now, I'm sure he would have a fit over my outfit. I'll have to deal with him later, but he won't be able to do anything but complain about it by then. My jean shorts are just shy of what I would consider normal. They cover everything but show a lot—and I mean a lot—of leg. My red tank top is tight and gives me just enough of cleavage.

I look hot.

Really hot.

My legs look amazing. Like, off-the-charts ahhhmazing. The shorts matched with my heels make them look longer than they are. Weeks of working daily at the gym and a few more pole dancing classes have them toned to perfection, and thanks to the sun, my tan is the perfect shade of dark. My long, chestnut locks are hanging down my back in soft waves, giving them that "I woke up like this" look even though it took me almost an hour to get each curl perfect. But my makeup might take the cake. Maddi did it before she left the house, going heavy on my eyes so that my green peepers would pop like crazy. I'm not vain, but I can safely admit that I look hot as hell.

It really is a shame that I look this good and I know it might not do any good. I'm frustrated. Ever since that day in my room, Cohen has been like a ghost. Any chance I thought I might have had to try to further our conversation was just kicked like a bug. He just disappeared.

Okay, he didn't disappear, but he didn't exactly make it so that we could ever be alone to have a private chat. Nope. If I tried, he just wasn't having it. He was hell-bent on keeping his distance, and that shit is ending tonight.

Nate pulls up to the event hall—a rustic, old log cabin—and grunts a few times when he looks over at me, clearly trying to tell me by his caveman speech that he isn't happy about my outfit.

"What is your problem?" I ask, crossing my arms across my chest.

His eyes narrow, and he grunts again.

I give him a few grunts of my own. What the hell? Maybe he'll understand what I'm trying to express verbally if I try to dumb it down to alpha speak.

"What are you doing?" he asks with his head tilting like a confused dog when I grunt a few more times.

"Well, dear brother, I'm trying to see if I attempt to vocalize as you and our father do that maybe you'll answer me back. Clearly, I have no idea what has your panties in a twist today. You've been all snappy snapperson since we left my house."

"You."

"Uh . . . can we add a few words to that, maybe a dramatic pause for flair and express a coherent thought that is well thought out and planned to make sense so that it can be understood and processed?"

"God, you can be such a bitch."

I smile. "Oh? You say that like it's a bad thing."

He sighs and looks out the front window.

"Seriously, Nate, what's going on?"

"It's nothing, Dani. I'm taking my bad mood out on you. Doesn't help that you're dressed like a tramp just to gain Cohen's attention."

I look down at my outfit again. I don't think it's trampy. Sure, it's showing my legs off and my top is tight, but I'm hardly indecent.

"Okay, tramp might be too much, but couldn't you have worn something that, I don't know, covers all of that under your neck?" He gestures wildly to my body.

"You're being ridiculous. And I'm not wearing anything *for* Cohen. It's summer, in Georgia, and, like, over a hundred degrees. I'm pretty sure this is considered overdressed by most."

Okay, so I'm lying. He knows it. It could be considered slightly manic in my desperateness to get some sort of reaction from him.

"You're only going to get hurt, Dani," he whispers so low that I almost miss it, and hearing him confirming my biggest fear brings tears to my eyes.

"You don't know that," I argue weakly.

He does know that though. Cohen's his best friend. Regardless of the fact that he probably doesn't like that I've always crushed on him, he's never tried to stop me. Until now.

"What do you know, Nate?"

He doesn't say anything for the longest time. He just continues to look out the window, taking in all of our extended family as they mill about the parking lot and outside the venue. I follow his gaze when I see it soften slightly and see Ember Locke waving at our direction. Her face falls when Nate doesn't acknowledge her and she looks over at me. I give her a weak smile but bring my attention back to my brother.

"He's bringing a date, Dani."

And cue heart stop.

It just drops right into my stomach.

In all the years I've loved Cohen Cage from afar, he's never, not once, brought one of his dates around the family. I'm not stupid. I know he dates. He practically has girls falling over themselves to get his attention. But throughout the years, he's never brought them around. And with everything that's been going on between us for over a month now, I really didn't think he would stoop this low just to get me to leave him alone. Maybe he didn't mean to leave a trail of hope in his little goodbye speech the other day.

"What?" I gasp.

"You heard me, Dani. Don't make me say it again."

"Is it . . . is it serious?"

"He's bringing her, isn't he?" He looks over, and I can tell he hates that he is hurting me right now. "I've only met her a few times. She's nice enough. I honestly don't know her or their relationship well enough to tell you any more. He's bringing Chance, too."

"Oh," I say, looking back out the window.

"Yeah, oh," he parrots, reaching over and grabbing my hand to give me a strong, reassuring squeeze. "Come on, little princess. Let's get this over with."

When we make it inside, things are predictably insane. Whenever we all get together, things tend to go that way. I love my family, but sometimes—like right now—they're just too much.

The room is huge, set up that way to ensure plenty of space for the number of guests they plan on attending. Numerous tables are scattered throughout the middle of the room, with some space for the food tables, DJ, a bar, and a huge stage set up across the room. It's typically used for small, local concerts and some wedding receptions. I guess you could consider it country chic, with the log cabin look from outside continuing inside. They've added crystal chandeliers to the vaulted ceilings and carried the décor to the table settings. Mason jars full of wildflowers are at each table, American flags sticking out the center of each, with a red-white-and-blue theme for each table. My attention goes back to the large stage, which takes up the whole back end of the room. It's covered in a thick, red curtain—and I officially decide that it will be my escape later.

Obviously, Mom, Dee, and Melissa went all out. I see Mom at the far side of the large room talking to Dee and Emmy. She's waving her arms around like a windmill, so she's clearly worked up about something. Daddy is standing by the bar with Beck and Asher. He looks up when we walk in. As always, he knows when one of his girls is near, and I have no doubt, judging by the way his eyes go hard, that he knows I'm upset. Or he's noticed my outfit. I give him a bright smile, which he doesn't buy for one second, and I move around Nate to go find Maddi.

She left the house almost an hour before me to come and help set up. The girls had spent the night back at their parents' house so that they could spend more time with their brother, so I knew they wouldn't be here yet.

Liam stops me before I even get two feet into my quest for Maddi to say hey and gives me a big hug.

"Are you okay?" he asks, not even breaking to say hello.

Another infuriating side effect of being surrounded by overprotective alpha males is their inability to leave well enough alone. They sense that one of the females in our group is upset and they just can't *not* try to fix it.

"Stop, Lee. Don't turn on your protector crap right now. I get it enough from Nate and Daddy. I'm fine. Just fine," I snap.

"Uh, right. I'm just . . . I'll just go find Zac and Jaxon now." He holds his hands up in a mock surrender and walks slowly backwards. Away from me and my special brand of crazy.

I watch him walk away until he stops where Asher and Chelcie's boys are standing with Cam and Colt.

"Aren't you a happy camper. You were fine an hour ago. How could your day change so swiftly?" Maddi laughs, coming up to my side and wrapping her arm over my shoulders.

I allow myself two seconds of soaking up her support before I duck under her arm, grab her hand, and drag her through the tables and out the back door.

"What in the hell," she mumbles, struggling to keep up with me. Which is laughable, really, with her long legs against my short ones.

I let the back door slam behind us and pull her farther behind the building and the dumpsters. No way I'm chancing anyone overhearing us.

"What has gotten in to you, Dani?" Maddi inquires when I finally drop her hand.

"Did you know that Cohen was bringing a date?"

"Do what? You're kidding, right?"

"Dead serious," I all but yell. "Nate just told me in the car that he was bringing someone. That's all I know. But, Maddi . . . surely it's serious if he's bringing her here! Oh my God, oh my God. I need to leave. That's what I need to do."

"Actually, you should probably just try and calm your shit down and stop acting like the world is over. It's Cohen. I'm sure that she is just a friend or something. I don't know, maybe she's homeless and he is bringing her so she can get a meal. Maybe she is part alien and using him to get to know our culture. Whatever the case may be, you freaking yourself out over it isn't going to do a bit of good."

"Why do you have to make so much sense?" I ask sarcastically after she stops talking.

She, in turn, gives me a glare that would make her father proud.

"Aliens? Really?" I laugh.

"Oh, shut up. And you know I make sense because I'm the smart one. Plus, with the twins not here yet, someone has to keep your ass from overacting. Oh! I know. Let's call Lyn. She'll know what's up."

She pulls her cell out of her back pocket, and after a few seconds of fiddling with it, she presses it to her ear.

"Hey," she says into the phone. "Are you alone?"

This is ridiculous. I should just leave now and save myself the gut-crushing pain of seeing another woman in his arms.

"Is Cohen bringing a date?" she whispers and looks around the side of the dumpster.

"No one is coming, Maddi," I whisper back.

"Then why are you whispering too, smarty pants?" she snaps and turns her attention back to her phone call. "I know that, Lyn, but Nate told Dani that he was and now she's freaking the hell out . . . I don't know where he heard it . . . No . . . Well, then who is she?"

Oh shit. It's true. I should definitely leave. Maybe if I cut through the woods to the industrial park, some nice trucker will take me to Mexico.

"Oh really? Oh . . . yeah . . . No . . . Shit. Okay. Bye." She looks down at her phone before looking up at me. Her eyes hold nothing but sympathy.

"It's true?"

"Looks like it," she whispers before pulling me into her arms.

"Okay, plan B. Let's turn this frown upside down. So he's got a friend with him. We don't know anything else, so let's just pretend they're friends and just friends. Lyn didn't know much. Just that her mom told her that he's brought her by the house a few times this last week. That's all she knows. Let's try not to stress about it, okay? You, my friend, look hot, so let us just enjoy the day. You continue to be hot, and aside from being polite, ignore him and his special friend. There will be plenty of other guys here tonight, so it's time to get your flirt on. Do you need me to go sneak you some booze?"

"Maddi, I'm old enough to drink. I don't need you to sneak me anything anymore." I laugh.

"Right. Well, it's time to act like you could care less and have some fun. Don't let this hang over you—not tonight. Tonight is about making sure Cohen knows his family loves him before he leaves. No sad faces or jealous eyes. This thing between you two will work itself out, I promise."

"Yes, sir, Maddi, sir." I salute her, and after a few giggles, we take off on a mission to practice my acting.

I've always been good at acting.

Even if I feel like my heart is breaking inside.

It isn't his fault I feel this way and he doesn't. Or I should say that I feel this way and he isn't willing to let himself.

One thing's for certain though. If Cohen Cage wanted me like I want him, he never would have let it go this long without taking it. Taking me and never letting go. Instead, he's just playing more games in his quest to keep me at arm's length. Because *he* is making decisions about the future without even considering that maybe I believe he's worth waiting for.

Time to put on my big-girl panties and pretend that the other half of my heart isn't going to be in the arms of another woman.

Chapter 12

Dani

"LITTLE PRINCESS, WHAT THE HELL are you wearing?" Daddy rumbles, taking my beer out of my hands. "No," he snaps, playfully slapping my hand and takes a sip.

"I don't think so," I laugh and grab it back.

He raises one dark brow but doesn't make a move to take my drink again. He had the hardest time when I turned twenty-one and could legally drink. He kept switching out my beers for apple juice the whole night.

"Want to tell me what has you down so I can go fix it?"

"Nothing is wrong, Daddy," I mumble into my cup.

"Right. You get that I wasn't born yesterday, yeah?"

"Oh yeah, I know that. You were born, like, fifty years ago."

I snicker to myself when he starts bristling. He hates to be reminded that he's over that fifty hump. I've seen pictures of him when he was my age, and honestly, if it weren't for the light peppering of gray, you would never know he was fifty-one. He's still one of the largest men I've ever met. He towers over Mom and me at six foot six, with muscles that have only gotten bigger and bulkier over the years. It's clear to not just me, but every friend I have had over the years that my daddy wasn't just hot when he was younger—he still has it.

"Don't think I didn't notice you going solid when the twins got here. Did you girls get into a fight? Does this mean you need to come home now?"

I roll my eyes and laugh. He's been trying to find reasons to get me to move home ever since he got back from his trip and realized I was gone. For a whole day, he wouldn't leave my living room. I think he would still be there if Mom hadn't shown up. All it took was her to whisper in his ear, and just like that, they were gone.

Of course the first conclusion he comes to is that the girls and I are fighting. He probably wishes we were. Which is really silly because one thing about Lyn's, Lila's, and my friendship—we don't fight. We never have and I don't see it happening any time soon.

Okay, well, time to divert his attention.

"Nope. We're fine. It was . . . uh, cramps, Daddy. You know, period stuff."

He looks horrified. Which was the goal. Daddy doesn't talk female issues. I asked him once to grab me some tampons from the store one day. He threatened to take Nate's car away if he didn't go instead. Nate came back thirty minutes later and threw the box at my head, cutting me right above the eyebrow and losing his car anyway for hurting me. To this day, I like to leave tampon boxes in Nate's car.

"Uh . . . yeah. I'm going to go over here with the guys and talk about football and boxing. You know, guy stuff."

I smile to myself when he walks away. God, he's too easy.

"Cramps, my ass," Liam laughs, throwing his arm around my shoulders and pulling me close. His strong hold makes it clear that I'm not getting away without talking to him.

I take a deep swallow of my beer and look up into his chocolate eyes.

"I don't think they're dating, if it makes a difference. He's hard-ly said one word to her, and she is sticking close to Chance's side. Chance, who I'm guessing isn't dating her either, looks like he would rather be anywhere else than glued to her side."

I look across the room where Cohen is talking to his brothers, Camden and Colton. As if he senses my gaze on him, his eyes meet mine, and he frowns when he sees Lee's arm around me. His eyes move back to mine, and even from the distance, I can see them heat. That fire that burns across my skin.

Okay, so he still wants me.

What the hell ever.

"Yeah, that right there. A man doesn't get jealous of someone he knows is just a friend if there isn't something else there, Dani. I've told you this a million times over: he's scared. Think about it and you know I'm right. His parents, your parents, all of the relationships mixed in that would go insane if you two got together. Sure, it could have a hap-py ending, but he isn't going to upset the fold. Not when it could just as easily go bad."

"It wouldn't go bad, Lee." And it wouldn't. I know it with every-thing I am that it would be a flawless love.

"You can't know that. Not for sure, anyway. Regardless of what your stubborn little heart tells you, you can't predict these things."

"Are you telling me I should give it up? Give him up?"

"Never, Dani. I would never tell you to give him or your feelings for him up. You know my parents' story. Dad never once gave up on Mom, even when it seemed fruitless. What I'm trying to get at, but clearly doing a terrible job of, is that if you believe with one hundred percent of your soul that he's your other half, don't you dare stop until you've had a taste of it."

Oh shit. My throat is burning. I swallow thickly and nod my head, not trusting my words.

"Do you think he knows how bad it is?"

"That you're in love with him and that you don't just want him to fuck you?" Liam guesses correctly.

"Yeah, that."

"He isn't stupid, Dani. He knows. Or at least he has an idea. Look, before, it wouldn't have been good for him to even entertain the thought. You were too young. I'm not saying that isn't an issue for him now, but you're almost twenty-two, so I don't think that's it. You know him. You know how important his family . . . this family . . . is to him. All I can tell you is to talk to him. He leaves tomorrow. Just talk to him. I know you guys talked before, but obviously, you didn't talk enough. Make him hear your points, and don't leave anything out. You say that he's saying no because he's leaving . . . well, don't let that stop you. If it's really that simple, then go for it."

"What about that girl?" I question, my mouth having a hard time getting the question out.

God, he's right. I'm eaten up with jealousy over her. She's pretty. Blond, busty, and tall. Everything I'm not. She is my complete opposite in every way.

"Who? The date? Yeah . . . something tells me you really don't have to worry about her. Seriously, Dani. She hasn't gotten up from that table he parked her at when he got here. If a girl were here with a man like him, you better believe she wouldn't be leaving his side. In case you haven't noticed, there are a few overly horny men in this room."

"You're so sick." I laugh and look up at Liam's smiling, handsome face. "What would I do without you, Lee?"

"Probably get lost in life, Dani. It would be tragic. Just confused and walking in circles around reality all of the time."

I throw my head back and laugh. How absurd the thought is. He knows I'm as independent as it gets. But he's halfway right. Just like without the twins, I would be lost without Lee in my life. My skin tingles, and I stop laughing to look around the room. Cohen's stopped talking to his brothers and is scowling over at Lee and me. His hand grasping his beer is turning white around his fingertips.

"Uh oh. Could the bear just come out of hibernation? Looking at his prey for the first time since a long, cold, lonely winter?" Liam snickers.

"Shut up," I hush, punching him hard in the stomach, only to pull my hand back when his rock-hard abs cause millions of little tingles to shoot up my arm. "Did your body just break my hand!?" I screech when the pain won't stop.

"The hell?" I hear growled, and before I can react, Daddy wraps me in his arms and looks at my hand. I let the familiar scent of leather and cinnamon calm me down, and I fight back the stinging tears and burn in my throat. "Liam Beckett, did you break my daughter?!"

"Oh come on. She hit me! I didn't break her. Well, my perfectly chiseled body might have hurt her slightly. But it wouldn't be an issue if she would learn how to keep her hands off of me."

"You little shit," I laugh over my father's shoulders.

Liam laughs loudly, "I'll go get some ice for the big baby."

"Don't call my little princess a baby!" Daddy yells after Liam.

"I'm fine, just hit him weird," I say to soothe his worry.

"How many times do I have to tell you not to hit like that? I could see your form was off all the way across the room. Should have gone for the crotch. Always go for the crotch, Dani."

Oh lord, here we go. He's been teaching me how to kick a man's ass since I was five and Zac stole my doll. Of course, his first lesson was for me to always go for the crotch.

"Daddy, I wasn't trying to hurt him. We were just joking around."

"Joking around? You aren't supposed to *joke around* with boys. I need to look into that island. Ship your ass off," he grumbles under his breath.

It's going to be a long night.

Four long-as-hell hours later, the parents have all left. Which was a relief. Not that it isn't fun to have everyone around, but I know we're all ready to let loose and enjoy the night. They wanted to keep the beginning of the evening just the close families. More intimate so that way we could all spend some time with Cohen. Through the hours, more of our friends came—some of Cohen's from school and some from Basic Training. Everyone is ready to make sure he enjoys his last night home for the next year. This is his second deployment, and I don't think it will ever get easy.

Cohen joined the Marines after he finished his football career at University of Georgia. He probably could have gone pro, but he's always wanted to follow his father's footsteps and join the Marines. Then again, for a boy who wore a cape for the majority of his childhood, it makes sense that the hero inside him would win.

The first time he went overseas, I was depressed for months. Worried, sad, and heartbroken. It was hard to watch his parents struggle with their worry and his siblings deal with the fear, and everyone in general just had a hard time knowing he was fighting in the middle of a war zone.

Like his father, mine, and the rest of the father figures in our close-knit family, Cohen was special ops, and when he was deployed, it was lights out for communication. It was months until we finally heard an update from him. In the thirteen months that he was gone, he was able to call home twice.

This time, he already warned his family that this would most likely be a longer tour. A longer tour and even less of a chance that he would be able to get in contact with us often.

I would be lying if I said that I wasn't terrified for him. Not because I have doubts in his abilities, but because of the very real fear that, no matter how trained he is, something terrible could happen to him over there.

"What's got that frown on your face, Dani-girl?"

God, that voice.

I suck in a deep breath when I feel Cohen sit down next to me. His smell instantly surrounds the dark haven I've escaped to. I thought I was doing a good job hiding back here. The party had gotten pretty rowdy when the parents left. Usually, I would be right there with them, but with Liam's words still floating around in my head, I just needed a moment to myself. To collect my thoughts and figure out a way to get him alone so I could force another talk.

When no one was looking, I walked behind the stage curtains, plopped my ass down in the middle of the floor, lay back, and let the vibrations of the DJ's music lull me and the darkness wrap around me like a comforting hug.

"Nothing, Cohen. Just thinking."

"Thinking about what?" he pushes.

"Are you scared?" I ask, sitting up on my elbows to look at him.

He turns his head but doesn't speak.

Given this opportunity to take him in, I don't waste a second. His dark eyes are looking directly into mine. Searching for what, I'm not sure, but one thing I'm certain of is that he isn't looking at me like a man who has a girlfriend should. Or whatever she is. His hair is freshly buzzed along the sides and slightly longer on the top, which makes me wonder who cut it for him since I know I didn't. He usually keeps it a little longer, perfect for all the times I've imagined running my fingers through it when I'm not in the middle of cutting it. The light beard he was sporting all year is gone, which allows his strong jaw to show. I love it when he shaves, but I also love the look of his beard. Every time he swallows, his jaw flexes in this sexy way I've never been able to control lusting over. Jaw porn. With Cohen, it's a very real thing.

I am staring at his lush, full lips when I realize I have been basically lusting over his face since he sat down. Shit.

When my eyes meet his, I expect to see humor at busting me, but all I see is the mirrored hunger I know is dancing behind my green eyes. His are heated, a deep fire blazing behind them. He isn't even attempting to hide his desire for me.

I hold my breath, waiting while the world stops spinning around me, and I go for it. Clearly, he's taken off guard when I all but leap off the stage flooring and into his lap. My legs fall on either side of his hips, my hands dive into that freshly cut hair—enjoying the prickle of the buzz against my palms—and my lips are on him before he has a second to figure out what my intentions are. He's solid and unmoving. If it weren't for his strong hands holding my hips in place, I probably would have gotten up and run away.

Pulling my lips off his motionless ones, I look into his shocked eyes and feel a heated blush of embarrassment wash over me.

"Oh my God. I'm . . . I . . . I shouldn't have done that."

He doesn't say anything, but he also doesn't let go of my hips when I try to move off him. It takes me a second for the reality to hit me—I'm sitting in the shadows, straddling a very shocked Cohen Cage.

Holy crap. Okay, so maybe I really was reading too much into the last couple of weeks.

"I . . . I don't even know what to say. I'm sor—"

My apology never leaves my lips, because in a split second, his hands tighten, pulling me harder against his body, and his thick lips crash down on mine. The feel of him, the reality of a kiss I've dreamt of since I was old enough to crave it, is so overwhelmingly perfect that I feel it all the way to my soul.

"We shouldn't be doing this here," I gasp against his lips, knowing that I don't mean a word of it. If he stops, I just might die.

"Can't stop, Dani-girl. Now that I finally know what you taste like . . . I can't stop," he moans when I shift my weight against his lap.

I can feel the truth in his words against my core, and I can't stop myself from rotating my hips against his hardened length.

"Jesus. I knew you would make me come undone."

His lips are back on mine. Caressing, lightly nipping between his teeth, before his tongue slides along the seam and demands access to my mouth. Our tongues dance together, almost as if they were made for each other. My breaths dance with his in a heated tango.

It.

Is.

Glorious.

"Your girlfriend," I pant, trying to pull back but knowing it will be impossible to let this go.

"Not my girlfriend."

I pull back and look into his hooded eyes, "She came with you, Cohen."

"*She* isn't with me. She came because she is the widow of one of the men from my unit, Dani-girl. She is here because she has no one else and she's had a hard time recently. But *she* isn't who I want in my arms. Good lord, woman. Shut up and kiss me."

Well, alrighty, then.

When I still don't move, his hands slide up my sides. His thumbs brush over the sides of my breasts, causing my nipples to harden painfully, before his hands cup my face. His fingers go into my hair, his thumbs lightly caressing my cheeks, while he studies my face. I have no idea what he sees there, but it must be enough, because seconds later, he pulls my face to his and devours my lips.

There is no other word for it. He takes my lips in a kiss so brutally perfect. His tongue duels with mine with effortless control.

It takes my sluggish mind only seconds to get with the program. Seconds, minutes, hours—I have no idea. It isn't long before I'm working his shirt over his head and his hand is working its way into my shorts.

"Dani, we need to stop," he groans as his fingers roll against my core, lightly pressing against my swollen clit before he pushes two thick digits deep within my wet core.

"Can't," I gasp against his mouth and dig my fingers into his shoulders. "Don't want to."

"Not here. Anyone could find us." He's right. I hate it, but he's right.

"Cohen Cage . . . I swear to God that I'm going to go insane if you're going to leave me like this."

He doesn't say anything. His eyes are back to searching my own.

"I've waited forever for this," I whisper.

His eyes close, and he drops his forehead against mine.

"Forever," I repeat.

"Shit," he groans. Then he pulls his fingers from my shorts, helps me right my clothing, and helps me stand with his hands against my hips.

I watch in confusion as he grabs his shirt and pulls it back over his head before he starts to pace around in the darkness.

Good job, Dani. Way to scare him off with your freakish admission that you've always waited for him to shove his hands down your pants. I bet he's trying to figure out the best way to run as fast as he can without hurting my feelings.

Well, too late for that.

"Listen, I'm just going to go . . ."

His head snaps over to mine, and within seconds, I'm back in his arms. He just holds me tight against his body. When his body starts to sway with the music coming through the stage's thick curtain, I struggle to keep up with his mood changes.

Until I hear the song the DJ is playing.

Brett Young's "Kiss by Kiss."

The same song I had my first dance to with him four years ago. The same song that has always reminded me of him day after day and year after year.

His lips go to my temple and he places a lingering kiss there before sliding his jaw down to rest it there. His breath against my ear is coming in deep pants as I hear him singing the song lyrics. Lyrics that will forever have a new meaning to me.

"And every time you look at me I just want to hold you. *All my life I've been waiting for you. Little by little falling for you.*"

Oh. My.

I pull back and look up into his handsome face. His lips curl slightly in a smile that seems to say, *Well, I guess the cat's out of the bag now.* His eyes hold mine as he waits to see what I'll do with his admission, and he pulls me deeper in toward his body. As if he's afraid I'm going to run.

As freaking if!

"I fell for you a long time ago, Cohen Cage. I've loved you my whole life."

His face relaxes, and he lets out his breath. When his forehead drops against mine, I brace myself for his rejection.

"Dani-girl," he groans like a prayer for strength.

Which is when it happens. When he realizes just who he has in his arms. And he starts to pull back. This is going to change everything between us. This final rejection. If the families find out—my brother, his siblings . . . Oh, God, Liam was right. This is going to be terrible.

"I have to go check on Megan. Make sure Chance can take her home."

And just like that, he's walking away from me, pulling the curtain to the side, and jumping down off the stage.

I didn't think it would hurt this bad. But having something I've wanted, desired, *craved,* in my arms for just moments only to have it ripped away is more painful than never having him.

Because no matter the obstacles we would have had to face, having him there, realizing that we really are just as perfect as I'd always imagined and knowing I'll never have it again feels like someone just died.

To top it all off, I was so close to what promised to be the most powerful orgasm I've ever experienced.

"Shit."

After dropping my ass back down to the floor, I curl my legs up and wrap my arms around them before laying my head against my knees.

Well, doesn't this just take the cake for shit outcomes?

Chapter 13

Cohen

ONE COULD SAY THAT I had a moment of insanity. An out-of-body experience that I was helpless to stop and just had to let happen. Maybe I could say it was the beer? No. No matter how I try to excuse what just happened between Dani and me, it would be a lie.

She was exactly where I wanted her.

She looked so beautiful when I walked in this afternoon. Her body showcased in those short-as-hell shorts. Those perky tits I love so much standing out in her tight tank. And those heels. God, what I wouldn't give to know what it felt like to have them digging into my back as I pounded into her.

It took everything I had not to rush her right then and there. But I stuck to my guns and kept my determination to stand back. If things were still there when I got home, then we would explore this.

"What am I doing?" I mumble to myself, jumping off the stage and into the party that had been going on around us, careful to hide the fact that my cock is about to claw its way off my body to run back to Dani.

Cam spots me and shakes his head. Colt, who's standing next to him, gives me a thumbs-up, which I return with my middle finger. He and Cam laugh so loud that I can hear them across the room and over the music.

It takes me a second to get through everyone and to the table I left Megan at. She looks just about as miserable as she was this morning when I stopped by to make sure she was okay. Jack should have been shipping off with us, and I know that's a fact that hasn't escaped her notice. It's been hard since we lost him, but no one has suffered harder than Megan. Well, maybe their four-year-old daughter, who keeps asking for her daddy.

A little over a week ago, she called me because she needed help with something around the house. When I got there and saw just how bad things had gotten, I stepped in and continued to stop by—just basically made sure she knew she wasn't alone.

"Hey, Megs," I say with a smile.

I drop down in the chair next to her and look over at Chance, who has been keeping her company—or as he likes to call it, "watch duty." Chance, like I did, served with Megan's husband.

I think I've always known that I would eventually join Corps Security. When my aunt Melissa got custody of me after my mom died—then, shortly after, met Greg—it didn't take long before I was adopted by both and calling them Mom and Dad. They have been a huge part of my life, and I honestly look at them both as my real parents. I was around three when they started dating. He has helped shape me into the man I am today. Since then, I've come a long way from the little boy who wore a cape everywhere and wouldn't shut up about dick piercings.

"Hey, Coh."

She looks at me briefly before turning her attention back to the people around us. I lean back and take in the room. Since all the parents ran out before things could get a little crazy, the makeshift dance floor is crowded with the pulsing bodies of my closest family and friends. The room is full of people enjoying life. That is all she would see. Happiness she doesn't have anymore.

"Are you ready to get out of here? I think Chance has been ready for a few hours now." I laugh when he nods an emphatic yes.

"I am, but I don't want to take you away from your family right now. You should enjoy your time home before you leave."

"And I will, Megs. I can come back, or Chance can take you home."

It takes me a little longer than I would like to get Megan to agree to go home with Chance. He'll make sure she gets home, takes a sleeping pill, and is okay before he heads back to our apartment.

I stop over with my sisters to let them know I'm leaving with the truck and to catch a ride with Cam and Colt. They don't pay any attention to me, but they nod their heads. After checking with my brothers one last time to make sure they know to take the girls to their house before they head home, I head to my last stop and that red curtain hiding my prize is just within my reach.

I might be crazy for this. Hell, if Axel found out that I was about to drag his little princess off to my apartment for a night of debauchery, he would cut my dick off. Or maybe chain me to the back of his big-ass truck by my Prince Albert. Not exactly a pleasant thought. I reach down and rub my poor junk at the thought.

"You sure about this?" I hear right before I'm about to walk up the side stairs that will take me back to the cloaked darkness behind the curtain.

I look over to see Liam leaning against the wall, his arms crossed over his chest, but no doubt he would push off and attempt to kick my ass if he felt I was about to hurt Dani.

"Liam, mind your business."

"Yeah, that's not going to happen. That girl back there, the one you left ten minutes ago, doesn't think you're coming back. I would have known that even if I hadn't peeked behind the curtain to see if she was okay. I'll give you this time because I can tell you had every intention of coming back to her, but you hurt her again and, friend or not, family or not, I'll fucking kill you." He ends his rant by stepping right into my personal space, and it's taking every ounce of control I have not to punch him right in the face. "She's my best friend, Cohen," he whispers. "You aren't stupid. You know how deep she feels for you, and if you would take two seconds to not be terrified about it going bad, you would be able to admit you feel the same way. Either do something about it or leave her alone so she can get over you."

"It's not that easy, Liam. I'm leaving tomorrow. Leaving. I know you know just as well as I do that I might not come back this time. Right or wrong, consequences be damned, there isn't much of anything that could make me stop now. Did I expect this? No. But that doesn't mean it isn't welcome. I tried to keep my distance. I denied us both, but I can't anymore. I won't hurt her. I could never hurt her."

"All right. I might take back my earlier assessment. You might be stupid after all. Make sure she is clear with whatever is about to happen and what it means to you, Cohen. Because if you don't, you're going to get her hopes up, and when you leave without making something, anything, clear, it will crush her more than just you being deployed will." He turns and walks off, grabbing Maddi on his way by her waist and playfully throwing her over his shoulder before marching onto the crowded dance floor.

It should be said for the record that I am far from stupid. I thought I was doing the right thing by denying us this. I thought that it would be easier for both of us if we didn't take this attraction any further.

One thing and one thing only is clear now.

I want Danielle Reid.

And right or wrong, I will have her.

I just need to make sure she knows I can't make her any promises about our future. Not with too much unknown standing in our way. When I get home, we can sit down and figure this stuff out, but for now, I need to find out if the fantasy of her lives up to the reality. I have a feeling that it will be even greater than I ever could imagine.

I don't know what I expected when I came back to where I left Dani, but seeing her sitting in some kind of protective ball definitely wasn't it. My Dani is strong. She wouldn't ever feel the need to turn in toward herself. Hell, if she weren't happy with me, she would have marched out there and kicked my ass herself.

"Dani-girl?" I implore, walking up to her still form and crouching down next to her. "Talk to me, baby."

She's quiet for a second, and just as I lean down to pull her into my arms, she catches me off guard with an elbow to the gut.

"You jerk. I told you not to leave me like that. I'm two seconds away from shoving my own hand down my pants to finish what YOU started."

Her eyes flash, giving me just enough time to prepare for her launching herself from her position. My arms go around her seconds before I fall back. Then I roll until I have her trapped under me with no way to get away.

Leaning down, I make sure she is focused completely on me before speaking. "I don't know what's gotten you worked up, Dani-girl, but I told you I was coming back."

"No you didn't, jerk-off. You said you had to go check on Megan. You said you needed to make sure Chance was taking her home. Now tell me how was I supposed to know in Cohen's world that mean you would be right back? You know what? Just forget it . . . Get off me so I can find my brother and have him take me back home."

She's lost her damn mind.

"That isn't happening." I push my hips against hers so there is no doubt in what I'm about to say. "For years—years, Dani—you've been parading around this flawless body and teasing me with something I couldn't have. For weeks, we've been dancing around this attraction. I've had a taste, and now, I need my meal. So what we're going to do is get off this damn floor, walk out the back door, and I'm going to get your sweet little ass to my bed quickly. I mean it, Dani. Years I've thought about what your pussy would feel like with my cock deep inside you, and I'm not giving that up now."

Her eyes widen hilariously. Those stunning, light-green orbs look at me with so much shock that, if I weren't so frustrated, I would laugh. Okay, so maybe I should have handled that a little better

Yeah, smooth I am not.

"What?" she breathes. "What happened to you saying this wouldn't happen?"

"I'm man enough to admit I was wrong and I'm open to discussing this again. Now get ready, baby. It's going to be a long night."

Chapter 14

Cohen

THE WHOLE TWENTY-MINUTE DRIVE TO my apartment is done with silence and sexual tension so thick that it's choking. My cock is testing the strength of its confinement. With every inhale, I can smell her arousal, her desire for me, and it's driving me insane with lust.

"Do you think we should talk about this, Cohen?" she asks weakly, like she would rather talk about anything else but knows it's smart that we at least lay some communication out.

"What do you want me to say here, Dani-girl?"

"The truth would be nice. Is this just some game to you? Or is this more? I'm not asking for the world, Coh . . . but I don't think that I can just give myself to you if it doesn't mean something to you. I'm so confused with your no-and-then-yes games."

I don't answer right away. I need to make sure she understands me, and there is no way I can get my point across if she is staring out the window and freaking out instead of looking at me. I need to see her eyes, to know that she is here with me and not running into her head to hide.

After parking the truck, I pull my seat belt off before reaching over and undoing hers. She looks over at me sharply before I grab her and pull her into my lap. My hands instantly go towards her face so I can hold her attention. My fingertips dance against her silky hair, her cheeks feel warm against my palms, and those stunning eyes stare out at me—she looks terrified out of her mind.

"You silly girl," I laugh. "What are you so scared of? I'm not the big, bad wolf. Although, I wouldn't be opposed to eating you up."

"Oh, God, that was corny," she chuckles.

"You would like that though, wouldn't you? Do you want me to eat you first, or do you want to be my Little Red Riding Hood and go for a long, hard ride?"

"Oh. God. Stop, Cohen. Those lines . . . They're terrible."

I snicker before leaning in and giving her a hard, bruising kiss. I don't take my time, but I do make sure that, with that one kiss, I dominate her mind.

"You wanted to talk, baby, so let's talk." Now that I've loosened the mood up a little, it's time to lay this out there so she doesn't have any confusion that I want her.

"I don't think I can. Not with you . . . with your . . . Jesus Christ." She starts to rub against my erection and drops her head back to rest in my hands, which are still framing her face.

"How about this?" I groan when she starts to grind down harder against my throbbing cock. "How about we get upstairs before I fuck you in my truck? I'm ready to play, Dani-girl, and there won't be anything quick about it. You either start talking now or get the hell up and in my bed."

"Bed," she pants, giving me another hard rotation of her hips against my lap.

I crush my lips against hers and help her ride out a few more rolls of her hips, pushing up against her to give her just enough friction to drive her insane, before pulling the door open and grabbing her hand.

"Last chance. Once I get you through that door, I guarantee I won't be able to stop."

"If you stop right now, Cohen Cage, I'm going to die."

I laugh and bend at the waist, and with a shoulder to her belly, she's up and over as I take off up the four flights of stairs as fast as I can with her giggles trailing behind us.

Chapter 15

Cohen

*I*T SHOULD BE SAID THAT I have fantasized about this moment for years. Right or wrong, it's the cold, hard truth. I've wanted this woman in every way possible, and tonight, I will finally get to stop craving and *take*.

Dani Reid has been the spotlight of every jack-off session I've ever had. Recently, those sessions have gotten a lot more play. She's consumed my mind. I keep picturing what color her nipples will be. How her pussy would glisten with her juices when I spread her legs wide. How it would taste to sink my tongue between those swollen lips. What kind of pussy would she have? Would it be bare? Maybe she would have a hint of that burnt-brunette hair I can't wait to wrap around my fist when I'm pounding into her from behind.

Every single image I've made up in my mind pales in comparison to the real thing. Seeing her body spread out against my black sheets, every inch of her tan skin covered in a slight blush, which I know isn't from embarrassment from being nude before me, but from her arousal. And Christ, the smell of her. When she stood before me and removed her clothing like she didn't have a shred of inhibition, I almost swallowed my tongue. Then she laid herself down on my bed, spread her legs, and let me take my fill. That was when her scent—that mouthwatering smell of her arousal—hit my senses. I take another deep breath and groan when my mouth waters.

"I was going to take my time and enjoy every second of this, but if I don't taste you right now, I'm going to go out of my mind. I need your pussy against my tongue and your come in my mouth. Tell me I can have you, Dani." I lick my lips and wait for her to respond.

Her eyes darken, that beautiful light green turning an emerald shade, and she nods her head. "I think you're a little overdressed though," she says confidently.

I feel my cock grow painfully hard when I watch her hands grab her small tits and pinch her nipples. If it weren't for the slight tremble in her hands, I would believe this fearless act.

"Baby, stop doing that or it's going to be over before it starts." I groan when she withers against the mattress. "God, that's hot."

Her eyes blaze. My words give her the push she needs. "Stop doing what?" she laughs. Then she trails one hand down her slim stomach and wastes no time dipping her middle finger into her core.

"Fucking hell," I grunt, reaching for my belt.

Her eyes burn with need with each move my fingers make as I deftly remove my belt, pull my shirt over my head, and start unbuttoning each button on my jeans.

Slowly.

So achingly slowly.

So slowly that I can feel each second as if it were a drum beating through the room.

She continues to dip one finger in and out of her soaked pussy. Daring me with each thrust to take her, finish what she's started. The hunger inside me is starting to take over, cloud my vision with one goal in mind.

Take.

Take and take until there isn't anything left for her to give me.

Her eyes widen when I pull my cock out of my pants and let them fall down my legs before I kick them aside. Those beautiful eyes of hers move from my cock and up to meet my eyes. Once, twice, and one final time before her movements still and she throws her head back and laughs.

Laughing at my cock.

Never has that happened to me before.

I look down to make sure that nothing's happened to him since I so carefully tucked him in this afternoon, but I don't see anything standing out. Same thick, tan skin. Same groomed manscaping.

And then it hits me. I drop my head, and with a heat of embarrassment flushing over my already fevered skin, I know what is going through her head, and it's just as funny as she thinks it is.

"You . . . Oh my God. You did it. Oh, wow," she hoots, choking on her words from laughing so hard.

"Can't say I've ever had a chick laugh at my cock before, Dani-girl."

"Well, I'm not just any chick! It's not my fault that . . . that . . . Jesus, Cohen, our parents tell stories about you always talking about that . . . well, THAT!" She finishes by pointing to my dick, which I'm still stroking even though she is basically laughing at the poor thing. "How many do you have, Cohen?"

"Enough." I smirk, sobering her instantly when she sees the intent in my eyes. "Enough that there is no fucking way you're going to be complaining when they're inside of you. You're going to love it, Dani. Each time I push in deep, you'll feel all four of them against your tight walls. You'll be begging me to take you harder so that the bar right here," I say, pointing to the one at the base of my dick, "rubs your swollen clit and the hoop knocks on your core. Each time I push in, you're going to feel them rubbing your tight walls. I'll have you begging for more, but for right now, it's just *enough*."

I bend down, grab her ankles while I pull her body to the edge of the bed, and spread her legs wide in the air. I hum my approval when I see just how wet her pussy is. She's practically weeping with her need for my cock.

"Dani-girl. Do you want my tongue or my cock?" I ask while trailing both of my hands down the legs I'm still holding wide. My fingertips lightly tease the skin behind her knees, traveling closer to where I want to bury my face—and then my cock.

She rolls her eyes back and moans but doesn't answer me. That's fine. I'll just give her both. Pulling her by her hips, I kneel on the floor. Then I smile up at her when she lifts up on her elbows to watch me.

"I'm going to eat you until you come in my mouth. Then I'm going to eat some more. And only then will I climb up this perfect fucking body and give you my cock. One thing you need to remember though, Dani-girl."

She holds my gaze, her skin flushed but her eyes alert.

"When I slam my cock inside your body, when my balls slap against your ass, when I finally take you, it means you're mine. Do you understand that?"

"God, yes," she pants. "Yes, anything . . . yes."

"That's good, baby," I hum and then lower my face to her pussy.

The first swipe of my tongue has her flavor bursting against my taste buds, and I groan before latching on and pulling her clit deep in my mouth. After playing with her until she's screaming and seconds from her release, I pull back, loving the feeling of her trying to push my head back down with her hands.

"You taste so fucking good," I moan, nipping her lips and the inside of her thighs with my teeth, causing her to scream out. "I can't wait to have my cock deep inside this cunt." And with that, I return my mouth to her body and I don't stop until she is screaming my name and coming against my tongue.

Only I lied and I make her go three times before I climb off the floor, grab her boneless body by the shoulders, and pull her with me deep into the bed. I don't give her a second to pull back before I drop my mouth to hers and spread her juices against her chin and lips. She kisses me with a hunger that matches my own, and I'm not sure if it's because she is just as worked up as I am or if the taste of herself on my mouth has her just that much hotter for me.

"Do you want my cock?" I ask.

"No," she pants. "I *need* your cock," she says breathlessly.

"Fuck yeah, you do."

Completely lost in the ecstasy of Dani, I absentmindedly stretch a condom over my cock, careful of the jewelry that was being laughed at earlier, and then I reach down, line up our bodies, and push myself balls-deep with one measured thrust. It isn't until she cries out, in pain and not pleasure, that I realize what I just did. Or better yet, what I didn't do, because if I had known I was her first, I damn sure would have had a little more finesse.

"Shit, Dani-girl. Fuck. Why didn't you tell me?" I take her head between my hands and will her to open eyes that she had slammed shut when I entered her body, and look at me so I know she's okay. My cock, still hard and deep within her tight pussy, is begging me to start thrusting. Demanding that I start to take her in the way my body has craved. But right now, I need to make sure she's okay, and there is no way that my body humping her like an animal will be anything close to okay. "Baby, look at me."

"I'm okay," she whispers, rolling her hips experimentally. "I just needed to get past that pain, but really . . . I'm okay."

"Why didn't you tell me?" I search her face, knowing she's brushing the pain under the rug. "If I had known . . ." I shake my head, because in reality, I was just so drunk on her that I'm not sure I could have stopped. "Baby, you have to talk to me."

She huffs out a breath, her cheeks getting red with embarrassment. "What would you have liked me to say? 'Hey, Cohen . . . before you *finally* fuck me, just thought you should know I'm a pathetic twenty-one-year-old virgin.' You know, stereotypical romance novel bullshit where the chick gets the guy only for him to freak when he realizes she is 'an innocent.' *Then* he runs as fast as he can because he wouldn't dream of ruffling a few feathers. News flash, bucko! I wanted my feathers ruffled. And I wanted them ruffled by you!" Her chest heaves when she stops talking, and her eyes go wide. "Did I just say all of that?"

"Yeah, Dani-girl. You sure did." I laugh and adjust my hips. My cock, still buried deep inside her body, twitches with the movement. "Just so we're clear here, I wouldn't have run the other way. I would have been more careful when I took you."

"Right. Well, can you shut up and fuck me now?" she whines when I shift again, and I feel the ring through my cock head brush against her womb.

I laugh, and her eyes narrow.

"Does it still hurt?" I ask with all seriousness.

"It wouldn't if you would move!" Her eyes are hooded and her breath is coming in quick pants by the time she finishes her sentence.

Her pussy clenches down when I shift again, and I drop my head to her neck to give her a little bite. She rewards me by hiking her legs around my back, hooking her ankles, and digging her nails into my shoulders on a moan. I pull back and rest my forehead against hers so that I can look into her eyes as I take her. Take what is mine and mine alone.

God, it feels better than I thought it would to know that no other man has ever been here.

I pull out just an inch before pushing back in and she doesn't flinch.

She is looking at me with complete love. I pull back a little more each time, and it isn't long before my body is thrusting into hers in quick successions. I wish I could make this better for her, but her pussy is so tight that it was milking my cock before I even started to move, and now that I have, I know I won't last long.

I reach down between us and start to put pressure on her clit. The second my fingers start to move in sync with my thrusts, her screams get louder, and it's only seconds before she throws her head back and my name is leaving her swollen lips as she comes long and hard around my cock.

Four thrusts later, with my balls against her ass and my cock as deep as I can go, I come, and with her eyes locked to mine, I realize that I was a fool to think I could have ever lived without this.

Chapter 16

Cohen

"WHAT HAPPENS NOW, COHEN?" SHE whispers into the darkness surrounding us.

She has one leg hooked over my hips with her thigh resting against my spent cock, the other lying against the bed. Her chest is pressed against my own, and her forehead resting against my neck. The hand she was using to draw circles on my chest for the last twenty minutes stills with her question, and I use the arm I was holding her close with to tighten my grip.

I knew she was working things out in her head, so I let her take her time and waited for the questions I knew would come. I have a few of my own that hit me like a burst of clarity while I stared into her eyes and felt her body take every inch of me. Things I thought I would be able to wait for when it came to her. Things I have no fucking clue how I'll be able to turn my back on and leave in the morning.

I have an inner battle warring inside me now. One side knows with no doubt that she is meant to be right here—naked in my arms with her heart beating against my skin. Then there is the other side. The logical side. The one that's afraid to take it past tonight, knowing how many other lives it will affect. It's not just the Cohen and Dani show. It's our families, siblings and everyone else in the tight circle.

Battle or not, the side that will win all depends on the woman in my arms.

"Let me see your eyes, Dani-girl." I dip my chin and wait for her to move her eyes to mine.

Her face is void of emotion, but her eyes aren't hiding a thing from me.

"Tell me, honestly, what you want to happen now."

"Honestly?" she questions.

"One hundred percent. One thing you need to understand about this from here on out is that, if you plan on telling me what I think— and hope—you are, then honesty is the most important thing. I can't go into this without knowing what's going on in that beautiful head of yours."

She's silent for a beat; all the while, her eyes never stop their hope- ful begging.

"I never want to let you go," she sighs, and I offer her a sad smile because we both know, come morning, she's going to have to. "I don't want you to leave, but I'll support you any and every way I can. I want to be able to be yours even when you aren't here but know that, when you come back, you're coming back to me. I want you to be able to go with the confidence that I'll be waiting for you if . . . if that's what you want, of course."

God, she couldn't be more perfect.

"Anything else?" I probe, moving one hand up to run my fingers down her cheek.

"I don't think we have enough time to get into everything that I want from you, Cohen. Let's just put it this way. I want you. I want you and everything that comes with it."

"Dani," I sigh. "I leave tomorrow, baby. I leave tomorrow and I can't even give you an estimate on when I'll be home. It wouldn't be fair for me to make you mine and demand that kind of commitment when I can't even be here for you. I won't even be able to contact you, Dani . . . How is that going to work? How is that fair to you? I don't want you to have to sacrifice for me—for us."

"When it comes to love, it's always worth the sacrifice. Always. One thing my parents taught me was that when you find the reason for your heart to beat, you don't ever let it go, and if, for some reason beyond your control, you have to, you fight with every breath in your body to have it back. You are worth that to me. You aren't asking me to give anything up, Cohen. I've loved you my whole damn life . . . What's a few more months of waiting if I know you're coming back to me?"

Each time she tells me that she loves me, it's on the tip of my tongue to return the words to her. I feel them, but I damn sure don't want her to think that I'm just saying them to parrot them back to her. Knowing Dani and the reservations she already has about my feelings towards her and with *us,* she would probably think that way too.

"What about our families?" I muse out loud. It needs to be addressed. I don't want it to become a big elephant in the room. Or, God forbid, her to want to hide this thing between us. First of all, with as often as everyone is together, it would be next to impossible. And I want to be able to show her off as my girl. Show her off and let the world know she is mine. I can't do that if she is worried about what will happen when we go public.

"What about them? Your sisters have been rooting for us to get together for years. Nate knows—or at least he knows about how I feel for you—and he's never said anything other than for me to be careful. I'm not sure that Cam and Colt care, to be honest. As for our parents . . . well, I don't know about them. What do you think?"

I give her a smile, and I'm instantly rewarded when her full lips tip up and she gives me one of her own. "Baby, I think that, when I get home, your father is going to kick my ass, because there is no way I can give this up. Here is my honesty. You ready?"

She nods her head.

"I want you to think about this from every angle, because that's what I've been trying to do. I would be damn proud to have you on my arm, in my bed, and to share my life with. I understand it's going to be a fight when it comes to your dad, but that's a fight I'll take if you're by my side. Our moms, yeah . . . that's not something you need to worry about. Trust me, baby. They'll start planning a wedding the second you and I let them know where we stand. My dad just wants me to be happy. And I guarantee you he will have my back when it comes to your dad. As for Nate, we don't need to worry about him either. I'll handle him. Sounds like my sisters aren't going to be a problem, and my brothers will be right there with Lyn and Lila."

I pause and shift our bodies so that she is lying under my body, her legs spread wide and her hips welcoming the pressure of my own. "The only issue I have here is knowing that I'm leaving tomorrow, and in doing so, I'm leaving you and what is most definitely starting between us. I'm not the type of man who likes knowing that his woman is alone, and if you needed me, I wouldn't be here. I don't like knowing that, if you're sad, I can't make it better. If you're sick, I won't be there to make you better. If you're scared, I can't chase away your nightmares. Bottom line, I won't be there for you, and that isn't something a man like me can stomach easily." I drop my head, give her a small kiss, and pull away, looking into her bright and hopeful eyes. "But, Dani-girl, I'm also a selfish man, because even knowing all of that, it doesn't make a difference. It's you and me, baby. You and me against the world."

I wipe the tear that leaks out of her eye before it can trail down her cheek to the radiant and very happy smile that has spread across her lips. Even when I drop mine to hers, the smile remains. And later—much later—when she is moaning my name, it still never slips.

My girl, my Dani-girl, is happy.

"You're mine?" she asks.

"Yeah, baby. And you're mine."

With a full but heavy heart, I hold her all night long. My eyes never once leave her sleeping—and still-smiling—face. I memorize every inch of her, from the way she feels in my arms to how she smells like wildflowers in the rain. When she moans in her sleep and huskily whispers my name, I know that, when I leave tomorrow, I'll be fighting every instinct I have to run back to her. It's going to be an uphill battle, but this will be one worth every second of yearning, because in the end, when I come home and she's right back in my arms, I'll be the luckiest bastard alive.

Chapter 17

Dani

I T'S HARD TO SEE THROUGH the tears clouding my vision. To see through the sadness my heart feels as I watch him get dressed. Watching him pack his things. Pull on his boots or grab his jacket. All the things I won't be watching again for months. Little, mundane tasks I'm trying to sear into my mind so I'll never forget. How his fingers look when he's hooking his belt through his jeans. How his brow furrows when he's trying to figure out how to get a little more space out of his carry-on. Even though I know he will come back to me, knowing that we're starting something so beautiful off with a big, ugly fog surrounding us has me in pieces.

He looks over when he finishes zipping the last zipper and gives me a sad smile. I'm sure my eyes are looking at him exactly as his are gazing into mine. Like this is it and if we don't see each other again, then we should make this second last a lifetime.

I bring a hand up and angrily swipe away a tear. I hate crying. It's a sign of weakness, but I'm helpless to stop them. My heart, while full to bursting with the knowledge that he is mine, is breaking.

"Dani-girl," he says on a sigh. "You're killing me with these tears."

He sits on the bed and pulls me into his arms. When his strong arms wrap around me and the comfort that always comes when he's near sinks into my skin, I only cry more.

"This isn't goodbye," he vows.

"Never goodb-b-bye," I stutter.

"It's 'see you soon'," he whispers.

"Every time I close my eyes," I promise.

We don't need words after that. What more needs to be said? I have to believe that, even brand new, we have the kind of connection that can beat anything.

He holds me in his arms for another ten minutes. Ten whole minutes that I feel complete. When his phone beeps, letting him know that his parents are on the way, he gives me a deep kiss before pulling back and standing from the bed.

"Stay as long as you want, Dani-girl. I like knowing you're in my bed even if I'm not here." He stops when I let out a big sob-like hiccup. Leaning down over where he placed me in the middle of the mattress, he gives me another long and deep kiss. "See you soon, my heart." With one more kiss, he stands, grabs his stuff and walks out the door.

I'm not sure how long I stay in the middle of his bed, surrounded by his scent and the memories of the night before. It isn't until Liam shows up and wraps me in his arms, causing my sobs to double in force, that I realize the sun has long since set and Cohen is likely gone by now.

"Wh-what are you doing here?" I ask when I'm finally able to calm down.

"Cohen sent me a text a little after nine this morning. Told me that, if I didn't see you by lunch, I was to go find Chance and get the key to the apartment. Lunch came and no Dani, so here I am. Come on, little princess. Let's get you home."

Lee turns his back when I move the covers off my naked body, throwing my shorts and one of Cohen's shirts over his shoulder. When I pull the cotton tee over my head, I know instantly that it must be the one he wore the night before. The scent of him, so fresh and powerful, almost brings me to my knees. I have to bite my lip to keep it from wobbling and victoriously keep the tears at bay.

"Here," Lee says with a smile. "I grabbed a few more and the body wash and the bottle of that shit he wears off the counter in his bathroom."

When I look at him like he's lost his mind, he laughs, throwing the body wash, cologne, and three shirts he was holding in my arms.

"What? You were standing there sniffing that one like you wanted to rub it all over yourself. Might as well make it so you can have some to last." He shrugs his shoulder, collects my purse from the floor next to the nightstand, and takes my hand before leading me out of the apartment.

Chance is fixing some food in the kitchen when we walk out. He gives Lee one of those manly head-jerk things and me a small smile.

"See you around, Dani."

I nod, but I know I won't see him around much. Not now that Cohen is gone.

God, he really is gone.

"Do you think she's dead?" the voice asks, and I feel something sharp poke my hip.

"No, but I think she smells like she is," another voice replies.

"It does smell . . . funky in here. I wonder, if we move her, what's going to be growing on those sheets."

"Ugh, Maddi—you're so gross!" Lila snaps.

"Shut up, you two," Lyn mumbles.

I feel the bed dip, but I pull the sheets over my head. "Go away."

"Fat chance in that happening. Time for some tough love, bitch," Lyn snaps before pulling my comforter off my body. "Seriously, Dani. It's time to take the shirt off."

"No."

"Oh yeah, it's happening. Either you can take it off on your own accord or I'll be forced to cut it off. Do you want me to cut the shirt? Huh, Dani? Do you want me to cut it into tiny pieces?" Lyn barks, standing from the bed and placing her hands on her hips.

"You wouldn't dare!"

"Try me. It's been three days since Cohen left. Do you see Lila and me moping around the house? No, you do not. You're acting pathetic, and it's time to snap the hell out of it."

What the hell? Who does she think she is?

"What the hell, Lyn! Who do you think you are to tell me that I shouldn't be upset?"

"I'll tell you who I think I am! I'm your best friend, but I'm also *his* sister. I get to live this right along with you, but I have the added benefit of watching you fall apart all the while I'm holding my worry about him in because I don't want to make you snap any more than you already have."

Oh.

"I love you, Dani. I'm so happy that you and Cohen had that before he left, but right now, you have to stop acting like he isn't ever going to come home because he will. He will, Dani. I swear." Her eyes start to water, and I want to kick myself for making her feel worse when I should have swallowed my upset and been there for them.

"I'm sorry," I offer weakly. And I am. It hurts still, having the memory of his body holding mine so fresh, but she's right. I'm grieving him as if he won't ever come back.

"Go get a shower and you can get your ass to work today so I don't have to deal with Sway going nuts over you missing another filming day."

I nod my head and climb out of the bed. When I go to pull off Cohen's shirt, I look over my shoulder to where she is standing. Maddi and Lila must have dipped out the door while we were talking. She raises one of her black, perfectly sculpted brows and looks down at my hand on the hem. I narrow my eyes and instantly decide that this shirt—and the others I'm sure she doesn't know about yet—will be hidden well.

And I'm not even ashamed of the smile I have when I drop some of Cohen's body wash on my loofa and start to get lost in the memories.

Memories that will keep me going long after he comes home.

Yeah . . . totally normal.

Ten hours of hell later, I'm ready to kill someone. I'm missing Cohen terribly, but that feeling was exasperated tenfold by Devon, his two idiots, and—God love him—Sway.

Devon wanted to know when "the romantic drama hunk" was coming in next, which was brought up when it was clear there wouldn't be anything show-worthy happening in the salon today. Lyn went nuts and threw one of her eye shadow pallets at him.

Devon's "assistants"—and I use that word loosely because I haven't seen them actually assist with anything—wouldn't stop being icky. The short one actually picked his nose, twice, and the second time almost had me throwing up my lunch when I saw him eat it. Then the other one . . . I can't put my finger on exactly what about him I don't like—but it's there. And his openly staring at every female in the room doesn't exactly give him any checks in the pro side.

And then Sway.

I might actually kill him.

Really.

I was in the back mixing some color for Jenna Nixon's pink touch-up when he came up behind me and tried to measure my bust. Like, full-on threw one of those measuring tape things around my body and told me to stop wiggling so he knew what size he needed to order for burlesque day at the salon.

I do not fucking think so.

And okay, I might have been a little overdramatic when I elbowed him in the stomach, but he crossed a line with the measuring tape.

Needless to say by the time the workday was over, I was more than ready to call it a night. If I'm this bad after just three days, I hate to think what I'll feel like as more pass.

And it's with that thought that I find it.

I find the reason I need to solidify that strength I need. A reason to smile again.

I'm not sure how I missed it earlier, but I wasn't exactly in the right frame of mind the morning he left—or each day after for that matter—so it makes sense that I didn't see it before. Tucked in one of the side pockets of my purse is a white envelope, sealed, with my name scrawled in masculine writing on the outside.

Not just my name.

The name only one person calls me.

My chin wobbles when I hold the letter that Cohen must have tucked in there at some point the night before he left. Part of me wants to rip into it and devour each word. But the sensible part of me wants to savor each word knowing that these are going to be the words I need to keep me going.

Dani-girl—my sweet Dani-girl.

You have no idea how long I've been watching you sleep. I feel like, if I stare at you for the rest of the night, it might be enough to last me until I came home, but even as I write this down, I know it wasn't enough.

It's funny how I've lasted almost twenty-six years without knowing what it felt like to have you in my arms. I've had your naked body against mine for one night and I know it was a feeling that I will struggle to be without. I don't know a better way to explain it other than it just felt like you were always meant to be there.

My dad used to tell me that your father used to get so pissed when we were kids because wherever I went, you weren't far behind, and whenever we were in the same room, I was always watching you. He told me once that, even back then, it was like we had some invisible cord pulling us together. I don't think I understood it until last night. I've always used excuse after excuse to push the feelings I had for you aside.

Anyway, my point is, while I was sitting here in the dark, watching you sleep, it hit me how much it's going to rip me in two when I have to walk away from you in the morning. Seeing you in my bed, sated and flushed from just taking you again, will be something I think about for nights to come.

It was unexpected, baby, but it was fate. It's our unexpected fate, and I have no doubt in my mind that this happened at the perfect time, for us, even if it sucks knowing I won't hold you in my arms for a while, I'll carry the memories of last night with me every second of every day that I'm gone. And when I come home, I'm not sure I'll ever let go of you.

Danielle Reid, you've burrowed your beautiful soul right into my heart.

Stay strong, my beautiful Dani-girl, and know that, wherever I am and wherever you are, I'll be thinking about you. Know that, when I get home, there won't be a second that passes that I don't show you just how much you mean to me. I was a fool to push this connection we have away for so long, and for that, I'm sorry, but now, it's you and me against the world and there isn't anything that could take that feeling away from us now.

Remember, I'll see you soon—every time I close my eyes.

Love,

Cohen

When I finish reading the letter, my eyes are wet with tears, but this time, they're tears of acceptance that I can and will make it through Cohen's deployment, and when he gets home, it's going to be him and me against the world.

And I can't freaking wait.

Chapter 18

Dani

Two months later

"DANI!" I HEAR LILA YELL up the stairs.

I smile to myself because I know what's coming. The same thing that's been happening every single Saturday at nine o'clock in the morning for the last two months.

I look at the red roses sitting on the corner of my desk and smile. I do the same when I pass the dozen on my nightstand, and then again when I reach the end of the hallway and see the other dozen that will be replaced today on the accent table right before the stairs.

For the last two months, like clockwork, I've gotten a delivery of a dozen red roses. There's never a card, but I don't need one. There is only one person who would send me such an extravagant gift every week. When the first delivery showed up, it was the morning after I had read Cohen's letter, and it was the fortification I'd needed. The girls didn't say much—not at first. Then, when it was clear I wasn't going to jump off the deep end, they took me off suicide watch and started in with the questions.

I told them what I could without giving them the intimate details of Cohen's and my relationship. We were together and would remain together until he got home. I explained to them that I wasn't going to mention it to anyone else past them and Lee. I didn't want to rock the boat. They don't understand or agree, but for now, they've left that alone. I think part of me is still worried that this is a dream. That Cohen will return and either change his mind or realize that it wasn't what he thought he felt. But also, I am selfishly waiting until I have his strength by my side before I tell everyone else.

And by everyone else, I mean my father.

"I went ahead and signed for you. That delivery dude is creepy as hell." Lila hands me the flowers with a roll of her eyes. "I swear my brother has gone soft," she mumbles under her breath as she walks away.

"Where are you headed today?" I ask while taking a big whiff of the flowers.

"I picked up a Saturday class for some extra credits."

"Damn, Lila! Aren't you worried that you're going to burn yourself out one of these days?" Flowers forgotten—well, almost forgotten—I look over at her with concern. She's been going hard for so many years that I really never stopped to think that maybe she might be pushing herself a little too much. "What's the rush, babe?"

"It's just something I need to do, Dani. I don't know how to explain it any other way. I just keep picturing all the kids that need my help and I don't want to give them anything less than one hundred percent."

I give her a smile before placing the flowers on the table just inside the entryway. Walking over to where she's picking at her nail polish, I wrap my arms around her and give her a big squeeze.

"You're going to be awesome, Lila. You would be awesome even without all these extra years of school, but with them, you're going to be unstoppable."

She smiles but doesn't acknowledge my words. "Do you want to catch some breakfast before you head off to meet Lee?"

"I'd like that. I feel like all I've been doing lately is working. Ever since Devon had to rush back to Los Angeles and he left Don and Mark in charge, things have been a little intense."

We walk down the hall and into the kitchen. Lila plops down on the barstool as I go straight to the fridge and start pulling out the ingredients I need to make French toast. Lila doesn't cook—ever. Not unless we want to be vomiting for weeks. The last time she tried to cook dinner for the house—when we had the brilliant idea that we should do a rotation so one single person didn't have to do all the cooking—she started a small grease fire, burned noodles, and made cheese toast without removing the plastic film over the slices.

Needless to say, with all her smarts, cooking just isn't something she can do.

"How are you doing with things?" she asks, breaking the silence.

"I'm okay, Lila. I really am. I know I got a little over the top when he first left and I'm sorry for that. It wasn't right for me to do that and not be there for you and Lyn. It's just—I can't even describe it. We've known each other forever. Been solidly on that 'just friends' line that I never imagined how different it would be to finally have him. Even if it was just for a few hours. Those hours . . ." I pause, remembering every second of my night in Cohen's arms. "When I was with him, it was like everything was right in the world."

"You sound like a cheesy Hallmark card," she giggles.

I laugh. "You're right. God, I'm pathetic."

"No, you aren't. I understand what you're saying, even if it is gross to think about it being with my brother."

"Do you think its crazy? This instant connection between us?" *I don't think it's crazy, but I know how others might see the swiftness of our relationship. I've been lusting after him for so long that I'm sure I* look pathetic to most. I know I never dreamt that he would return my feelings.

Lila studies my face for a beat, her expression giving nothing away, before she speaks. I don't know why, but between her and Lyn, I have always thought that Lila didn't exactly want Cohen and me to get together.

"I don't think it's crazy, Dani. But I'm worried about you. He's my brother, but you have always been like a sister to Lyn and me. I'm worried that things might get . . . sticky."

"Meaning?" I push hesitantly.

"What's going to happen when he comes home?" she asks, not answering my question.

"The same thing that would have happened if he were still here. We're going to tell everyone together and then, hopefully with their blessing, continue to see where our relationship goes."

"Okay. Well, what's keeping you from telling everyone now? I'll be honest, I don't agree with your wanting to keep a lid on it."

I'm trying to keep my temper in check. I know she's just trying to think logically, but that doesn't mean I'm not allowed to get frustrated with her lack of faith.

"You're afraid he's going to change his mind, aren't you?" she asks when I don't say anything,

"Never," I spit venomously. "Look, I don't want to fight with you, Lila, but I have faith in your brother that he never would have even opened this can of worms if he didn't mean it. But I will admit that I can see where you're coming from. It might be easier for me to say something now and deal with calming my dad down while Cohen is home. I know one thing for sure: when he comes home, I want to be able to focus on us becoming us without having to worry about hiding and being scared of what others might think. So I guess I'm not going to keep this to myself." I sigh and try to suck down the small panic I have from knowing what kind of chat that will be with my dad. "I'll tell my parents about it next weekend at dinner." I nod a few times before stopping. God, I must look like a bobblehead.

Her eyes widen. "You're going to tell your father—the same father that locked you in the house when Toby Gilbert tried to take you to the movies when you were seventeen and chased the kid out of the house with a chainsaw—that you and Cohen are together?"

"Hey—the chainsaw wasn't on," I laugh, remembering how embarrassed I was.

"Dani . . . he still chased a man down with a freaking chainsaw and all Toby wanted was to take you to a movie. We're talking about telling your father that you and Cohen are together *together,* and I'm pretty sure no one is going to believe that you two have something that doesn't involve touching."

"I know, I know," I sigh. "But I figure it would be better to tell him now and give him a while to get used to it before Cohen comes home."

"Oh, God. He's going to kill him. You know that, right?"

"He wouldn't kill him knowing it would hurt me. Hey! What's with the back-and-forth crap here? Five minutes ago, you were questioning my logic on not saying anything. Now, you don't think I should."

"I think that's before I realized what telling Axel you're dating his best friend's son would do to said best friend's son."

"It'll be okay. It will."

She gives me a weak smile, which tells me that even she doesn't believe my lie to myself.

God, this is going to be a nightmare.

Lee came over later that night with my brother. We were supposed to go out to a local sports bar for dinner, but by the time they got there, I was so tired that all I wanted to do was crash. I feel like I've been running on empty for the last few weeks, grasping at any kind of sleep I can find.

We're all camped out in the living room. Lee and I are sitting on the couch, my head in his lap while his fingers brush my hair, pulling me halfway to dreamland, when my phone rings for the second time in five minutes.

"It says 'private,' Dani," Nate says from the recliner next to us. "Want me to answer it?"

"Yeah, whatever," I mumble with a wave of my hand, not really caring. Anyone who needs me that bad could just call the house.

"'Ello?" Nate booms into my phone. "The fuck?"

Something in his tone draws my attention, and I look over at him. His eyes are locked on mine, but other than the sharp look he's throwing my way, he appears to be relaxed.

"Yeah. Sure thing, *bro.* I think you might want this, Dani." Nate extends his arm with my phone and waits for me to take it, looking at me like he can't figure out what's going on.

"Hello?" I question, trying to shake the lingering fatigue away.

"Dani-girl," I hear, and my eyes shoot to Nate before closing tightly and letting his voice wash over me.

Oh my God!

"How . . . how are you calling me? Did you call your parents? Your sisters or brothers? Oh my God! Are you okay? You're calling because something happened, aren't you?"

"Slow down, baby," he laughs. "I missed you. That's all."

Well, so much for holding my shit together. Those three words almost cause me to come undone. I give Nate another look, begging him not to freak out until I can talk to him. He gives me a hard one back but doesn't say anything.

"I miss you, too," I breathe while getting off the couch and walking out of the room.

Right when I'm about to shut the door into the front bathroom to get some privacy, I hear Nate boom at Lee, "Did you fucking know about that shit?"

"I'm guessing I have some explaining I need to do to your brother when I get home," he laughs, completely unconcerned about Nate's freak-out.

"That's an understatement at the moment," I laugh when I hear something thump on the other side of the door followed by Lee's whine of pain. "Don't worry. I'll talk to Nate."

"You shouldn't have to deal with that alone, Dani. I hate that I've left you in that position." He pauses, and I can hear his breathing pick up. "Fuck, I hate this. If you want to wait to say something, I won't hold that against you. I meant it when I said it was you and me against the world."

"I can handle it." And I can. Plus I wasn't joking when I told Lila earlier that it would be best for me to soften the blow a little when it comes to my father.

"To answer your earlier question, no. I haven't and won't be able to call anyone else. I'm going dark, baby, and I know this might be the last chance I get to call home—I needed that call to be to you. I couldn't go without making sure I told you some things. Things I should have said before I left. God, I sound like a fucking sap. I can't explain it better than me needing to get my head straight before our next mission and the only way I could accomplish that was to talk to you."

Ho-Lee-Shit.

"Oh . . ."

"Is that a good 'oh'?" he laughs, the connection getting a little fuzzy.

"If your sisters find out, they're going to kill me."

"No, they won't. If they do, you just tell them that their brother loves his girls, but he loves his woman more."

Wait a minute.

"Do what?"

He laughs again, the sound like a balm for my soul. "Dani, what do you think we're doing here?"

"Uh, talking?"

"Yeah, baby. Talking. You going to tell me how much you love me?"

"You already know how much I love you," I jest.

"I do. And now you know I love you."

"Even if I didn't, the weekly flowers are sure doing a good job at showing me."

He's silent.

Silent for so long that I pull my phone away from my ear to make sure we didn't have the connection drop.

"Dani. I haven't sent any flowers."

"Don't be silly, Cohen. Of course you have. They've been coming every Saturday since you left. Who else would send them?" I feel what can only be a described as a flash of fear wash over my body. Oh my God. If Cohen isn't sending them, then who is?

"Flowers . . . yeah, those aren't my thing, Dani. They look beautiful for a little while and then they start to stink before they die. When I show you how much I love you, it damn sure won't be with something that's going to die in a week."

Oh. My.

"Put your brother on the phone. Now," he barks.

I jump at his tone, the fear I started to feel only seconds before rushing into my system, and I almost drop the phone because my hands are shaking so badly.

I rush out of the bathroom door and almost tumble over my brother, who is standing there, looking guilty, with a cup in his hand. A cup I'm sure was just pressed against the door like the ghetto little spy he is.

I mutely hand Nate the phone and step back until I bump into Lee. He looks down at me with concern, and I just shake my head, not trusting my words.

I listen through the roaring in my ears as Nate responds to what Cohen is saying in clipped tones. His eyes shoot to mine a few times, the anger that was there at first now turning to concern.

"I'll take care of it," he snaps and hands me the phone again.

"H-hello?"

"Don't worry, baby. Your brother knows what to do, and he'll take care of everything. Is Lee there too?"

I nod my head but then remember he can't see me. "Lee's here."

"Good. Ask him if he can stay with you for a while."

"I'll do that."

"I love you, Dani-girl. No one is going to mess with that. No one. Don't worry, okay?"

"I'm not worried." And I'm really not worried. I'm not. I am terrified.

"Liar," he whispers. "God, I hate that I can't be there to protect you. This is killing me, Dani. It goes against everything I feel to not rush to you."

My heart breaks, the fear I felt instantly dimming. "I'll be okay. I promise. I'll make sure I'm not alone and the guys will watch out for me. I'm . . . I'm going to tell Daddy about us and, well, this. He won't let anything happen to me, Coh."

"That's a good idea. Might mean he kicks my ass a little harder when I get back with all that time he will have to stew on it, but it will be worth it to know that you're safe." He doesn't even hesitate. Not one second, which would have made me think he doesn't want this.

"Tell me you love me, baby. I have to go."

"I love you, baby." I smile.

"Yeah," he sighs. "And I you."

"See you soon," I whisper.

"Every time I close my eyes."

I don't move the phone away from my ear. Not when I hear the click or when Nate starts to ask his questions. I just smile to myself and let it sink in.

Chapter 19

Dani

PREDICTABLY, THINGS GOT A LITTLE insane after that call. Nate demanded to know what was going on between Cohen and me. I was honest with him, and in the end, he didn't have a problem with it more or less, just that I had kept from him.

Okay, that might be a stretch. He knew how I felt, of course, but he was shocked that Cohen had taken it that far without at least talking to him first. Then I had to explain to my irrational older brother that he isn't my keeper.

Don't ever tell a man who was raised by alpha males that he isn't the keeper of his baby sister. It isn't pretty and there is usually something that gets broken in the process. This time, it was my coffee table when I pushed the big ape over for telling me that I should be locked away on an island of Barbies and Big Wheels.

Yeah. I'm always going to be the baby sister.

That being said, justifiably, what he did have a problem with was the unexpected and unknown sender of the weekly flowers. I told him everything I knew about the delivery guy and how many had come, showing him the ones that were still around the house. Each of the vases held a big, black bow tied to the center of the glass vase. Black wouldn't have been my first choice, but when I'd thought they were from Cohen, it hadn't bothered me. Now, it makes me skin crawl.

And that was before Nate had found the first microscopic-looking wireless camera in the arrangement.

"You're moving home," he booms through the room. "That's fucking it. No. You're not staying here one more second, Danielle!" He starts pacing around my bedroom, his hands clenching in tight fists at his sides. Bringing out the full name is his way of showing me that he's serious.

I don't think so. No. I finally got out from under my father, and there is no damn way I'm going back. Especially now, it would only be a million times worse.

"I'm not leaving my home, Nate."

"Don't be irrational, Dani!" he screams in my face.

Lee, who was quiet until now, steps between us. "Be pissed, I get that, but don't you dare talk to her like that."

I give him a squeeze before things get too intense between him and Nate. Won't be the first time, and it damn sure won't be the last.

"Look," I start and step around Lee so that I can make sure Nate knows I mean every word I'm about to say. "I'm not going to leave. First of all, if whoever is sending the flowers is watching me, they'll see that and follow. I'm comfortable here. We're safe here. Lee can stay for a while, right, Lee?" I turn and wait for him to nod. "And I'll tell Daddy what's going on. I won't be put out of my own house because of some stupid flowers."

"Flowers with goddamn cameras in them, Dani!" he yells.

"Tone, Nate," Lee reminds him.

"Shut the fuck up, Lee."

"Would you both shut the hell up?!" I scream.

"What the hell is going on here?"

Oh great. I look over at my mom and smile sweetly. She narrows her eyes, and I know she doesn't buy it for a second.

"Do you want to tell me now or wait until your father gets in from unloading the car? He's always freaked me out with that sixth sense he has when it comes to his children. Imagine my shock when I'm trying to enjoy a glass of wine and a nice game of Candy Crush when your dad comes rushing in the room and demands we leave *right this second* because he knew you needed something. Of course, he couldn't tell me what it was you needed, so we had to stop off for just about everything he could buy at Walmart, the only damn store that's open at eleven on a Saturday. So . . . before he gets in here and I have to hear him gloat about being right, why don't you tell me what has your brother doing his best Axel Reid impression? Hey, Liam," she finishes with a smile. "Don't you look handsome tonight."

Jesus Christ, it's going to be a long night, and all I want to do is go to bed.

"Don't worry. His bark will be a lot worse than his bite," Lee whispers in my ear on a laugh. He's quick to move away before my dad walks in the room though.

"Hey, Daddy," I smile when he pushes into the room. "Shouldn't you be in bed by now? You know, past your bedtime and all?"

"Don't be a smartass with me. What's going on?"

"What makes you think something is going on? Nate and Lee were just watching a movie with me. Normal boring night."

"What makes me think something's going on? Besides the fact that a father always knows when his little princess needs something? How about your brother over there?" he states and points to Nate.

Nate, who is standing farther away in the middle of the living room, pacing back and forth and muttering to himself. His fists are clenched and his face is flushed with anger.

"Oh . . . poor guy. I told him that 'N Sync wasn't getting back to-gether. He took it really, *really* hard."

Lee lets out a boom of laughter. My mom snickers to herself and rubs her hand down my dad's back.

"Dani," Nate warns. "You tell them or I will."

"I don't think—" I start only to be interrupted by Nate when he drops a bomb in the middle of the room.

"Why don't you fucking start with you and Cohen and then get to the flowers and cameras, *Danielle.*"

"The hell is he talking about?" Daddy rumbles.

"Uh, about that."

"There better not be any of *that* to be *about,*" he fumes.

"What does that even mean?" I ask.

"Don't you be smart with me. Start talking."

I sigh and look at my mom for some help, only to get a small nod and smile. Lee isn't much help either. He walks over to the couch, sits next to Nate, and waits—the popcorn we forgot about in their hands.

"Shit," I mutter.

"Mouth!" Dad explodes.

I narrow my eyes and have to resist the urge to stomp my feet.

"Start. Talking."

"Ugh! This is ridiculous. Well, this is definitely not how I saw this going. Thank you, Nathanial. You might as well sit down, Daddy."

"I don't want to sit down," he argues.

"Now who is acting like they're a child," I tease.

His face softens for a second before he remembers why he's upset.

"Okay. So it's probably best if I just rip it off like a Band-Aid, right?" No one speaks. "So . . . Cohen and I talked before he left and we decided that, when he comes home, we're going to see where we stand."

Daddy looks at me, his eyes blinking a few times as my words float around in his mind. I can see him trying to figure out what I just said, and then I watch when it finally sinks in. His tan face turns beet red and his nostrils start to flare. His eyes go even harder before he explodes.

"THE FUCK YOU SAY?"

Oh boy.

"Axel, baby, calm down."

"I won't calm down."

"She's an adult. You *know* Cohen, and I know that he would never do anything to hurt her. Ever. So your normal excuses of them being up to no good aren't going to work. Not with him. You've known that boy since he was three years old. If there is anyone you shouldn't have to worry about, it would be Cohen Cage."

"I also remember all that boy would talk about was his dick, too!"

"I think you're twisting those memories slightly. Plus, it was his father's dick." Mom burst out laughing when Lee and Nate start choking on their popcorn.

Serves those little shits right for trying to enjoy this clusterfuck.

"Izzy," my fathers warns.

"Good lord, Ax. You were never this over the top when we were their age." She laughs and then walks over to where I'm standing. Her arms come around me and her mouth goes to my ear. "He'll get over it, but don't back down."

I get a big squeeze before she walks over to Nate and slaps him over the head.

"Don't laugh at your sister."

"Where are the girls?" Daddy asks when no one makes a move to further the conversation.

"Maddi is spending time with her sister. She said she's been missing her lately. The twins are out. And before you even think about it, yes, they know and they're completely okay with it."

"I don't like this," he grumbles.

"And you don't have to. But it won't change anything, Daddy. I think it's time to let me live my own life and stop acting like I'm a little girl."

"That's not going to happen. I'll work on it, but I won't make any promises that I won't be having words with him when he gets his ass home. Long words, Dani. Words that may or may not involve me showing him my gun collection. Now sit down and tell me the rest."

"Actually . . . I think YOU might want to sit down for this part."

Chapter 20

Dani

TWO NIGHTS AGO, I HAD to vaguely tell my father that I would be dating when Cohen came home. I think that, if had it been any other person, he wouldn't have accepted it as well as he did. Well, I say, "accepted it," but I heard him when he stepped in the kitchen to "get a beer" and boom into his phone at who I can only imagine was Cohen's dad that his son was "going to violate my daughter and that shit better not happen."

That conversation went a lot better than the flowers and cameras one went. To say that my father lost his shit would be a vast understatement. It took my mom offering him God knows what for him to finally leave. I try to tune them out when she starts whispering in his ear to get her way.

Not something I want to think about.

Nope.

Never.

So here I am, two days later, and I feel like I'm about to climb out of my skin.

Daddy has decided to appoint himself as my personal bodyguard.

And if that isn't enough, the lingering exhaustion I've been feeling for weeks has hit an all-time high. Or I guess it would be low. I've been falling asleep at work. In the shower. You name it. I was eating dinner, which was cooked by Maddi and delicious, the other night with the girls and fell asleep in my bowl! In. My. Bowl! Who does that?

I'm over it.

At least he agreed to let Chance accompany the girls and me to the Loaded Replay concert tonight in Atlanta. God, I would have killed him if he had shown up. He pulled whatever strings he has and our shit tickets have been swapped out with V.I.P., front-row tickets. Of course, his stipulation was that our group of five—me, Lyn, Lila, Maddi, and Stella—turn into a party of six. Chance was going or we weren't.

For tonight, Chance will be an honorary chick because I am not missing this show.

Loaded Replay hit the scene huge a few years ago. They're a mix of old-school classic rock and new-school flare. There isn't a single band out there currently that has what they have. Of course, it doesn't hurt that their lead singer is a chick who is smoking hot and she's backed up by three damn fine men.

Maddi has been *in love* with their drummer, Jameson Clark, since the first day she saw a picture of him. Tall, built, blond Adonis. He really does look like a rock god. Lead guitarist Weston Davenport, brother of lead singer Wrenlee Davenport, is the fan favorite though. He looks like a rock-n-roll version of Liam Hemsworth, right down to that killer smile. I've always thought that their bassist, Luke Madden, was fun to watch. He has that boy-next-door look to him, but his eyes just scream trouble and mischief. Bottom line—you can tell there is something about Loaded Replay that just screams badass.

To say we're excited would be the understatement of the year.

"Thanks for agreeing to this," I tell Chance when we load into his Expedition to head over to the arena.

The girls are in the back, going on and on about how they're going to get the attention of one of the band members. I tune them out and focus on picking at the frayed holes in my jeans.

Where Lyn, Lila, Maddi, and Stella decided to go with their Slut Barbie looks, I kept it simple with skinny jeans, a flowing chiffon shirt, and my favorite knee-high, leather boots. I looked good, but I also looked like I wanted to be comfortable and not pick up potential bed-warming friends.

"Yup," he rumbles.

"You don't talk much, do you?"

He looks over briefly before returning his attention back to the road. "I don't think you've been around me enough to make that assumption."

"True. But so far tonight, I've said hello and gotten one of those man chin-lift greeting thingies. I asked you how you were and you grunted. I asked if you liked Loaded Replay and I got another grunt, and when you were ready to leave, all you said was, 'Truck,' and walked away. So you're right—I don't know you that well, but I think I actually can safely make that assumption correctly."

He looks over again. This time, his stoic face is grinning. "I can see what the attraction is now."

What an odd thing to say. "Excuse me?"

"I never could understand why Cohen would go on and on about you—no offense—but I get it now. You've got some fire under all of that innocence."

Oh. "Wait. Cohen would go on and on about me?"

"Clueless," he laughs. "You're right about one thing: I don't talk much. But that doesn't mean I don't watch. That guy has been watching you for as long as I've been around. And I don't just mean looking at you a few times when you walk in a room—the second that you walk in, his eyes never leave you. Always thought he was crazy, but I get it."

"Uh, I'm glad?" What am I supposed to say here? *Thanks for understanding why he is attracted to me?*

He shakes his head and continues to drive with his smirk in place. Such a weird man.

Since we were a little late to leave, when we finally get to the arena, they have already started letting people in. Every inch, from the ticket-holders at the entry to the ushers standing at the seating doorways, is crawling with fans. No, crawling would be a bad word for it. There literally isn't an extra inch to move. Everyone is yelling, beers are spilling, and the air around us is full of excitement to see one of, if not the, hottest bands in the country. Most of the chicks are in various stages of slut. Because Wrenlee Davenport, with her undeniable beauty, which is matched with one hell of a set of pipes, there seems to be an even mix of both men and woman milling around. A group of teenage shits almost cause me to drop to the ground when they go running through the crowd. If it weren't for Chance catching me at the last second of my stumble, I would have been on the ground.

No one even bothers to talk. It wouldn't do any good. Chance grabs my hand, I turn and grab Lyn, and I watch until we're all connected. This should be fun. Lyn gives me a look that tells me that she won't be letting go even if we go down. She wouldn't, either. If she goes down, the heifer will take everyone down with her.

Ten minutes later, we finally make it to our seats—best freaking seats in the house—and that's only because Chance finally had enough and started shouldering his way through the crowd. He isn't a bulky guy like my brother, but he is tall, and what he lacks in bulk, he makes up for with his general attitude. I probably would have gotten out of the way, too.

"I'm so fucking pumped!" Maddi screams, waving her fist in the air.

"Me too! Oh my God. Do you think we can get the guys attention? I'll probably piss myself if Weston looks my way. Like, legit piss myself." Lyn starts to fan herself with her hand, and her eyes roam around the stage just feet in front of us.

"That's disgusting," I laugh.

"Nope. I wouldn't piss myself. I would probably come in my pants though!" she exclaims.

"Jesus Christ," Chance grumbles.

I laugh and continue to look around the packed venue. Everyone around us is vibrating with the same crazy energy I've felt since we pulled into the parking garage. It's hard to contain the excitement you feel when you know you're about to see a group so huge perform. I tune out the girls, ignore an uncomfortable Chance, and just soak it all in. My earlier exhaustion is long forgotten.

The lights dim thirty minutes later, and the opening act, an all-female rock band called Carnage, is now working the stage. I'm not a huge fan, but the girls are, so while they jump and scream, I join in the fun. Honestly, I just can't wait to see Loaded Replay.

"Holy shit! Here they come!" screams Maddi and Lyn.

As if they heard them scream, all the lights go off, and after a small pause, there is a heavy drum beat that fills the air. Just *thump, thump, thump* fills the space and takes the excitement in the crowd to explosive levels. It doesn't last long as a solo beat until I hear and feel the bass line that makes my skin breakout in goose bumps. And seconds later, the electric guitar rift that lights the air around us has the girls next to me acting like they're hormonally challenged. The second the lights stream onto the stage, lighting up the four members of LR, Lyn and Maddi have tears streaming down their faces—the freaks. Stella is bobbing her head in tune with the beats, her long, brown hair swishing around her angelic face. Lila is laughing at her sister's and Maddi's antics, but she keeps peeking at the stage.

Elbowing Chance, I try to get his attention to let him know I need to use the restroom, but his eyes are transfixed on the stage. Well, not the stage. He's looking dead on at the stunning lead singer. The same lead singer who is holding his gaze with a wicked gleam in her bright eyes.

I must be the only one in the whole damn place who isn't acting like a bitch in heat.

Whatever. I don't want to miss more of the show than I have to, but if I don't pee now, I'll be pulling a Maddi and really embarrass myself. Chance doesn't even notice that I'm leaving until I'm already through the row of screaming fans and turning to walk up the ramp. I look back and catch his pissed eyes before I give him a sassy wave and walk off. Hey, when a girl has to go, she doesn't wait around.

Okay, so leaving the man who is supposed to be watching me for the evening wasn't my brightest move. I'm sure I'll have to deal with him being pissed when I get back—or worse, I'll have to deal with my father if he tells him. I've always been an independent person, so having to rely on someone else to babysit me isn't my favorite pastime.

I make it back to the seat, having only missed one song, but predictably, Chance is fuming.

"Don't pull that shit again, Dani. I like my balls right the fuck where they are. Your father wants me here for a reason, so don't act like a child and ignore that."

He's right. I know he is.

Wisely, I nod my head before turning my attention back to the show.

But I also don't mention the weird feeling I got when I was walking alone through the arena.

Chapter 21

Cohen

FUCK ME, I HATE BEING here.

I hate every day I'm away from home and stuck in this fucking sandbox.

Every day I'm here, I feel like I lose a part of my soul.

My worry for things at home have hit an all-time high, and if it weren't for my training, I would have been dead days ago when we hit an ambush of gunfire and bombs.

The only thing that is keeping me going is the knowledge that it might be over soon. We got word a few hours ago that, if things start to turn around, we could be home as early as two months from now. Two months is a whole hell of a lot better than the seven months this mission was projected at.

God, I can't wait to get home.

I've felt this pit in my gut since Dani told me about the flowers that have been showing up at her place. This feeling I'm helpless to correct. A feeling that has been screaming at me to get my ass home as quickly as I can because something is wrong.

My girl needs me and I'm completely fucking helpless.

Chapter 22

Dani

THE LAST THING I WANT to deal with on a Monday morning is camera crews and a manic Sway. No. That's not right. I don't want to deal with them any day, but today, I'm in bitch mode and I just can't seem to shake myself out of it. Every look someone gives me, even if it's just a smile, has me wanting to punch something. I can't decide if I just need more sleep or if I should kill Maddi for keeping me up all night with the noises that were coming out of her room.

I had considered going over to Cohen and Chance's place. I've escaped to Cohen's bed more times than I care to admit since he's been gone. More so since the Loaded Replay concert two weeks ago. I'm sure my family and my roommates are starting to notice my lack of attendance here lately. Chance isn't exactly the best company either, but we've become good enough friends that, between the grunts and hard looks, he's kind of fun to be around. Okay, fun isn't exactly the right word for what he is. He fills the void of loneliness the girls just can't. He talks to me about my concerns when it comes to Cohen and his "going dark," and since he's lived that life, it's reassuring to hear from him that it just means Cohen is on mission and needs to stay focused.

So here I am. After a night of no sleep, contemplating if I would be able to get away with murder.

We're on filming day two million seventy-five—okay, I kid—and I'm about to shove these cameras up Sway's ass. Of course, it doesn't help that Lyn decided to call out because she was partying all night long, causing me to have to spend almost an hour rescheduling all of her clients. The new chick, Samantha, was a no-show, and Sway has been doing fucking cartwheels around the salon because of some heels that went on sale at Saks.

Yeah. I'm officially just having a crappy Monday.

And Devon is still gone, so Don and Mark have been up my ass all day. Okay, I take that back. Don has. He doesn't bother me as much as he did when we first met two months ago, but that doesn't mean he doesn't annoy the ever-loving shit out of me.

Mark, on the other hand, is silent and broody, and he generally makes it his life mission to let me know that I'm not working the camera like I should be and how the show all depends on us following the scripted points Devon wants us to hit. That is usually followed up by me reminding the idiot that it's a reality show, not a scripted sitcom.

But together, they both give me the creepiest vibes ever. I can't decide if Mark and his silent "I hate the world" vibes are worse than Don and his creepy little winks and smiles.

Today freaking sucks. I look over at a scowling Mark and think, again, how many ways I could make his death look like an accident. His newest scowl is because I wouldn't ask my last male client out on a date and make it look like I had been pining after him for months.

As freaking if.

"What has gotten into you, sweet girl?" Sway asks when he is finally able to stop dancing around.

"Just feeling a little low today," I mumble and continue to stock my station.

"Do you need me to kick the cameras out today?"

I look over at him, shocked, because Sway would never kick the cameras out. He loves every second of this reality show crap. His handsome, caramel skin is etched in concern. Dark, perfectly sculpted brows are pulled in, and his eyes show love and compassion. He runs one of his—manicured, of course—hands over his buzzed hair and waits for me to answer.

"I'm okay. Promise. Just keep that one away from me," I tell him and point over at Don.

"You got it, darlin.' Just promise Uncle Sway that, if you start looking any more blue, you'll take that skinny ass home." He wraps his arms around me, his silk blouse cool against my cheek.

"Promise," I sigh, soaking in the comfort I didn't realize I wanted or needed.

In all honesty, for the last two weeks, I've just started feeling . . . weird. I think a lot of it has to do with the fact that I miss Cohen and hold some resentment towards life because he was taken away from me right when we had finally gotten somewhere. Everyone seems to be doing just fine and I'm little miss broody. I hate feeling this way, but it's almost like I'm helpless to stop those thoughts.

I just want him home.

"Well, hello, my sweet child."

I smile to myself when my mother's soft voice enters my brooding.

"Hey," I sigh and let all my stress drain from my body when she wraps her arms around me and gives me a tight hug. "What are you doing here? Did I miss an appointment?"

"Since when do I need an appointment to come and take my only daughter out to lunch?" she smarts.

"Oh, my bad," I laugh. "Sway called, huh?" I correctly guess. That man can't help it. He hates seeing any of his girls upset.

"He sure did. He also told me he would handle your next two clients and that I wasn't supposed to bring you back until I've checked out the new sales at Lenox Mall. He also told me that, if you argue about missing work or upsetting clients or whatever of your 'outrageously cockamamie' excuses are, I'm supposed to tell you he has your father on speed dial and won't hesitate to call him." Her smile is huge, her jade-colored eyes flashing with humor.

I peer over her shoulder and look at a smiling Sway. He gives me a wink before spinning on his heels and returning to his conversation with Don. God, he's such a meddler.

"Well, I guess, since the boss man has spoken, I have a free day to spend with you."

She laughs softly. "Go ahead and do what you need to get ready, baby. I'm going to go bother Sway for a little while."

"Stay away from the cameras, Mom. You know Daddy would shit himself if you ended up some weird, fake twist in the story line. Knowing how these idiots work, you would end up being Sway's new lover and the reason that he is leaving his husband and daughter. Scandalous stuff. Just downright indecent!" I throw my hand over my chest and mock outrage.

I make quick work of cleaning up my station and making sure I have everything together for tomorrow's clients. Mom is still busy laughing and chatting with Sway when I walk up to the front desk. Don is nowhere to be seen, but Mark is standing next to one of their camera crew members with his arms crossed and a scowl firmly in place. I'm sure he's pissed that I'm leaving in the middle of a film day. Well, what the hell ever. I know it's childish, but I can't stop myself before I stick my tongue out.

I win this round.

"God, I'm stuffed," I laugh, pushing my plate of wings away from me before I can grab another one. This happens every single time Mom talks me into coming to Heavy's, her favorite barbeque place in town. From the way Dad talks, she's been hooked on this stuff like crack since before Nate was born.

"Well, give it here. No sense in letting those wings go to waste."

I laugh when she pulls the plate I just discarded in front of her and finishes it off in record time.

"I have no idea how you stay so tiny. You should really be at least five hundred pounds."

She looks up, her eyes shining. "That's because I work out every night."

"Yeah, right! I've never seen you step one foot in the gym . . . Oh. My. God. Don't say anything else. Some things can't be unheard, Mom!" Ugh! I do not want to think about how she works off all this damn food. Nope. Not thinking about it.

"What?" she says in shock, but she still has that devilish smirk. "Your father bought me one of those stair thingies."

"An elliptical?"

"Yes?"

"You don't even know what it's called! I bet it's not even out of the box," I laugh.

She wipes her fingers off on the wet napkin and laughs at me. "Moving on, sweetheart. Why don't you tell me what is going on with you? I called the house the other day and Lyn said you were out. I thought . . . Well, I thought that you and Cohen . . . I guess I'm just wondering what's going on."

"Why does everyone keep asking me what's going on? I'm fine. I was a little upset—okay, a lot upset—when Cohen left, but I'm fine. Really."

"Dani, you aren't fine."

I look at her—really look at her—and notice how concerned she looks. All the humor she held on her beautiful face is long gone and she's looking at me like she can see right through me.

I sigh. "I miss him, Mom. It really just is that simple."

"I see."

"I know we haven't talked about it since Daddy freaked out, but are you really okay with this? Cohen and me?"

She reaches out and takes the hand I was resting against the table. "Honey, I couldn't be more thrilled. I only ask because you haven't seemed like you're handling this separation well, and trust me—I understand."

I give her a sad smile because I know all about how well she did not handle the separation from my dad all those years ago.

"It's just . . . The girls mentioned that you haven't been sleeping at the house, and even though I know it isn't my business, I guess I'm just concerned and being nosy."

One thing I love about my mom is that she is super easy to talk to. I know that, when I tell her that I've been sleeping over at Cohen's apartment, she might not like the idea, knowing that Cohen doesn't live alone, but if anyone will understand where my head is in all of this, it's going to be her.

"You promise not to tell Daddy? *You* will understand, but him? No, he most definitely will not."

Her brow furrows, but she nods her head. I know she doesn't like keeping things from him, but I hope she can keep this to herself.

"I've been sleeping at Cohen's place."

She doesn't say a word.

"In his bed. It's just . . . Okay, I know this is going to sound insane, but there's just something inside me that makes me *have* to be near him. I never imagined I would miss him this much, and being in his space, his bed, surrounded by his things . . . It just makes this emptiness

I constantly feel a little easier to bear."

"Oh, sweetheart." Her eyes start to water, and I know it's only seconds before she turns on the waterworks.

"Please don't get upset. I really am okay. It's just been a little of an adjustment. I haven't been sleeping well, and it just all caught up on me this last month, but when I'm in his bed, I sleep like the dead. I swear it makes no sense. We had just come together and decided to take a try at a relationship. Our time was so limited before he left that it might as well have just been seconds. How is it possible to miss him so much?"

She doesn't waste a second. My chin starts to wobble a little, so she is instantly on my side of the booth and pulling me close to her.

"You know about when your father left for his tour? I was a mess, Dani. Not just because of everything that happened after—losing my parents, our first child—even though those were enough to send me over the edge into the deep end. I was a mess because I didn't have the one person who gives my heart a reason to beat. Don't for one second downplay that feeling or its significance. Let me ask you this. If you think that you're having a hard time without him, how do you think he's handling everything? Do you think it would do him any favors to know that you're suffering when he isn't here?"

"No, Mom, I don't think it would." And honestly, it wouldn't. If he knew how upset I was about his being gone—knowing that was one of the major reasons he didn't want to start this between us—then it would do nothing but cause a distraction. "Of course he doesn't *know* that, though, and doesn't have a way of knowing how I'm doing."

"My silly little girl. I'm sure you don't realize this because this is really the first time you've loved someone with so much power behind it. When your other half is in pain, you always know."

"How am I supposed to just not miss him?" I ask.

"You aren't supposed to stop missing him, Dani. But you can't let that desire to have him near take over your life. You're pushing away your friends, you aren't coming to family dinners, and hell, you haven't even talked to your father in a few days. Something that I promise you he hasn't missed. You have to keep living your life, but living it in a way that you have that knowledge that he's coming home to you and this separation isn't forever. I lived twelve years thinking that I wouldn't ever see your father's face, Danielle. I know pain, and I know what it feels like when you feel like you have no hope left. These feelings you have aren't even close. You and Cohen, darling girl . . . You two have been fated from the beginning, and there isn't a damn thing that could take that away from you."

"What does that mean? We've been fated from the beginning?"

She takes a deep, shuddering breath and lets it out on a whoosh. "Let me tell you a little story. One that I hoped I never had to tell you, but one I think will help you understand why I am certain this thing between you and Cohen is much bigger than you even understand."

She takes the next thirty minutes to tell me all about her first marriage, one I knew she had but never ever knew the terrible details. Daddy doesn't like to talk about him, her first husband, and now that I know the hell my mother lived through during those years, I completely understand.

"You see, when I finally left my ex, I really didn't think I had hope left, Dani. I had Dee in my life, and she probably would have been my savior for the rest of my days, but I still felt empty. Then, when we moved here, to Hope Town, that was when Greg came into our lives. He had known Dee for a while, and as you know, he served with your daddy. I always used to ask myself why God was so cruel to make me spend all of those years without your father, to take our first child away, and bring all of that pain. It wasn't until years and years later, when I was sitting on the back porch during one of our family parties, that I realized what the big picture was. And let me tell you, I would have lived through all of that again if it would end in the same outcome."

"I don't understand," I tell her.

"Let me finish, sweetheart." She shifts in her seat and pulls something from her jacket pocket. "I took this that day. The sun was so beautiful that I just had to get a good shot of it. It was bouncing off the lake and outlining the dock and the trees around it, God, it was stunning. Here," she says and holds something out to me.

I look down, not sure what to expect, and gasp. I don't remember the moment. I was too young, but I recognize us instantly. She's right. The picture outlines the dock and the trees surrounding their property line to perfection. It also highlights the two figures sitting at the very end of the dock. I must have been around six or seven in this picture. It was the year I convinced my mom it would be a brilliant idea to cut my long, thick hair to my chin. Cohen, even at eleven, was so much larger than my tiny frame. We're sitting close, our heads touching temple to temple, and his scrawny arm is wrapped around my shoulders. I have no idea what we were doing or talking about, but it's clear in that picture that there was something so loving about the two of us.

"Even at a young age," she continues, "he was always drawn to you. If you were hurt, he was there. When Nate was being . . . well, Nate, he was always around to make sure whatever upset you was fixed. And the same went for him. Even as a baby, if you knew he was around, your sweet, chubby face would light up. You and Cohen have been a long time coming, and I know that everything that has ever happened in the past was to make sure this moment, every moment since then until now, was going to happen. It's fate, baby. I used to think it hated me, but I just realized that it works with the bigger picture. I never would have met Greg if it wouldn't have been for everything I went through, but I also wouldn't be able to be the mom you need—the one with the experience of what you're going through—if I hadn't lived it myself."

"Oh, Mom," I gasp and choke back the sob that so desperately wants to escape.

"I guess my point is, you might not feel whole right now, and, sweetheart, I understand why, but you will soon. Fate won't keep you two apart when it's been so clear that together is where you're meant to be. Hold strong and don't let this pain of missing him make you push everyone else who loves you away."

Clutching that picture to my chest, I let her words sink in and vow to do better at this whole "missing someone" business.

Chapter 23

Dani

FTER ALL OF THE EMOTIONAL heaviness at lunch, we decided to spend the rest of the afternoon shopping. Even though it's a pastime I know my mother loathes to an extreme, she knows that it's something I love. I didn't realize how much I needed some mother/daughter time, and now that she's opened up my eyes to how well she knows what I'm going through, it's easier knowing that I have her to talk to about everything I'm feeling with Cohen being gone.

The sun is starting to fall behind the trees by the time we make it back to the complex where Sway's is located. Even with the late hour, the parking lot is far from empty.

Mom pulls her car next to mine and gives me a big hug. "I want you to come to me if you start feeling down again, Dani. Don't let it fester until you're being dragged down with exhaustion. Miss your man, but don't mourn someone who's coming back to you."

"Promise. I love you," I respond, feeling lighter for the first time in weeks.

I don't think I realized how much I needed this. I just don't feel like I can talk to the girls about this knowing that they're missing their brother just as much as I am. Lee doesn't understand even though I know he would try. And Chance is just . . . Chance.

"I'm going to go and see your father before I head home. Do you want to come with me? I know he would love to see you."

"I'll be over in a little while. Let me drop all of these bags in my trunk and head in to tell Sway I'm going to take tomorrow off. I think I just need a mental day. One that's away from those damn cameras."

"All right, baby."

She walks away, waving at Sway through the floor-to-ceiling windows on the salon and heading through the door to Corps Security, my dad's company he co-owns with the rest of his buddies. It's not lost on me that he probably loved it when I started working right next door so that he could keep his eyes on me.

Absentmindedly, I walk behind my car and toss in the bags that hold the clothes I did not need to buy. My mind is still on the afternoon and everything my mom and I talked about. It isn't until I step between the cars that I notice the piece of paper sticking out from the driver's side door, flapping against the window with the light breeze.

Reaching out, I snag the slim paper and look around. Shrugging off the feeling of being watched that crawls up my spine, I unfold the paper and almost lose my lunch.

> YOU ARE SUPPOSED TO BE MINE, BITCH. YOU TAKE MY FLOWERS WITH A SMILE ON YOUR FACE, BUT SPEND YOUR TIME CRYING OVER SOME MOTHERFUCKER THAT ISN'T EVEN THERE. I HEARD YOU TODAY! YOU ARE MINE, DANIELLE! IF YOU THINK SOME OTHER MOTHERFUCK WILL HAVE YOU WHEN YOU BELONG TO ME—YOU ARE DEAD FUCKING WRONG.

I must be screaming. That's the only thing that makes sense, because not even seconds after my shocked and terrified hands dropped the note, I see my daddy, who is followed by Greg and Maddox, barreling through the door of his office and charging across the parking lot. Right as my head slams against the ground, I feel my body being lifted and cradled in his strong arms as he rushes away from that piece of paper, which is now being clutched between Greg's fist as he and Maddox look between each other with trepidation written all over their faces.

"She's going to the fucking hospital and that's the end of the discussion, Izzy. You didn't fucking see her, Izzy! Her head slammed against the ground, goddamn it!"

Damn, my head hurts. I push myself up from the couch in my dad's office and look around at the worried faces. My dad is crouched down on his knees in front of the couch, and my mom sitting on the armrest above where my head was just resting, her hand lying on his shoulder. I'm sure she is trying to calm him down. Maddox is leaning against the desk, and Greg is pacing the room.

"I'm okay," I say, but it comes out like a moan when my head starts to feel like it's spinning. "I think."

"See! She doesn't even fucking know if she's okay. Let's go, little princess. Time to go see the doctor." He jumps to his feet and goes to grab me before my mom reaches out one slim hand to stop him.

"Calm down, Ax. Let her speak for herself before you go crazy." She turns to me with concern etched on her face. "Sweetheart, is your head bothering you?"

"A little." I stop and look up to Greg, the last person who saw the message. "Do you have it?" I ask him.

"Yeah, baby girl. Don't worry about a thing, okay?"

A look I don't even attempt to process passes between him and my dad.

"I think it might actually be a good idea to go get checked," I moan. Then I lean over and lose my lunch all over my dad's feet.

Dad freaks out. He's convinced that I'm broken and someone needs to fix me. My head is hurting more from his continual barking at the staff at the urgent care clinic. My mom just sits back and lets him do his thing. She told me a long time ago that she learned her lesson when it came to him. He's going to over-parent and be protective to a point of annoyance and there just isn't a damn thing that will change him.

"Hello, Ms. Reid. I hear you took a nasty spill this afternoon," the young doctor says when she stops in the room. She smiles sweetly at me before looking over and seeing my parents. Her face instantly goes hard. "Mr. Reid, I presume?" At his nod, she continues. "I hear you've been giving my staff a hard time today."

I giggle, and Mom snorts a laugh out.

"Hello, Dr. Webb," I say after reading her jacket and effectively cutting my father off before he can start in on his rants. "It wasn't that bad. Just a little bump when I hit the ground. Lingering headache."

"Don't forget you threw up, Dani. Remember."

"Yeah, Daddy, I know. I was there." I roll my eyes and look up at the doctor.

"That's what they said. Your scans look fine, and aside from the contusion and obvious concussion, I would say you're fine. I'm going to write you a prescription for some low-dose pain meds that will be safe to take in your condition."

"Jeeze, Doc. You make it sound like I'm dying." I laugh and then wince when my head throbs.

"Oh, I'm sorry. Bad habit I guess. I know pregnant woman don't usually like us to refer to them as having a condition." She laughs, looking down at her chart, and doesn't even notice that the room has gone electric.

"I'm sorry?" I whisper. "What did you say?"

She looks up, noticing my expression before looking over at my parents. I don't know what she saw there since I'm absolutely terrified to look at my father.

"Oh, I am so sorry. I didn't realize. With your lab work and the date listed as your last menstrual cycle . . . I'm sorry. I just assumed."

"What are you saying, Doctor?" my father spits out. I can literally hear the force he had to use to get the words through his lips.

"I'll need to talk to you daughter in private, and then, when she's ready, she can choose to share the information we discuss as she sees fit. I do apologize, Mr. and Mrs. Reid."

I don't move my eyes from my lap. I keep my head down even through the struggle of my mom physically pulling my dad out of the room. I don't move when I hear him yelling out in the hallway or when I hear something crash. Not even when the door clicks loudly when the doctor shuts herself in the room with me.

The whole time, my mind is spinning.

Pregnant?

Surely, she's wrong. She must have someone else's chart. I remember the question about my last period. I just opened the app on my phone and put what it said. My periods have always been erratic, so I never even gave it a second thought.

"Danielle? Is it okay that I call you Danielle?"

"Dani," I mumble.

"I'm sorry?"

"It's Dani. I've always hated Danielle. Sounds like a mouthful, so I go by Dani. It works. I don't get any annoying nicknames. I'm just Dani. Dani Reid. That's me. Holy shit, am I freaking pregnant?!" I end my verbal vomit on a scream that makes me wince.

"I take it this is a surprise?"

"Very much so," I tell her, starting to freak out a little.

"How about I go get our portable ultrasound machine and we get a little look. Might ease your mind and make it seem a little more real. Well, once the shock wears off." I nod my head, but I don't speak.

Pregnant.

Holy shit. Cohen is going to freak.

And my daddy is going to go apeshit.

Chapter 24

Cohen

THE NIGHTS ARE SO LONG here.

I'm left with nothing but longing to be home with my family and with Dani in my arms.

It gives me nothing but time to sit and think.

Think about the time I lost with Dani because I was too busy pushing her away.

Time I'm losing now because I'm over in this fucking hell, hunting terrorists.

And the worst feeling of all is that growing ache in my stomach that tells me I have to get home soon. I can't explain it any other way. It's a daily struggle to push the feeling aside so I can concentrate on my job and make sure I don't get blown the fuck up in the process.

One thing is for certain in all of this. This time away from Dani has proven one thing to me. That one night I had with her in my arms will never be enough.

I roll over on the hard ground and close my eyes, and just like the night before and every one since I've been here, I see her smiling face.

Chapter 25

Dani

THE DOCTOR COMES BACK IN the room, dragging some weird-ass computer behind her. She flips the light off before she has me lie back on the exam table, and she puts my shirt over my stomach before I can get over my shock. My leggings are wiggled down until they are resting just above my crotch. And then I let out a yelp when she squirts some goo on me.

"Sorry, Dani. I don't usually run the ultrasounds, so I must have grabbed the gel that wasn't in the warmer," she mumbles more to herself than to me.

I look down to where her hand is moving some wand-looking thing around in the disgusting goo. This is so nasty. All of this work for her to tell me that she read something wrong.

I have almost convinced myself that there was no way she could be right. Hell, Cohen used a condom every time, so surely there is no possible way for me to be pregnant. I haven't been throwing up. Everything has been normal. Just because I don't have a regular period doesn't mean I'm knocked up.

I am about to open my mouth and tell her just that when the oddest sound echoes through the small room. "What the hell?" I question at the noise. It sounds like thundering hoof beats.

"Well, that, Dani, is your baby."

She sounds so pleased that I can't help how my eyes narrow before the shock hits again. Jesus, it's just the night for shocks.

I hesitantly look over at the monitor she's pointing to before my heart stops for a beat before picking up. I have no idea what the heck I'm looking at. I just know it's the most beautiful thing I've ever seen in my whole life.

My baby?

Cohen's and my little miracle.

The doctor starts pointing to everything and explaining what I'm looking at. Every word she speaks, I soak up like a dying woman. Already head over heels in love with the child I was convinced only seconds before couldn't even be possible.

Holy crap. I'm going to be a mommy?

Even through I'm scared out of my mind for what this means for my future—my future with Cohen—I let the love for this child wash over me and smile the brightest smile I've probably ever had.

"So . . . surprised but happy?" she asks.

"Very." And I am. I really am.

"The baby's father? I can print these images for you."

"He's overseas. But I would love to have a few copies so that I can show him when he gets home."

"Of course. Do you know when he is expected to return? If you would like, just come on by when I'm on shift and I'll make sure you guys are able to sneak a peek at this little one. You're measuring right at twelve weeks, so unfortunately, it's too early for a gender screen. But come back in a few weeks and we can see if that little one wants to give you an early show."

"Thank you," I breathe roughly when she hands me the printouts of my baby and moves to turn the lights on. "Hey, Doc?"

"Yes?" She looks over after she washes her hands.

"Do you know if there is a back entrance you can sneak me out?"

She throws her head back with a laugh and shakes her head. "I'm sorry."

"It's okay. He's just a little . . . overprotective."

"I noticed." She laughs. "I'll step out and give you a minute. Congratulations, Dani. I want you to be careful. You shouldn't be alone tonight because of the concussion. You also need to follow up with your gynecologist later this week. Is it okay to have your parents come back in now?"

"Uh, yeah. Can you mention to my dad about my headache or something? It should keep his temper in check if he knows he can't freak out. Gives me a day or so to let this sink in."

She laughs but agrees.

When the door opens five minutes later and my mom walks in, she immediately wraps her arms around me. I can tell she's crying, but I wasn't expecting to see a huge smile on her face when she pulls back. She leans in and gives me a kiss on my forehead.

"I love you," she mouths.

I look over her shoulder and see my daddy. All six feet six inches of him, his tattooed arms crossed over his chest, and every vein bulging in his neck. His face is beet red, and his breathing is erratic.

Daddy is pissed.

"I love you, Daddy."

"And I love you, my little princess," he says, deflating some. Then, almost as if he remembered why he was so worked up, he stands tall again and his veins pop back out. "But I'm going to kill that motherfucker who touched you."

Mom gives me a squeeze, and I stay silent. Because really, what am I supposed to say to that?

Predictably, Daddy wouldn't take me home. He didn't say a word, even through all my complaining. Mom just giggled in the front seat. My head was killing me, so I wasn't willing to put up the fight. But I wasn't staying. My plan to call Lee the second we got over there was foiled when he answered and said that he was on a date.

My father thoroughly enjoyed watching me stew in my anger over being held hostage by him.

"Fine. I'll call one of the girls."

"The fuck you will, Dani! You might not remember how this night started, but I sure as hell do. Until we figure out what is going on with these flowers and now that note—you aren't leaving my sight."

"I'm not staying, Daddy. I'm perfectly safe at home. And if it's a problem, then Lee can stay with me."

"Liam doesn't own as many guns as I do," he snaps, crossing his arms over his chest, again, in his international Axel sign for "don't mess with me."

"Lee is also a black belt and could kick even your ass."

"Liam wouldn't be able to do shit against a knife or gun, Dani. You're safe here. I can keep you safe."

"I'm safe at home!" I scream.

"I know you're not going to argue with me, your father, who happens to own a fucking company that specializes in fucking security, that you're going to be better off without me watching over you. News flash, little princess: there isn't a single person that I trust to keep my little girl and future grandbaby safe."

His eyes soften slightly when he mentions the baby, and I just know that, despite his anger, which I'm sure will make another appearance, he's going to love this baby just as much as he loves Nate and me.

"Don't you look at me like that, Dani. I'm still going to kill that asshole who knocked up my little girl."

I'm not sure what it was in his tone that made me look back over at him. "What? I can tell you have more to say."

"I didn't want to get into this while everything that happened today is still so fresh, but I have to say . . . I'm disappointed in you, Dani. I never thought that you would do something like this to Cohen. I just hope that, whoever that bastard is, he's worth the trouble he caused. I might not have told you, but I couldn't have picked a better man for you to end up with than Cohen, and when he finds out you're pregnant with another man's child, I don't see how that can end well."

He turns and walks out of the room. His words hit me right in the gut before they slam directly into my heart.

Another man's child? What in the hell!

I don't even take a second to process my anger. I grab my cell out of my purse and search for the number I need. It doesn't take long for the call to connect.

"'Lo?"

"Chance? Can you please come get me?" I hiccup through a sob.

Chapter 26

Dani

CHANCE DIDN'T ASK ANY QUESTIONS. He pulled into my parents' driveway thirty minutes later and honked the horn. I didn't even pause. I got my purse, grabbed the bag with my meds, and walked out the front door. I could hear my dad yelling when I jumped in the passenger seat and slammed the door before locking it.

Chance looks at me with questions in his eyes before he looks past me to where I'm sure my father is fuming.

"If I drive out of here right now, is it going to get me killed?" he asks.

"Possibly."

"Right. Well, seeing as I like being alive and I plan to keep on breathing for a while longer, I'm going to step out of the truck and have a chat with your dad."

Before I can stop him, he opens the door and steps out.

Shit!

I can hear them talking, but not what is being said because the window is up and the hum of his engine is drowning them out. Hesitantly,

I reach over and press the down button until the window is cracked slightly.

"... just came because she called me and sounded upset. I owe it to Cohen to make sure she's okay, sir. No offense, but if she isn't okay here, then I'll step in."

"Is it yours?" my dad barks.

"Is what mine?"

"The baby."

Chance looks over his shoulder at me. His face is stoic, but his eyes flash in warning. Warning of what, I'm not sure.

"I was unaware that Dani was expecting, sir."

"Cut the bullshit, Chance. Are you sleeping with my daughter? With your roommate's girl? Do you think I don't know about the nights she's been sneaking over to your place?"

Holy shit. This is bad.

"Axel!"

I look between the two men standing toe-to-toe in my parents' driveway to see my mom running down their porch steps.

"You need to step away right now. This, all of this, is none of your business, and as much as it kills you that it isn't, it's time to shut the hell up before you cause your daughter more pain. We will have words later about what you're accusing her of."

God, I love my mom.

Chance doesn't give him a second to reply. He steps away, turns, and walks back to the driver seat.

Mom calls his name and gets his attention before he can shut the door. "She needs to be watched tonight after her fall. Wake her up every few hours. I trust you to take care of her?"

"Yes, ma'am." He shuts the door and backs out of their driveway.

I can tell he has plenty to say, but he's keeping quiet.

"I'm sorry, Chance," I whisper.

He doesn't speak, but he reaches out and grabs my hand, holding it tight in his and giving me just what I need at the moment.

Someone else to be my strength.

The second we got back to the apartment, I took off to Cohen's room. By the time my head hits his pillow, I was ready to crash. Chance gave me the time I needed—and wanted—to be alone. The only time I saw him was the two times that he woke me in the middle of the night.

I can't believe that my own father would think so low of me. Even through my hurt that he would even say such a thing, I can see where the thought sprouted. Cohen's been gone, and by his own account, he knows I've been coming over here. It makes sense, even if his lack of faith in me is heartbreaking.

I don't realize I'm crying until I feel the bed depress.

"You want to talk about it? I'm not good with the chick shit, but I can try to help."

"I think you've guessed that I'm pregnant?"

"Figured as much when your dad was about to rip my head off and assumed I had slept with you. I thought he knew you and Cohen were together?"

I sigh. "You should know him well enough to know that, when he's mad, he gets . . . irrational. I guess he didn't consider that it was something that happened before Cohen left. And everything that happened today, with the note and then the baby bomb, I guess he just lets his emotions get the best of his."

"I won't insult you by questioning if this is Cohen's or not, but you do realize that it's going to be on the top of everyone's assumptions that this baby isn't his?"

"I've waited for him my whole life, Chance. Everyone who knows me knows that. I just can't believe my own father . . ." I trail off and leave it hanging. No sense in beating a dead horse.

"Why don't you tell me about the note? Then give either your girls or Liam a call. You need your friends around you, and honestly, Dani, I like you enough, but I don't know how to be the shoulder you are bound to cry on at some point."

I laugh and take a deep breath, willing my hurt feelings not to fester into tears. "Yeah, okay." I tell him all about the note and what I remember it saying, which isn't much, but he promises to check with the guys at work to get more details. In the end, I feel a little better just having someone to talk to, but I decide that he's right and I need my people.

Not knowing what to say to the twins yet, I pick up and dial Lee, knowing that he can help me sort my head before I call them. Having just dropped his date off, he agrees to head on over to the apartment. I can tell he wants to ask questions, but he hangs up with the promise to be over shortly.

"Well, you really managed to go all out in the drama tonight, Dani," Lee says, leaning back against the headboard and opening his arms so that I can rest against his chest.

"Can you believe I'm pregnant, Lee?"

"Honestly? I can't say I'm shocked. I mean, it's Cohen."

"What the hell does that mean?" I laugh.

"The man wore a cape for, what . . . like, twenty years. He's some super-secret black ops marine. I'm pretty sure he could kill me a million different ways—the man is just born to have super everything."

"We used a condom, Lee."

He gags. "I love you, Dani, but I don't want to talk about that shit. Let's just leave it at shit happens and his super sperm battered down the shield."

I slap his stomach. "God, you're disgusting." I settle back down for a second before I push up and spin to look at him. "Do you think Cohen will think the same thing my dad did?"

Lee doesn't say anything, which doesn't help the trepidation I already feel. "I'm not going to lie to you, Dani. From the outside, without all the facts, it looks shady. But you said it yourself. Your dad didn't even know how far along you are."

"I would never betray Cohen like that."

He smiles. "Yeah, I know that. It's a shitty situation, Dani. Wait until Cohen gets back before you start to worry about it. I will say, I wouldn't keep this from the girls."

"I didn't plan on it. I just need to process things. I'll call them tonight."

"Sure thing, babe. Come on. Let's get some rest. I came straight here after a night out with Stacy. I'm fucking beat."

Lee and I managed to get a good few hours in before the knocking started. Chance left a note that said that he was over at Megan's and would be back later. He's been spending a lot of time with her lately. I teased him about finally dating, something I've never seen him do, but he told me that it isn't anything other than helping her out with her daughter. I push back my normal embarrassment and guilt when I think about my first impression of her. Now, having met her, I know she is just a grieving woman who needs her friends.

I step out of Cohen's room and walk to the door. When I look through the peephole, I smile and shake my head at the noise four fists can produce against one door.

Well, that didn't take long.

I open the door right when Lyn is about to bang on it again and just barely dodge her fist.

"Damn, Lyn!"

"About time, bitch," she snaps.

"Hey, Dani." Lila gives me a hug and follows her sister into the apartment.

"Where's Lee?" Lyn asks, looking around.

"Right here. God, could you be any louder. I was out with the screecher before I came over here, and God, my head hurts."

All three of us look over at Lee and gawk.

"I can't believe you went out with her crazy ass again," Lila snaps. "The last time you went out with her, didn't she go on and on about how many babies she wanted to have with you AND detailed out their names and what they would look like?"

"Christ, you must love crazy," Lyn mumbles.

"Oh, shut up. It wasn't that bad. Plus, I was horny."

"You're disgusting," Lila sighs.

"All right. Enough of this shit. What's going on with you?" Lyn says.

"What makes you think something's going on?" I hedge.

"Don't play me for a fool. First of all, you don't come home at all last night. You don't answer your phone. Your car is still at the salon! And if that isn't enough, when we went home to Mom and Dad's for dinner, Cam was going on and on about how he and Colt overheard Dad telling Mom about how you got some fucked-up letter after work today. *Then* he said that you had to go to the emergency room. If that's not enough to know something is most definitely up with you, then you're insane." She takes a deep breath, and for the first time, I see through her anger and the worry she must have had all night for me, instantly making me feel guilty.

Taking a strengthening breath, I point to the couch. "You two might want to sit down."

Chapter 27

Dani

"SO LET ME GET THIS straight. You got some fucked-up letter at work and proceeded to pass out. You went to the doctor, found out my brother knocked you up, and then your dad flipped his shit and accused you of basically being a slut?" Lyn finishes her rehashing of my last twenty-four hours with a dramatic sigh. "Wow. When you decide to go for the shock factor, you really put your all in it."

"I'm going to be an aunt?" Lila says breathily.

"Holy shit, we're going to be aunts!" Lyn screams, and I wince when her loud tones hit my ears.

"Did you just register that little nugget? What part of 'my brother knocked you up' didn't register that fact?" Lila smarts.

"Oh, shut it, Lila! I'm in shock here."

"So . . . I take it you two don't share my father's immediate reaction?"

They both stare at me with a mix of outrage and sadness. Like I've lost my damn mind, which is a feeling I share with them both at the moment.

"You've been in love with my brother for years, Dani. Even if that weren't the case, you aren't the type of person who strays when you're in a relationship. Regardless of where the other person is, you're loyal to your very core."

I smile at Lila's words. I didn't realize how badly I needed to hear that they believed me.

"I'm sure he regrets it, Dani. You know your dad. He's hotheaded, and as protective of you as he is, I'm sure the 'whole letter on the car, falling and getting hurt, and *then* finding out he's about to be a grand-father' took a toll on him. Yeah, I think it's safe to say he was probably tipping over the boiling point." Lyn reaches over and rubs my hand. "That doesn't excuse it. You have every right to be upset. I just can't figure out why you wouldn't call us." She gives me a sad smile, but there's no judgment in her gaze.

"I needed to be around Cohen. I'm not even sure I realized it at the moment, but the second I got here—surrounded by his things—I don't know how to explain it. I just felt like I was . . . home."

Lila has a big dopey smile on her face, and Lyn is looking at me in complete understanding.

"You still could have called us, Dani. We would have been here in a second. Did you think we would be upset or something?" Lyn pushes.

"It has nothing to do with that. I promise. I was still wrapping my head around it all myself. I wanted to be here, alone, and spend time with Cohen the best I can without him being here. My God, I sound like a complete nut job," I groan and drop my head into my hands. "He left here thinking he had one type of girl and he's going to come home to me being a complete basket case. Who comes over to their boy-friend's place so they can sniff his shit and hug his pillow?"

They both throw their heads back and laugh. The tension is broken just like that.

My girls get me. They always have, and that will never change.

"How about we spend the rest of the night doing girly shit and binge-watch some old One Tree Hill shows?" Lila asks as she stands to give me a big hug.

"At the risk of sounding even crazier . . . can we do that here?" I ask.

"Sure thing. I mean, I don't think smelling my grungy brother will be quite as comforting for me as it is for you, but I'm down." Lyn laughs. "We need to get some junk food too. Fatten you up already! I can't wait for you to have a cute little belly. Oh my God! I still can't believe my niece or nephew is cooking away in there."

I stop, causing them both to bump into me in the middle of the hallway. My jaw goes slack and my eyes wide.

"Holy shit. I'm gonna get fat!" I spin, grab the nearest body, and shake her shoulders. I can hear Lyn laughing her ass off behind an equally shocked Lila. "I'm going to be a big freaking whale by the time he gets home. He left me all skinny, toned, and hot, and he's going to come home and I'll be like, 'Oh hey, big boy, guess what? I ate a whale and you knocked me up!'"

Why are they laughing so hard? Can't they tell how much I'm freaking out here? There is no damn way he's going to want me all fatty mcfat fat.

"This is going to be terrible," I groan and turn my back on two of my best friends, who are losing their sanity with how much they're laughing. When I hit Cohen's room, I crawl back in the center of his bed and wrap my arms around one of his pillows.

"You're a mess, Dani. Cohen isn't going to just stop loving you because you have a belly. Plus, I hear some guys actually find it even more attractive. Stop freaking out over something you have no control over. Warning though, he will be shocked. I know my brother, and he might just pass out when he finds out."

I gasp and shoot up to my elbows to glare at Lila. "Do what?"

"Do you really think he's going to not even be a little shocked when you tell him that he gave you a little going-away present? No man would be able to take that kind of news without a little shock, Dani. Don't worry about it. It's all going to be fine. One thing about Cohen, and you know this, is that boy was made to be a father. He's always looked forward to when he will settle down and start a family. I think it comes with the whole idolizing our dad thing."

"What the hell are you talking about?" I question her.

"Just ask Lyn. When we were busy planning our weddings and what big, bright futures we would have as kids, Cohen would always tell us about how he couldn't wait to get older. He would be a hero just like Dad and have a house full of kids and a woman he loved to warm his bed. Of course, I never understood the last part." Lila finishes and sits down next to me, pulling the pillow from my body and shoving it behind her head. "He's going to be so happy it's you, Dani."

I look at her for a beat, letting her words sink in, before I feel a big, crazy smile take over my lips.

Well, that all sounds like a dream come true.

Hours later, we are still sitting in Cohen's bed. Junk food is spread all over the comforter and season two of One Tree Hill is starting on Cohen's television. Thank you, Netflix, for making girls' emotional television binging so much easier.

Lyn and Lila did what they do best. They took my thoughts out of my head and made me stop freaking out. Every time I got quiet, they would knock every doubt I had out of my head.

We spent time looking at the ultrasound pictures and talking about baby names and what he or she would look like.

I am hoping for a boy who will have his father's strong features and gorgeous, brown eyes. The girls are hoping for a girl so that we can dress her up in all of these adorably cute outfits they already started looking for.

"Look at this one, Lila," Lyn squeals and turns her phone to show Lila whatever new outfit she found online.

"Hey, Dani," I hear from the front of the apartment, and I almost jump out of my skin.

"Holy shit, he scared the crap out of me," Lyn says with her palm pressed to her chest.

"You and me both." I climb over Lila and make my way down the hallway to where I think I heard Chance's voice. Right when I come out of the hallway and into their large, sunken living room, I halt in my tracks and feel my body lock up with tension.

Chance walks my way and gives me a reassuring squeeze on my shoulder before he continues down the hall. I turn and see him step into Cohen's room and shut the door behind him.

Well, I guess that means the girls won't be coming to my rescue.

With a deep sigh full of dread, I turn, square my shoulders, and face my father.

"You look like you're ready for battle, little princess," he says solemnly.

"That's because I feel like I'm gearing up for one."

"Dani—" he starts, going to take a step towards me . . . until I hold up my hand to pause his movement.

"I think it would be best to stay over there, Daddy. This can't be fixed with a hug."

His eyes close, and I can tell how much it's costing him to hold himself back. I have no doubt that he regrets what he said, but the fact remains that, however fleeting, the thought went through his head.

"You all but called me a whore, Daddy. Your own daughter. The one you raised to believe in the power of love, and despite your over-the-top protectiveness, I found that love. That once-in-a-lifetime soul mate connection you and Mom have. I never, not in a million years, expected that from you."

His face softens, "Baby," he sighs. "I'm so sorry."

"Do you really believe that, after loving Cohen for as long as I have, with the first hurdle our relationship is faced with, I would run to another man?"

He shakes his head, his eyes never leaving mine.

"I can understand that you're having a hard time with the fact that I'm not a baby anymore. I haven't been one for a long time, but I always knew you would struggle with letting me go until you literally couldn't hold on anymore. But what I can't understand is why you reacted the way you did."

"Please, my sweet little princess, let me hold you."

I'm not sure if it's the slight tremor in his deep voice that causes the first tear or if it's the one of his own sliding down his face, but the second that tear falls, there isn't a thing I can do to keep him from crossing the room.

"I needed my daddy," I sob into his chest. "I needed you and all I got were accusations I never in my life thought you would throw at me. I needed you to hold me and tell me that everything would be okay and that you loved me. But you pushed me away and it broke my heart."

"God, Dani. Please stop." His arms tighten around me, and I feel my feet lift off the ground. His head drops to my shoulder, and I feel him take a deep breath.

"I can't breathe," I gasp and squirm against him.

He gives me another squeeze before he lightly drops my feet back down. When he pulls back and I get my first look at his red-rimmed eyes, my heart breaks a little.

"I don't know how to forget what you said to me, Daddy," I sigh. "I expected your shock. I expected your anger at Cohen. But most of all, I expected your love."

He clears his throat. "Sit down, little princess. I think, maybe, I can help with that."

I follow behind him and sit down on the worn, leather recliner. Daddy sits next to me in the matching one, and I wait for him to talk. I have no idea what he thinks can give me—maybe some insight on how he reacted to my pregnancy—but I wait.

"I don't think I can explain just how it feels to grow up with shit parents, Dani, but the ones I had—they were as shitty as it gets. I never wanted you or your brother to know how bad it was for me when I was growing up. Never wanted that for you, but I think you need to hear some of it . . . to understand why I am the way I am."

I lean back and wait for him to continue. It's his show now.

"My parents . . . They were never sober. They were never not high off some drug. They never talked to me with anything other than hate. That was my life until Social Services took me and I ended up in the system. That wasn't much better, but I wasn't beaten and I ate enough that I didn't starve. But it was lonely, Dani. It was terribly lonely. Until I met your mom. Trust me when I tell you that I know exactly what you mean when you talk about a once-in-a-lifetime soul mate. That was and is your mom for me.

"You know about me being deployed and what happened to me and your mom during those years and the ones that followed. But I don't think I've ever told anyone, outside your mother, what it felt like when, years later I found out that our baby didn't make it. God, Dani . . . To hear how your mother suffered killed me, but to know that part of us had died gutted me. I know the rational side of it. I went to a few therapy sessions with your mom to have those quacks throw it out there in terms I could understand. For a child who grew up the way I did, to live that lonely life void of love, a child with the woman I loved more than life, was my second chance. I remember the day your mom told me, all those years after, and sitting on the dock behind the house, vowing to God that, if I was blessed with more children, I would never stop protecting them. I would give them the love, safety, and life I never had."

He stops and wipes a tear that escaped my eyes. I don't speak. We sit in silence while I wait for him to compose his thoughts.

"I know I take it to a level that is just too much when it comes to you, Dani. I look at you, seeing so much of your mother, and I'm reminded of that sweet, stars-in-her-eyes woman I left all those years ago. That I left to a life of hell for years. I see the pain I couldn't protect her from, and it makes me hold you just a little tighter. I think I rationalized with myself that, if I just held on as long as I could, you would never know that kind of pain."

"I still don't understand how you could even think that I could do something like this to Cohen, Daddy. How I could cheat on him?"

"I don't think that, baby. I didn't think it then, and I don't think it now. There is no excuse for what I said. I'm not disappointed in you. I'm disappointed in me. I was scared, Dani, and that's the simple truth. I was terrified when I heard them say you were pregnant. All of those old wounds just sliced right open, and what I felt all of those years ago came back tenfold. Only this time, it was my girl, my little princess, and I was terrified to my core."

Never in a million years did I expect that from him. My father? The big, bad Axel Reid was scared? Nope. Never.

"The second you left and I realized what I'd said, I wanted to chase you down, but your mom said that I should give you time. Well, actually, she screamed at me for being a jackass. I'm always going to look at you as my little girl, Dani, and there isn't anything that could change that. I'm damn proud of the woman you've grown to be, and I love you more than life itself. I can't tell you enough how sorry I am for letting my emotions and temper get the best of me."

"You hurt me," I tell him.

"I know, and it kills me."

After hearing where he was coming from, my heart settles a little and I understand where he was coming from. Even if it still hurts, I know it's more because the words are still fresh in my mind. He's always been hot to the touch when he feels things deeply. That's just how he's wired. And honestly, if I had been thinking clearly, I probably would have anticipated a reaction like his. Doesn't make it okay, but I can't hold a grudge because he was blinded by the pain of his past.

"I love you, Daddy."

"I love you too, little princess."

"You have to let me fly now," I whisper.

"I know I do. I know. I don't want to let go, Dani, but at least if I have to I know you'll be in good hands."

"You're really okay? With Cohen and me . . . and the baby?"

"Yeah, sweetheart. I really am. I'm scared, I won't lie about that, but I'll work on not projecting that on you. Just don't expect me to change overnight. My little girl having a baby of her own? Jesus, Dani." He pauses, stands, and pulls me up so he can give me a kiss on my forehead before wrapping me up in his strong arms for another hug. "I'm still going to kick his ass. You know that, right?" he says, his voice rumbling against my ear that's pressed against his chest.

"No, you won't."

"Oh really? And why is that?" he asks and pulls back to look at me, his green eyes shining.

"Because you won't hurt me like that."

"I'm still going to yell at him. Maybe even throw shit," he counters.

"Yeah, now that I can see."

He doesn't stay long after that. I know the girls are probably about to bust down the door to make sure I'm okay. I walk him to the door, my heart feeling so much more whole since he came by. With the promise to come over for dinner the following night, he leaves me with a hug.

With a smile on my face, I walk back down the hallway, feeling much lighter than I did earlier. Things aren't just going to be magically easier from now on. There's the small fact that Cohen doesn't even know he's about to be a father, but I have no doubt in my mind that he will be able to see this miracle for what it is.

At least, that's the hope I will wrap myself in until he returns.

Chapter 28

Cohen

EVERY FUCKING DAY, I START to resent the life I always thought I wanted. Fighting a war I don't see ever ending is starting to pay its price on my sanity, and my heart is starting to feel heavy with every passing second I am away from home.

I miss my family. My parents, sisters, and brothers. I hate knowing that they are at home worrying about me and my safety. I know every time I'm away in training or deployed that my mom doesn't sleep well and my dad has nightmares. My sisters do better, their belief that I'm invincible helping that. And my brothers hide their worry in beer and sex.

But worst of all, I miss Dani.

It's hard to believe that something I never knew I was missing would take root and make it impossible to imagine leaving her again. I know without a shadow of doubt that this will be my last deployment. When it comes time to reenlist, I won't regret my decision to stay home and start my life with her.

It sounds fucking nuts, but after all of this time away, I know where my future is, and it damn sure isn't in a big fucking sandbox, getting shot at daily.

The second I get home, I'm going to pull her father aside and beg for her hand in marriage. Then make my girl mine forever.

I smile when I think about the future we're going to have. That right there has been the only thing that's kept me sane. Years, so many damn years, I pushed these feelings away, and there's no way I'm going to waste a second more before I make sure she knows how I feel.

"Yo! Cage, boss man told me to make sure you got this. Came over urgent a second ago."

I look over when Ferguson hands me a folded piece of paper. I unfold it and realize it's an envelope with just my name on it.

"The hell is it?" I snap, wanting nothing more than to get some sleep.

"No clue. He took a call, took some notes, then stuffed it in here and told me to find you ASAP. So I found you and did what I was told. Now, take the shit so I can get some grub."

I snatch the envelope from him and walk away. I've never cared for Ferguson, but he's a damn good soldier.

We were lucky tonight. Things were winding down here, and we finally made it to base camp after having been gone for three weeks on another mission from hell. I will be able to have a shower and actually eat food that doesn't taste like hard shit.

Walking away from the mess hall, I quickly look for the building we were using as mission control for our unit. After shutting the door and enjoying a second of silence, I open the letter.

I had hoped you would be home by now, but I'm assuming this was a multiple-mission assigning and you're looking at closer to a year.

Fucking sucks, brother. Wrap up what you can and get home. Your girl needs you. I don't want to fuck with your head over there, but I can't impress it harder. I wouldn't be bothering with this if I didn't think it was necessary. Do what you need to do. Wait it out and hurry it up, call or fucking write. But she needs you and it should be something that's handled sooner than later. I'll keep her in my sights the best I can, Cohen. Stay safe. -Chance

With trembling hands, I refold the note and try to calm myself down. I've known something was wrong. I've felt it since the day I left. That feeling has turned my gut into a constant pain. Feeling like I've been needed at home is nothing compared to knowing I'm needed and not being able to do a damn thing about it.

"Fuck!" I roar and slam the door open hard enough that the very foundation the room is build on is sure to feel its force.

I set off for my CO and pray that he can tell me how the hell to speed this bullshit up so I can get home to my girl.

I'm not sure what I look like when I approach my CO, but he is more than accepting that I need to get a call home. Typically, we don't get the opportunity to contact anyone back home. Our missions are like that. We need our focus to be spot-on. Anything else would result in one thing. Our death. We're out "hunting" for weeks and months at a time. Searching for our target, sleeping with our backs against each other, hiding whenever we can. Crawling through the desert in conditions that are as bad as it gets. We eat, sleep, and breathe with the single-minded focus of a warrior. A killing machine. When situations at home cause our focus to waver, they're willing to do whatever it takes to point our focus back into the tunnel-vision mindset of a robot. Which is essentially what we're trained to be.

And with my mind spinning with a vague-as-fuck message from home, things would end up dire if I were hunting. Chance fucking knows better than to send some fucked-up shit like that. He knows that the only thing it would do is take my mind from the mission and make me become consumed with worry. Something I can't afford to have happen.

CO Krajack has me stuffed into a room with a secure line home in minutes of my handing him Chance's letter. My first call—Dani.

With each ring that goes unanswered, my heart starts to pick up speed, and my palms are so wet from the dread I feel pouring out of me that I almost drop the phone.

"Mother FUCK!" I thunder through the silence surrounding me.

"Breathe, soldier. Pick someone else and fucking call them," Krajack grinds out from the doorway behind me. "Won't do a bit of good to sit there acting like a little girl. Try your father."

CO Krajack and my dad served together. They spearheaded our unit, and Krajack made it his life's goal to see it turned into the baddest of the bad. Having him know Dad didn't make life easier for me when it came time for training. If anything, he pushed me harder than anyone else. But he's also the only one who would know me well enough right now—and correctly guess that I am way too fucking close to tearing the shit out of anything that gets in the way of me finding out what's wrong with my girl.

I nod, grabbing the satellite phone and pressing the buttons I need to in order to connect me with Dad's cell, praying that he answers.

"Cage," he barks.

"Dad," I say in a way I know he will instantly know I need him.

"Son?" His tone instantly alert.

"Tell me why I got a letter from Chance telling me to get the fuck home because Dani needs me? You know I can't deal with this shit. If she needs me home, I'm going to be wrapped up in that and—god dammit! You know, Dad. You fucking know how my head is going to be if I don't know what's going on." I feel Krajack place his hand on my shoulder and give me a firm squeeze.

"C-man, I don't know. Mom and I just got back in town the other day. I know something happened when she left work the other day, but Axel hasn't briefed me yet."

"Fucking shit," I mutter.

"You got the call. Call Axel, son. As much as I miss my boy and would love the time to talk, you need to get your head on straight so you can get the hell home. I love you, son."

"Love you too, Dad."

He rattles off Axel's cell and, after the promise that I'll keep my focus, says goodbye.

I hang up, give Krajack a stressed look, and make another call—hoping and praying for answers this time.

It takes one ring for Axel's cell to connect.

As if he's been waiting for my call.

The dread in my stomach intensifies instantly.

"Cohen."

Not a question. He's been waiting.

"Had Chance call an hour ago. I figured you would have called sooner than this."

"Don't play games with me, Axel. I know you have your issues with me right now, but do not play games with me. I don't owe you an explanation, but my first call went to Dani—where it should have gone. Then Dad, who couldn't give me shit, so here I am, calling you and hoping you shut the fuck up with the warnings about your daughter and give me what I need to know. Is my girl okay?"

He doesn't waste a second. "Respect the hell out of you right now, Cohen. It's not a secret that Dani means the world to me and, if I could keep her under my wing for the rest of my life, I fucking would. But," he sighs, "I was reminded that it's time to let go and let her fly. Pleased as fuck that she's flying to a man I admire and that I believe is man enough for my girl. Just fucking remember, she was my girl before she was yours. There are things going on here that are much bigger than you and me. Things that I have no right in passing on to you, but I can't stress it enough that you need to either get home or get ahold of Dani."

"Ax—"

"I know what it's like to be over there, Cohen. To make sure your focus doesn't waver and that you don't end up dead. I've lived that shit, so I fucking *know*. But I wouldn't have gotten word to you if I didn't feel it was needed. Dani's threats have picked up in a sense. Flowers stopped, but she got a letter the other day that makes me believe things are more than just an admirer. As much as it kills me, she doesn't need or want her father right now. I know how Krajack works. You'll be over there for years if he doesn't wrap shit up. He picks your missions wisely. Some to keep your training sharp and some that are more than needed to help stop this motherfucking war. What I can't stress enough is that what doesn't serve a purpose need to be dropped so you can get back stateside. Move your missions up in order of importance and get home to my girl. She's safe and I won't let that fact change. Not now and not ever."

"What the fuck! How is that not supposed to mess with my head, Axel?"

"That wasn't the purpose, but you need to know that shit's going down that doesn't look like it's going away any time soon. You need to know that your clock isn't going to just keep ticking and that it's time to get the fuck home."

"You're telling me that I shouldn't be worried some freak is after my girl and that I should be home?"

"What I'm telling you is that you need to turn into that little invincible shit you were as a kid. Do your job and do it quick. Then get the fuck home."

"You have to know this isn't going to do shit but make me worry about her."

"*I* won't let shit happen to her," he vows.

"You better not, Axel. I know you love her. That can't be argued, but I would die for that girl. I would die for her and kill any motherfucker who harms a hair on her head. I'll talk to Krajack and see what needs to be done to cut our time here down."

"You do that," he says, and the line goes dead.

I drop the phone on the table, more confused than I was before I called home. All of these vague hints and half tells. Not one thing I can grasp that makes me feel confident that she is okay until I get home.

"He's right, you know?" Krajack says from my side. "We pick and choose between training exercises that serve no purpose other than to sharpen your skills and those that eliminating the enemy. I was hoping to have four to seven more months left with you over here, but with this intel, I'll do my best to cut that in half. Best I can do. Keep your head where it needs to be, Cohen. I can't afford for you to lose your focus."

"I appreciate that, sir." I sigh with resignation that I'm stuck here and my girl needs me.

This is going to be the hardest next few months of my life.

Chapter 29

Dani

Three months later

THINGS HAVE BEEN A LITTLE easier these last three months. I still miss Cohen, but shortly after I found out about the baby, he was able to get a message through e-mail that he would be home soon. Of course, his soon was in the next few months, but that was better than the unknown timeframe we had been working with since he left.

With the push of strength that his short e-mail gave me, I felt like I could face the world. We still didn't know exactly when he would return, but we knew it would be soon.

Things at work have been easier, too. When I got back after my fall, Sway was predictably in his extreme mothering mode. He would only let me work half days, and those days that I did work were always light. No coloring or heavy treatments. I was restricted to cuts and the like. Actually, now that I think about it, he hasn't let me do a color in almost a month. Every single time, he intercepts my client.

Devon wasn't too happy about losing his star drama maker, but he worked it in as me being too depressed to work because of my lover having broken my heart.

Whatever.

Surprisingly, Don's been the annoying one this time. He seems to think my sole purpose in life is to make his job easier by making sure I do things for ratings alone. He wants certain shots, or for me to do one of the lines he has written to give the show more drama, or the one time he asked me to fake a fight with Stella and fake slap her.

I don't fucking think so.

Mark's actually been the voice of reason this time. He joined me for lunch in the breakroom a few times before they left to go back to California, and I like to think we had some sort of a friendship. I gave him some pointers on how to win over the girl he's been dating. I guess you could say I have a soft spot for the guy now.

Of course, they haven't been around for almost two months. There was apparently a big issue with Devon's production team back home. Some big-time embezzlement stuff with the higher-ups, and until they could recover some funding that was stolen, they had to pause filming. Last we heard from Sway was that today would be their first day back. I am looking forward to seeing them. I hope that Mark was able to use some of my tips to get closer to his girl.

Unfortunately, one thing that didn't stop in the last three months was the weekly flower deliveries. They picked up about two weeks after the letter that was found on my car. So far, they've been impossible to track, always paid for with a prepaid Visa, and the order placed online. Maddox, the IT guru at Corps Security, has been struggling to actually nail down a location since whoever is actually placing the orders is smart about covering his tracks. So far, the orders have been placed in different locations all over the globe. Well, according the IP addresses, that is.

Needless to say, things have been a little on edge with no answers. Between Lee and my brother, there has always been someone

sleeping at our house. Dad had what already was a top-of-the-line security system replaced with one I still needed a manual to figure out.
He's gotten even worse since I started showing. It's like my belly's
growing—the sign that the baby is in fact very real—kicked his protective tendencies into overdrive. That tangible sight was all it took. He
went as far as to steal my car keys two weeks ago and demand that I let
him pick me up for work from that day forward. That was short-lived
and got him in the doghouse with Mom for almost a week.

Never a dull moment with him.

Another thing that has changed is my new friendship with Megan.
I really feel terrible about my first impression of her when I thought
that she was dating Cohen. She's become a huge support and go-to
person for advice. Chance told me that my friendship and the bond she
can give me over my pregnancy has given her something to focus on,
and he thinks it's helping her heal. She has her moments, but I think
he's right.

"What are you going to wear today? Planning on showing off that
adorable little bump for the cameras?" Megan asks from where she's
lounging on my chaise lounge in the corner of my room.

I look over at her in the mirror I'm using to fix my makeup. She
has Molly, her adorable four-year-old daughter, bouncing on her feet
with a smile dancing across her beautiful face.

"I think so. Now that I'm over that weird 'I'm not fat—I'm pregnant' stage, I find myself wearing the tightest things I can find just so I
can show it off."

"Dani?" I hear Molly say in her singsong voice. She sounds like a
little angel. "Can I play with your jewsree?"

"Sure thing, tink." I ruffle her blond curls when she skips towards
my dresser.

"You know she's going to destroy your jewelry box again," Megan
laughs.

"Eh, let her have at it. I moved all my valuable pieces after the last time. I swear she broke my heart with those tears. I almost told her she could have my grandmother's hand-me-down pearls!" I tease.

"Tell me about it. I would probably give that girl anything she wants with just the smallest tear. God help me, she's spoiled rotten."

"Nah, she's just well loved." I give her a smile and pull on my tight, black blouse. It hugs my belly perfectly, and the pencil skirt makes my legs look great. I've been putting on a little weight in my thighs, but now that I look closely, I just look curvier. My breasts, on the other hand, have really benefited from my pregnancy. I actually have cleavage without having to use a damn good expensive bra to get. "How are you doing, Megs?" I ask, pulling on my black silk blouse.

Today is the second birthday of her late husband since he passed away. It's a testament to how far she's come since the sad girl who was at Cohen's going away party. She's smiling today when I fully expected her to be locked in her house, crying.

"I'm doing a lot better, Dani. Really, I am. It gets easier every day that passes. I still miss him like crazy, but I'm trying to follow your lead and see the beautiful things in life and focus less on the things that I can't change. I was a mess when he was deployed during my pregnancy with Molly. I still don't know how you're able to wake up every day with such a positive outlook."

I look over at her with a small smile. "I don't know if it's so much of a positive outlook or the knowledge that, regardless of what life throws at me, I've been blessed with what life I've lived. I can't spend my life worrying about what might be or what could have been. I lost a lot of time with Cohen. We had one brilliant, eye-opening night together, and it might sound ridiculous, but if that was the last night I ever have with him, I'll cherish it forever."

She gives me a nod, and I know she understands. We've talked about her holding on to her happier memories and letting go of the hard ones. She understands where I'm coming from.

I know it sounds stupid. One night of us being an "us" was all it took for me. I could have had an hour and the outcome would have been the same. He's the other half to my heart. It's been like that for as long as I've known him, and no time frame could change that.

I look over my bed at the photo I had blown up and framed in a huge display of just how much I miss the man.

The image my mother gave me months ago—the one of Cohen and me sitting on my parents' dock almost twenty years ago. The one that proves that we've been building this connection for longer than we both could even imagine.

I spend a little more time with Megan and Molly before I have to head into work. After hating the cameras in my face for so long, it's going to be weird embracing them today. Megan was right. Now that my bump is one hundred percent recognizable, I want the world to know about my little baby.

"Hey, Sway," I say when I walk into the salon.

He spins on his solid-gold—with glittered embellishments on the heels—stilettos and gives me a big smile.

"Oh, darling girl, come and let Sway rub that belly! My lord, I love babies. Stella!" he screams, and I watch her wince.

I swat his hands away when he tries to open the top buttons of my blouse.

"Yes, Pops?" she responds with an eye roll. "God, leave her tits alone! Sometimes, I wonder if you're not really straight."

"Don't you give me that 'tude! I'll go get your dad next door and have him remind you that you're supposed to be sweet to me. I'm just trying to make sure little mama gets her tips. She's got four male heads to work on today." He gives me a wink.

"I'm always sweet to you, you weirdo."

I laugh at them and move around Sway and into the madness of the salon. Looks like a full house today, too. All eight stations are busy—minus Sway's and mine, of course.

"Where are the cameras at, Sway?" I call over my shoulder as I head to the breakroom to throw my purse in my locker.

"On the way, little mama."

I manage to get myself in order and a good head start on Mrs. Cartwright's highlights—without Sway seeing me doing color—before I hear Devon bang his way through the door.

"Ah! If it isn't my favorite home away from home! Are my little bees ready to buzz today?"

I roll my eyes in the mirror, causing Mrs. Cartwright to giggle.

"Hey, Dani," Don says from right over my shoulder. "We're going to need you to look over these story lines."

I spin on my amazingly kickass black heels and look down at Don. Yeah, down at him. My heels make me *maybe* right at five foot five and he's still shorter.

"I've already told you, Don. I don't do fake. If you want someone to beef up your show, then hire an actor."

"Holy shit, did you swallow a beach ball?"

Oh no he did not.

I might be rounder and my belly might be a very noticeably pregnant, but I am not *that* big!

He's looking at me with the strangest look on his face. As if he's mad about me being pregnant.

"What did you—" I stop talking when I hear a crash in the front and turn my head to see what happened. Mark is bent over to help the cameraman who looks to have tripped and dropped his equipment up.

"Son of a bitch, Troy! Do you have any idea how expensive those cameras are?" Don yells and walks away from me.

"God, what's up his ass today?" Maddi says, sidling up to my side. She drops a makeup brush and bends over to get it before giving me her attention. Her hand, as usual—it's always her first reaction when she's near me—goes to my belly for a small rub. "Maybe he's worried about the camera adding ten pounds and you looking like a whale," she smarts, and I give her a shove.

"Shut up. Stop using my paranoia to mess with me."

"Incoming," she says oddly and moves back to her station.

I give Mrs. Cartwright a look before glancing up in my mirror and seeing Mark walking over.

"Hey, Mark," I say with a smile.

"Dani. Uh, you're pregnant?" He's looking at my stomach like it's about to jump off my body and smother him.

"It would appear so, Mark," I laugh. "I didn't get a chance to share the news with you before you left."

He clears his throat, looking pained.

So weird. "Everything okay?"

"What?" He shakes his head. "Oh, sorry. Just a lot on my mind. Things back home were crazy. That girl I was telling you about? Yeah, not sure if it's going to work out. She wanted . . . well . . . ." He points to my stomach, and it hits me. She wanted kids and he must not have.

"Oh, I'm sorry, Mark. Don't worry. There's tons of fish in the sea. Hey, how about we grab lunch today? Catch up and all that?"

The whole time I am talking, his eyes keep wandering back to my stomach. Damn, the guy must really have an issue with kids.

"Probably not today. Lots of stuff we need to catch up since we were gone for a while. Hey, did Don talk to you about the story lines we want to try and hit with this round of filming? They would probably jack up the drama, good for ratings and all that."

What the hell? He knows how I feel about that crap.

When I don't answer, he looks down at my stomach again before sharing a look with Don and walking away without another word.

So. Freaking. Weird.

I look over at Maddi, and she looks just as confused as I am. She shrugs one shoulder and then turns back to the young girl she's giving makeup tips to.

I return my attention to my job. It isn't long before I realize the day is wasting away and I still haven't eaten a thing.

"Hey, Maddi? I'm going to order some Chinese. You want in?"

I walk around and get orders from a few more people before placing the call. If I don't eat soon, I'll most likely take off my arm between clients. I would rather just go out and get it myself, but Dad was clear that I'm not to leave the salon alone—for anything.

I am in the middle of cleaning out my brushes and wiping down the area in front of my mirror when I hear the door ding and I look up to see the blessed food delivery.

"I could give you a kiss. I'm so hungry," I tell the young Chinese man.

He doesn't say anything, just roughly shoves the heavy bag in my hand and thrusts the receipt in my hands. I sign it, add the tip, and shove it back. Maybe a little harder than I intended, but damn. What's it take to get a little friendliness?

"Have a nice day," I mumble.

Of course I'm ignored and he's right out the door a second later.

I look around, thinking that maybe I have some sort of "don't talk to me" vibe since there isn't anyone near me except for our receptionist, Kat.

"I'll be in the breakroom if anyone needs me. I think I have about forty-five minutes before my next client gets here."

"Sure thing, Dani."

I drop the bag down in the middle of the breakroom and make quick work of pulling off the staples and opening the large, brown bag. Expecting to find our lunch order, I'm momentarily shocked by what I see inside. Then, when what I'm looking at sinks in, I jerk my hands back towards my body.

I feel like I'm drowning. The sound of my blood pumping ferociously through my body is making my ears cloud. My eyes tear up and my vision gets foggy. I must be screaming something fierce, because the next thing I know, the door is slamming open and Sway, along with half of the other stylists, come barreling in.

Sway grabs my shoulders and tries to get me to talk through my hysteria. "Child! Good heavens. What has gotten into you?"

I go slack, and I feel him adjusting his grip to keep my body from falling to the floor.

"Stella? Talk to me, ella-bella!"

I focus on Stella over Sway's shoulder, and the look of terror on her face does nothing to help my panic. I start to gasp and struggle against Sway. I have to get out of here.

"Someone go next door to CS and get some help."

I don't hear anything else after that. My body decides that it's had enough and just shuts down. My cries silence, my tears dry up, and I just go slack.

My focus stays straight ahead, but I don't see anything. My mind is too busy focusing on what I saw inside that bag.

The baby doll snapped apart with red letters against the torso.

Their words forever branded in my head.

An image I will never, as long as I live, forget.

YOU WILL PAY WITH THAT BASTARD BABY'S LIFE.

Chapter 30

Cohen

GOD, IT FEELS GOOD TO be home. I've been back stateside for the last week, having to debrief up north before I was able to get my ass back to Georgia. It was an impossibly hard week because I knew I was within a few hundred miles of holding my girl. I didn't have time to call and check in with Dani. I knew that, the second I heard her voice, it would be game over, so I stayed the course and checked in with my dad and Axel as much as I could. So far, nothing's changed.

My first stop home should have been Dani's, but I figure she is at work, and that gives me some time to get a shower, change out of the clothes I've been traveling all day in, and get to her for what I hope will be a welcome surprise.

I pull my truck up to the apartment and lean back with a deep sigh. Fuck if my body doesn't relax within seconds of parking my truck. Especially now that I know there will be no more of this leaving shit. I officially have been let go from the program. No more gone for months, going dark with no chance of talking to the ones I love back home. And most important—no more leaving Dani.

We can finally focus on growing our relationship. Making her mine. And I'm never going to fucking let her go. In the back of my mind, I've worried that she's had enough waiting, given up on us before we could even get off the ground running, but I've pushed it aside and kept hope.

There is no way that, after all of this time, when we finally have our shot and it will be over before we even get started.

Reaching over the back seat, I grab my bag and climb down from my truck. Then I pause to stretch before I bound up the stairs two at a time. I drop my bag, dig for my keys, and open the door.

The smile on my face dies instantly when I walk into the living room. Every single fear I've had since I left comes back but with a soul-crushing force.

My girl.

My fucking Dani-girl is wrapped up tight in the arms of the man I've considered one of my closest friends for years. Her back is to me, her head is tucked into his chest, and his arms are wrapped around her tight. He looks up when the door opens, and I can't even look him in the eyes because of the red haze clouding my vision.

I didn't think it could get worse. Nope. Never in my wildest nightmares did I think it could be worse than seeing her in the arms of another man. But when she turns at the noise and I get a good look at her, my world stops spinning. Right here, it just stops with an intensity that rocks my foundation.

"The fuck?" I bellow, the sound booming through the room, bouncing off the walls, and making Dani flinch.

"Huh?"

I look from her stomach—her slightly rounded and very obviously pregnant tiny bump of a stomach—and I feel my lip curl in disgust.

"And here I figured you would be waiting with your arms wide open." I throw my bag down and turn my back on them both.

I hear her gasp just as the door slams behind me. I don't even pause. The lump in my throat is burning and my eyes are watering. I blink, willing the show of emotion to stop, and thunder my way back down the steps and into my truck with a swiftness that shouldn't be possible given the way I'm feeling right now.

I just left my heart on the floor up there while my future fell around me.

After hours of driving around, the sun setting in my rearview mirror, I find myself pulling up to the one place I know will give me some peace.

My parents' house.

Cam's and Colt's trucks are gone, so at least I know I won't have to deal with them. As much as I would love to see my brothers, right now, with my mind as volatile as it is, it would be a reunion they don't deserve.

Dad's truck is parked right next to Mom's minivan. The lights are shining brightly out the windows and onto the front lawn. I sit in my truck for the longest time, still trying to calm my mind.

My throat still locked down with a lump the size of Texas.

I don't even know how to process what I saw when I walked into my apartment. Dani looked so lost—until she turned to see me—and I still can't place the emotions that crossed her face, but she almost looked guilty. A feeling I never thought I would see from her. I've struggled with the way I've felt for her for so long, but never once did I feel guilt.

Then, when I saw her belly . . .

Even with the flash of betrayal, I couldn't help but notice how beautiful she looked with that sign of life growing on her tiny frame.

All the dreams I used to get me through almost seven months of deployment of the future we would live—together—gave me the focus

I needed to push through the pain of missing her. All of it, just like our start, is over before it began.

I jump when I hear a knock on my window and look up to meet my dad's concerned, blue eyes. I'm not sure how my mind knew that he was what I needed, but the second I see him, I let the emotions that were threatening to burst through tear through me.

"Dad," I lament. My shoulders start to shake, and I don't even care that the tears are starting to fall from my tired eyes.

His eyes narrow and he pulls the door open. I climb out, slap my arms around his back, and, for the first time since I left home, let him be my strength.

"Jesus, C-man. What in the hell is going on?" He pulls back, runs his hand over his thick, graying hair, and then grabs my chin, forcing my eyes to his.

"I just left the apartment," I sigh, getting a hold on my emotions. "I'm sorry. I was doing a good job at keeping my shit together."

He just looks at me, confused, before a flash of understanding flickers through his eyes. "I see. I know it must be quite shock. I'll admit your mother and I were just as surprised." His tone gives nothing away, clearly letting me run this show.

"I don't understand. I can't even seem to wrap my mind around what I saw, let alone everything that I'm feeling right now."

He gives a soft laugh. "Yeah, it was a shock for me, too, when it happened to your mom and me."

I'm explaining what seeing Dani like that did to me when his words register. "What?"

"When I first found out she was pregnant, shock was my first feeling, hands down, but then, when I realized what our love had created . . . Fuck me, that was one of the most incredible feelings in the world. I'll admit it even made me cry, son. No shame in how you're feeling."

"What?" I repeat, shocked.

"Christ, Cohen. Did finding out you're about to be a dad knock you stupid?"

"What?" I offer lamely, that feeling I had finally rid of in my gut returning.

"Uh, so I take it you didn't just see Dani?"

"Yeah, I fucking saw her—wrapped up in Chance's arms," I snap.

His brows crinkle and he looks at me, waiting for me to continue.

"Wrapped in his arms, Dad. What more do I need to give you. They looked cozy enough that I didn't stick the hell around."

His eyes harden, and he shakes his head. I wasn't expecting the hard hand against my head.

"The fuck!" I shout at him.

"The fuck about sums it up. I never thought I would say this to you, but damn, you sure did fuck things up big time with that idiot move."

"What the hell are you talking about?" I ask, rubbing my head. "That hurt, old man."

"You really thought she's with Chance? Had been with Chance? Son, she's six months pregnant. Do the fucking math."

"Yeah? I left almost seven months ago."

"Did you even pay attention in school?"

My mind starts spinning, trying to remember what little I know about the female reproductive system. When the truth hits me—hard—I have to stabilize myself with one arm on the truck.

"Yeah, son. Some stupid shit about the adding two weeks here, taking the time of conception and then adding some weeks—I don't really know how the hell it works, but I assure you that she is very much pregnant with your baby. Trust me. It was a shock to us as well, but not once did we lose the faith you did in your girl."

"I fucked up," I exhale deeply.

"You sure did. Come on. I'm shocked your mother hasn't broken down the door to see you, and we need to give Dani some time to cool off before you rush over there. I guarantee you, if she's anything like her mother, the lack of trust you held for her will piss her off, maybe more than it will hurt her. Either way, you have some serious making up to do."

He walks away, muttering something about raising me better than acting like a douchebag.

Chapter 31

Cohen

"MY HANDSOME BOY!" MY MOTHER screams when I walk in the door. She slams herself into me and gives me a hug tight enough to knock the wind out of me. Then she follows it up with a slap on the side of my head that rivals my father's in pain.

"Dammit, Ma!" I exclaim and move away from her vicious hands before she can get another slap in.

"I heard every word, you silly boy. How could you even think that?" She jabs her fist on her slim hips and gives me a hard look. "I can't even imagine what she's feeling right now. Not after the day she had."

"What does that mean?" I ask.

"Oh no, you don't. She's fine where she is. For now, you're going to tell me how in the world you could even think that she had been unfaithful."

Jesus. Where do I even start?

I follow my parents into the kitchen, where Mom starts a pot of coffee. Thirty minutes later I have it all laid out.

My rush to get home, the exhaustion that months of stress and worry had placed on my shoulders, and the feelings that seeing her with another man had rushed to the surface.

"I snapped. There isn't an excuse, but fuck. I let my jealousy get the best of me."

"Not an excuse, but it's forgivable, Cohen. It couldn't have been easy being away when you knew that you're needed at home. I get what you're saying, but that still doesn't explain how you rushed to the thought that she was with another man," Mom says with a sigh. "It wasn't right, but given everything you've been through, I understand."

"You need to talk to her, son. Don't let this fester," Dad adds when she finishes talking.

"I know. I know."

It's been four hours since I walked in and assumed the worst. The fact that *I'm* about to be a father hasn't even settled in now that the relief that I was horribly wrong is still fresh in my system.

"Do you want to talk about it, son? How you're feeling? I know it's a lot to take in."

I look over at my dad and sigh. Not for the first time, I realize just how lucky I am that he found my mom and, in turn, found me. He's been my rock since I was three—my hero—and the man I've always hoped I could just be half as good as.

"I'm going to be a father," I gasp, holding on to the countertop with a white-knuckled grip. "Holy shit," I breathe.

Dad laughs, and Mom smiles. It isn't lost on me that they're excited about this news.

"Do you know if it's a boy or girl?" I question.

Dad opens his mouth to respond, but Mom beats him to it. "I talked to Izzy about it last week and she said that Dani had refused to find out. She said that she didn't want to know unless you were right there with her to find out at the same time. She held strong on that she didn't want to know until you were home—or obviously if she went into labor. Izzy said that Dani believed that you were going to be missing so much that she didn't want to take that away from you." Mom smiles and leans against my dad's side.

"Shit," I puff, once again feeling the extremes of my rushed judgment.

Even through everything she's been going through alone, she still put me and my feelings ahead of her own. I'm sure she wants to know what we're having, and that she wanted me there badly enough to wait for something that huge is humbling. And it makes me feel like an even bigger jackass for even thinking that she had been with another man. The girl saved herself for me for almost twenty-two years.

"I think I need to go to my girl," I state. "Shit. What if she's so pissed she isn't even willing to hear me out?"

"Son, the one thing I know from experience is there is no problem too big for true love to conquer. Just take a look around you. Everyone you know has been faced with a challenge in their relationships. Challenges that, even at the time, felt unbeatable, but if what you had—for however brief before you left—gave you even a sliver of promise that I think it did, then you don't stop until you fix what's broken."

When I don't speak, Mom picks up where he left off. "You've been pushing her away for years, my sweet boy. I know you struggled with how you felt for her, so it was no shock for me when I found out that you two had finally come together. I hurt for you—so badly—when you had to leave before you two even got started, but I knew, I just knew, that you two had that 'staying power' kind of love that I felt when I met your dad. Nothing—and I mean nothing—can change that. You're going to screw up—that's a promise—but all that matters is that you work your hardest to fix it." She walks over and wraps her arms around me. Standing on her toes, she kisses me on my stubbled cheek. "You, my darling boy, need to stop thinking that you aren't allowed to feel the way you do for the woman you love. It was only a shock to her hardheaded father, but according to Izzy, he's admitted how to-the-moon happy he is that his baby girl has found a man he truly thinks is worthy of her love."

That feeling I had in my throat earlier comes back, but this time, I'm able to clear my throat and push it down. Hope is blossoming in my chest at her words.

"I know you're eager to go find her, but I think we need to address a few things before you leave, son . . . alone." He gives Mom a look, and she returns it with a small, worried nod.

"I'll leave you two. I love you, Cohen. I'm so happy that you're home safe."

I give her a hug, bend to kiss her cheek, and follow my dad into his office.

He shuts the door behind him and walks to lean against his desk. "You aren't going to like this, Cohen."

"I figured as much when you mentioned this needed to be done without Mom. I'm guessing she doesn't know?"

"She knows enough that she's aware of the issues that have been going on. However, she doesn't have a single clue at how dire they've become as of today. I've got to say, you have incredible timing, son."

He takes a deep breath, and without thought, I steel myself for whatever news he has to share with me. I'm guessing that it has everything to do with that ominous message from Chance and the chat with Axel. The one that was instrumental in having Krajack rush my assignments and my ass back home in record time.

"You know about the flowers. The first note she got was shocking enough that it's had everyone on high alert. She hasn't been alone, not even for a second." He walks around the desk, hits a few keys, and turns the computer so I can see the scanned document.

> YOU ARE SUPPOSED TO BE MINE, BITCH. YOU TAKE MY FLOWERS WITH A SMILE ON YOUR FACE, BUT SPEND YOUR TIME CRYING OVER SOME MOTHERFUCKER THAT ISN'T EVEN THERE. I HEARD YOU TODAY! YOU ARE MINE, DANIELLE! IF YOU THINK SOME OTHER MOTHERFUCK WILL HAVE YOU WHEN YOU BELONG TO ME—YOU ARE DEAD FUCKING WRONG.

My skin crawls in outrage and anger when I read the words. When I think about how Dani must have felt when she saw this, my heart starts to beat wildly. Fuck. I should have been here for this. I should have been here to protect her from harm and I wasn't. That is my burden to bear and one I'll work every day for a lifetime and then some to make up for.

"Is this the last of it?" I ask through clenched teeth.

"Not even close."

"Explain," I spit, my mind going into survival mode, and the *hunter* I've been trained to be fights for control.

"After the note, she passed out." He holds his hands up when I open my mouth to explode. "Stop and listen, Cohen. Don't go off half-cocked until you know all the facts. Now that you're home, you need to know what you're up against."

"Keep going," I rush out.

"The flowers didn't start up right away, but they didn't stop. We were able to intercept enough of them that Dani doesn't even know just how bad it continued to be. Axel was concerned about her being in the early stages of pregnancy and what the added stress could do to her and the baby. Understandable considering his and Izzy's past. We've tried, but thus far, we have been unsuccessful in tracking down the origin of the purchases."

I can feel myself becoming angrier and angrier. The need to protect what's mine is starting to manifest into a craving to kill whoever is threatening her safety.

"I promise you, Cohen. She was never alone. Either there was someone at the girls' house or she was at work. The few times she went out with everyone, there was always Liam, Nate, or Chance with her. As much as Axel hated it to begin with, her wanting to stay at your place so that she could be near you, whatever that means, gave us a little peace of mind because we all know that Chance is more than capable of protecting her. They've formed a friendship since you left and that's all it is—a friendship."

"I get that now. What else is there?"

"Today, she was at work and ordered some lunch. I think she had been there for about five hours before she placed the order. According to the surveillance cameras we have placed in the doorway and on the salon floor, there wasn't anyone alarming. Clients that Sway has confirmed are regulars and no new ones. The stylist and staff. The camera and production crew for that Sway All the Way show. That's it. Dani ordered Chinese, and when the order came, the delivery person brought in the food, had her sign, and left. We lost her when she went into the breakroom to eat, but I've seen what she found when she opened the bag . . . and what it did to her. You aren't going to like this," he warned.

"Just fucking tell me so I can get to her, Dad." My anger becomes a palpable thing.

"What you need to do is calm down, because as pissed as this is going to make you, you need to be there for her. I have no doubt that what you saw was a terrified woman being comforted. Sway sent someone over for help, but with Axel and Beck out of town and Maddox up to his elbows in case backlog, Chance and I were the ones who showed up. Chance took her out of there while I waited for the police and secured the scene."

"What. Did. She. Find?" I grind out forcefully.

He sighs and returns his attention to his computer. Within seconds, the monitor is turned my way and I have to fight the urge to throw up.

My God! What in the fuck?

"Someone has their sights on her, Cohen. This is one of the first times that she's actually dressed to show off her stomach. Normally, she wears baggy clothing, and honestly, I wouldn't have been able to tell until today. She dressed up—according to Megan, who rushed over to help Chance earlier—to show off her pregnancy because she knew the cameras would be back after a two-month break. Whoever this is, they honestly didn't know about the baby until today. That I'm almost positive about."

"They've been watching my woman, Dad. Watching her close enough that this was a clear threat. You read that first letter. We're dealing with a fucking lunatic. Someone who views her as theirs. What do you think is going to happen now that I'm home? Just by being with her, I'm placing her and my unborn child in danger."

He studies my face for a beat. "But your being gone is killing her. Plain and simple, Cohen. It's not been easy, despite the brave face she's kept. You can protect her. You *will* protect her. Don't let some stupid thought that she's better off without you even enter your brain, son. I raised you better than that shit."

I shouldn't be surprised that he so clearly read me.

"I need to go to her." I state.

"You need to go to her," he agrees.

I give him a quick hug and all but rush out the door.

With a renewed sense of confidence and the feelings of over-whelming fear for her and our child, I speed through the streets and make my way to the woman who I, just hours before, wronged.

I have a lot to make up for, but my parents are right. When you feel something as powerful as what Dani and I share, you don't ever stop fighting for that. I'll be damned if I let some crazy fuck threaten the future I will have with Danielle Reid.

Chapter 32

Dani

I DIDN'T EVEN CRY WHEN Cohen stormed out of the apartment. The shock from the day still held my tears at bay. I wanted to. God, how I wanted to. But I managed to keep my shit together. When that door slammed shut, I stepped away from Chance and, without a word, locked myself in Cohen's bedroom.

I should be angry. I should be so mad that I leave and never look back. I should be a lot of things, but what I am is numb.

Never did I think I would have that kind of reception from Cohen when he returned. I had envisioned it in my head over and over. The homecoming I would give him. How happy I would feel when I was able to tell him about our child. The love I would feel from him.

I don't know why I didn't even stop to consider that he would look at me with distrust and accusations. I guess I just believed him to be better than that.

I sigh and turn to my side, my nose burning with emotion but my eyes still dry. My hand carelessly rubs against the light kicking coming from my belly. I squeeze my eyes shut, willing the memories of this afternoon out of my head when I once again think about the terrible image that met me from the lunch sack.

When I open my eyes again, I realize that I must have fallen asleep. The sun, which was been dropping when I laid my head down, is long gone, and through the window, the moon is casting a soft glow around the room. I can hear Chance moving around outside of the room. I should go talk to him. Ask him to at least take me home. But even with the earlier events, I don't want to leave the one place where I've felt close to Cohen.

I hear the doorknob shake, and it's followed by some scratches. And then the light from the hall filters into the otherwise dark room.

Looks like Chance got sick of waiting for me to emerge.

I keep my body still, waiting to see what he'll do next. Chance isn't exactly a man of many words, so I'm guessing I'll get a quick, "Let's go."

I almost jump out of my skin when I feel the bed depress. I move to leap out of the bed when two steel bands carefully wrap themselves around my body and I'm pulled back against a hard, warm body. I struggle, panicking with the thoughts of Chance being in Cohen's bed with me. That is, until the familiar scent of Cohen invades my senses and my body instantly deflates. The tears I was doing such a damn good job at holding off rush to the surface when I feel his body—a body I've missed for so damn long—hold me even closer.

"Dani-girl," he groans.

His head drops to my neck, and I feel his lips against my skin before his arms let up slightly. But only long enough to travel from my chest and for his warm palms to stretch out against the small bump that holds our child within.

"God, Dani," he breaths out with a slight tremor.

That right there is all it takes for me to hiccup once, twice, and a third time before a huge sob vibrates through my body.

"Baby," he exhales. "I'm so fucking sorry, Dani. More sorry than you could ever imagine."

It takes me a second to calm down, but when I do, I shift and turn in his arms, instantly missing the feeling of his hands against my belly.

"You thought that I . . . that Chance and I . . . Cohen, you believed the worst in seconds. I haven't set eyes on you in months, and the second I do, you actually believed that I had been with another man—Chance of all people."

He drops his forehead to mine and doesn't speak for the longest time. He runs his fingertips through my hair, down my face, and over my lips. His eyes follow every movement his hand makes. He doesn't stop until his fingers are pushed into my hair and he's holding my head in his hand. I wait until he locks eyes with me, unwilling to back down about how his reaction made me feel.

"You have no idea what it's been like to be without you this long, Cohen. My heart felt like it was only beating half beats. I felt like I was missing a part of myself for so long. I craved the day that you would return and I would feel whole again. I had that feeling for one night—*one night, Cohen!* I knew within hours of being with you that I would stop Heaven and Earth if it meant that I could just have one more second. I didn't doubt in the power of that . . . the power of us. So please tell me how in the world you could take one look at me after all of that and think what you did."

His eyes close tight before he opens them and looks at me, his lids filling with unshed tears.

My mouth drops in shock. I have never seen him cry. Never. He's always been someone who holds his emotions close, but not in a way that keeps him closed off. It's just how he's wired. So seeing him let me in so effortlessly and letting me physically see how much this is costing him is huge.

"I can't justify how I felt away with excuses, Dani. That is all it would be—one giant, fucking stupid excuse. I've been running on fumes since I got word that there was trouble brewing at home. Running on fumes that would bring me home to you, baby. I lived the knowledge that, if I just hurried up and finished my shit, you would be in my arms—where I could keep you safe. It's been the only thing I could see for months. Months. The second I got back, I did what I needed to do so that I could get home to you. Drove through the night and into the day with one thought on my mind. You. When I walked in and saw you in Chance's arms, I didn't even see anything other than someone other than myself touching you when I haven't been able to for fucking months. My jealousy got the best of me, and I can't apologize enough for that."

I narrow my eyes at him. "I saw your face, Cohen. You looked at me and saw my belly and thought the worst. Don't even deny it. I got the same look from my own father, so trust me when I say that I know exactly what that looks like. I didn't even dream that I would get that from you."

His eyes flash, and I see the remorse dancing behind his sorrow. "I'm not proud of it, Dani. I'm fucking ashamed that I even let the thought, however brief, cross my mind. Nothing I say can make that up to you. Nothing. But I promise, baby, that I don't think that you were unfaithful to me."

"Yeah, Cohen, you do. Somewhere deep inside of you, you felt that."

He shakes his head. "No, baby. I don't. I promise you that. What I did feel was every single emotion and helpless feeling I've had crash into me at once. The pain of being away from you when I knew you needed me. The worry that I wouldn't be here when you needed me. Everything that has haunted me day to day and week to week. That and the crash of adrenaline I had been riding high on since I got back stateside just got the best of me. My jealousy got the best of me and turned me into someone I'm not proud of. I've never felt this way towards someone, Dani. It's all new to me, and I guarantee you I'll fuck up again, but I'll spend my life making it up to you. God, Dani . . . please fucking tell me that I didn't let my temper get the best of me and ruin us."

One tear escapes his eye, which is followed by another, and another. His breathing is picking up, and his chest is rising rapidly under where my palms are resting.

"You hurt me."

"I know, baby. I know," he sighs.

"I've been dreaming of the day you would return to me and I would feel whole again. Dreamed of it, Cohen. Every night that you've been away from me, I've pleaded with God to bring you home in one piece."

"Fuck, Dani-girl," he chokes out, his eyes closing and again tears leaking down his handsome face until they disappear in his stubble.

"It's been the only thing that's kept me from falling apart with the shit life has thrown at me. You and your love."

He doesn't look up, but his arms lock even tighter around me and he pulls me closer to his warmth.

"Even though you hurt me—and, God, did you hurt me—the only thing I craved since seeing your face again was this feeling right here. This feeling of your arms around me, your heart beating strong and healthy against my palm, and the life we created moving between us. Through all that pain, the only thing I wanted was the one person who'd caused it."

"Stop, please, Dani," he begs.

"I've loved you for a lifetime, Cohen. A lifetime doesn't just give up when the other part of me makes a mistake. A lifetime takes that mistake and turns it into a building block for an even stronger foundation."

His eyes snap open and his hopeful gaze locks with mine. "Baby?"

"I love you, Cohen. That will never change. But don't ever hurt me like that again. I'm strong, baby, and I'll make as many building blocks as we need until the day my last breath leaves my body, but don't make me build them out of pain."

His eyes flash, and in seconds, his lips are against mine.

Hard and demanding.

He takes my mouth in a bruising need that steals the breath right out of my lungs.

"I love you, *my* Dani-girl. I promise you that I will never doubt what we have. Never again, baby," he mumbles against my swollen lips before he takes control of my mouth once again.

His hands trail down my back, grasping my hips, as he rolls onto his back while taking me with him. My skirt rides up instantly when my legs are spread to make room for his hips. I use my hands against his chest to push up so I'm straddling his lap and looking down at his brown eyes, which are so full of love.

I sit up straight and let out a slight moan when I feel his erection press against my panties. His eyes flash when I take his hands, which were resting on my hips, and move them around to the front of my belly.

"This," I stress, pressing his hands against the thumping our child is making against my belly. "This is our child, Cohen. One that was made with a love so powerful even I struggle to understand it. A love that was formed over a lifetime and solidified with one night that I will forever remember as one of the best of my life. We've been fated for this moment since before we were even born, baby, and I'm beyond fortunate with this unexpected fate that's been given to us."

His eyes darken with each word I speak. I notice the second that my words register and he realizes the words I used.

The same words he used in the letter he left me all those months ago.

"I love you, Cohen."

"And I love you, Dani-girl. And I you."

I drop my head and take his lips in a slow, deep kiss. Our tongues move together as our breaths mingle. We take the kiss as deep as we can without physically fusing together.

He flips us so that he's on top, and his hips rock gently against my core. He's careful not to put his full weight on my stomach, but he makes sure every inch that can touch is touching.

"Wrap your legs around me, baby," he demands, breaking from the kiss for just seconds until I do what he's asked. "Just like that," he says, and I feel him grow even harder against me.

He moves against me until I'm seconds away from coming undone. My whole body is feeling as if it's burning as my climax slowly starts to crawl up my spine. Right when I pull my lips from his to cry out in what promises to be a powerful climax, he stops.

"Oh, God! Don't stop. Please don't stop," I beg on a sob.

"Never," he declares.

His lips start leaving a trail of fire across my jaw and down my neck until he reaches the fabric of my blouse against my chest. He leans back onto his knees and trails both hands along my collarbone until they rest in the V of my cleavage. I catch his intentions only seconds before he takes a fist of silk in each hand, and with a firm pull, my blouse is ripped right down the center. His eyes darken even further when he takes his first glimpse of my bra-covered chest.

He doesn't speak a word. His fingers continue to light their fire along the cups of my bra and over the swells of each breast. He flicks the front clasp but doesn't move to unhook it. His fingers dance in twin caresses down my stomach until he's cradling my rounded stomach between his strong palms.

"This right here makes me the happiest man in the world, Dani. Seeing you swollen with my child. Knowing that part of me is inside of you right now is one of the hottest things ever. God, I fucking love you," he groans.

His hands roll over my stomach before those sinful fingers move back up to my bra. In one deft move, the clasp is flicked and my breasts spill free.

"These tits. Fuck, Dani. I'm going to fuck these tits," he promises before he bends down to take one nipple between his teeth for a light nip before soothing the pain with his tongue. "I'm going to fuck them until I come all over your chest, baby. Then I'm going to eat you until your juices are running down my chin. And when you're begging me for it, I'll give you my cock." His mouth returns to my other nipple, and he flicks his tongue over it before pressing his lips around the tight bud and sucking it deep.

"Shit," I moan, feeling my pussy clench and literally weep for him. "I need you," I beg.

"Not yet," he says around my sensitive nipple. His breath causes me to shudder. "I'm gonna fuck these tits first."

He leans up and squeezes each globe together a few times, pressing them tightly together before letting them go, and he licks his lips when they bounce to the side. "Yeah, I'm going to fuck these tits."

I cry out when I feel his hips leave mine. My eyes widen when he jumps off the bed and all but rips his clothes off. When he moves his hands to his waist and pushes his jeans and boxer briefs off in one swift move, his cock springs out and bumps against his stomach. His long, thick length is swollen with need, and I can see the drop of semen rolling down the hoop through the head. He pumps his cock roughly as his eyes trail over me.

"You need to be naked, baby. The second I feel your body against mine, I won't be able to stop. And those"—he points to my skirt and panties—"will be in my way," he growls.

I yelp when he jumps onto the bed and causes me to jolt. His fingers go to my waist, and I feel him roughly pulling the fabric from my body. He gives my mound a quick kiss that leaves me begging harder before he straddles my body and starts to climb up. His cock is pointing angrily at my face as he carefully moves over my rounded belly, his hands bracing the headboard to ensure that no extra weight falls on me. I bend my head and lick the top of his cock, and he groans long and low.

"Yeah, I'm going to fuck the hell out of these beautiful tits," he says. "Squeeze them tight, baby."

I do as he requested and push them together so that his cock is nestled between them. He closes his eyes and drops his head forward. Beads of sweat roll down his face and drop from his chin onto my chest.

His hips start to rock, slowly at first, until he picks up his thrusting. "Squeeze your tits harder," he grinds out. "Fuck me. Been so long," he says on another groan.

I never imagined that being titty-fucked would be so hot, but with each thrust, the piercings through his hard cock rubbing against the inside of my tits and the tip of his cock just a breath away from my mouth, I find my mouth filling with saliva and just begging to take his length in deep. The quicker he moves, the more my fingers squeeze each nipple until I'm only seconds from coming.

"God damn," he breathes.

I lean my head down and open my mouth so that, with each thrust up, the head of his cock is inside my mouth. His movements start to falter after that, and with one powerful groan, he pulls back and takes his cock in his hand. After a few pumps, I feel his warm semen coating each tit and hitting my chin. I reach up, swipe at his come, and stick my finger deep in my mouth, watching his eyes burn as I lick away every drop.

"I want my come on your tits while I eat you, Dani," he demands before moving his body down and latching his mouth firmly against my swollen and weeping clit.

"Fuck me!" I scream.

"I will," he rumbles against my core. "I fucking will and you're going to be begging for it until your screams are shaking my windows, Dani."

"Now, please," I whine, not even ashamed at the pathetic tone my wanting has brought forth. "God, please . . . I need to be full of you."

"Fuck, that mouth. Now I want my cock in your mouth." He moves his mouth from my sensitive clit and gives me a long lick before nibbling along my swollen lips. Each bite of his teeth has me whimpering louder.

"Give it to me . . . Give it to me . . . Please," I pant.

He ignores my begging, sucking along the seam and licking the wetness that leaks from my pussy. He feasts on my body like a starved man. When his tongue probes into my body, my walls clamp down, looking for anything to grab hold of.

"So tight," he murmurs on a groan. "I'm going to pound this pussy, Dani. Pound you until your ass is red from my balls slapping against them."

Oh, God. I'm going to die. If he doesn't fuck me now, I'm going to die. My body is strung tight, every muscle just waiting to snap, and the nerves are firing sporadically throughout my whole body. I whither against the mattress, my fist clutching the sheets as my body heats with arousal so powerful that my back lifts off the mattress and a whine-cry-scream noise shoots from my mouth. His fingers, which were holding my knees apart, trail down until he's grasping my thighs and his thumbs are rubbing on either side of my wet core. I can feel my wetness dripping down my crack and onto the mattress below. I should be ashamed of what my body is doing, but it just turns me on further.

"Please, God, please!" I shout.

He dips two thick fingers deep into my pussy and curls them, hitting me in a spot that has my eyes rolling back and a scream so loud bursting from my lips as I clamp down and come on his fingers. My body is locked tight as I cry out his name over and over again.

When I finally crash back down to Earth from the power of my orgasm, I look down my body and lock eyes with his. They're full of sinful promise, and my body quivers when he lifts his mouth slightly so I can see him roll his tongue over my clit, causing little quakes to shift through my limbs.

"You're going to give me another, Dani. You're going to come again and soak my chin. I want to feel your body cry out to mine." He bends, sucks, and looks back at me. "When I fuck you with that fucking wetness coating your virgin ass, you're going to beg me to take that too. Aren't you, baby?"

He doesn't give me time to answer him. He bends his head and gives making me orgasm again all of his focus until, just as he said I would, I cry and scream and claw at his neck and shoulders to get him to stop.

"I fucking need you . . . Need you so bad," I pant breathlessly. "I need your cock, Cohen. Please give me it, fill me, and fuck me hard. It's been so long, baby, please . . ." I trail off, mumbling who knows what about how desperately I need him.

He gives me another lick before he trails kisses up my body. When his mouth takes mine in a hungry kiss, the taste of myself on his mouth has me moaning deeply.

"Please," I mumble against his mouth, the word slurring.

"Are you ready for my cock?" he asks on a grunt as he reaches down to rub the head of his cock against my pussy.

The feel of his piercing rubbing against my fevered skin causes me to whimper.

"Do you want me here?" he asks, pushing just the tip into my weeping core. "Or do you want me here?" His hand leaves his cock, and I feel his fingertips against my asshole.

I tense, and his eyes heat until they're almost black.

"Does my girl want my cock in her ass?"

"Fuck, yes . . . anywhere. I need it, baby," I gasp when he rolls one finger in the wetness that is seeping from my body.

His soaked finger trails down from my pussy, and I feel him press against my ass again.

"Relax," he pants. "Relax and let me in," his says with an evil grin. "I'm so fucking hard for you. So hard that it hurts."

"Yes," I sigh and then yelp when his finger breaches my tight asshole. "Need it," I gasp.

"Fuck yeah, you do." He continues to push his finger in until I feel him stop, his knuckle-deep finger causing a delicious burn.

"More," I plead, not even sure what I'm asking for. My nails dig into his shoulders, and I almost pass out from the sensations that wash over my body when he pushes in deeper.

He shifts so that he is lying against my side, his rock-hard cock pushing against my thigh, and after pulling his finger from my tight hole, he returns to my soaked pussy, coating not one, but two fingers. When he trails down to my rim again, I'm ready for him and push out when his fingertips touch my tight opening.

"Fuck me. My girl is begging for it. Begging for my cock in her virgin ass. I want your pussy, baby, but I need this too. I need to take you here."

I nod my head, panting with need that is so great it has stolen my speech.

"As wet as you are, I would almost think you didn't need lube, but there is no fucking way I'm taking this ass without getting you ready. I want to hear you fucking scream, Dani. Beg. Me. For. It."

He doesn't wait for me to respond. He rolls to his side, I hear him rummage through his drawer, and then he's back. His wicked grin makes his handsome face flash with a dirty promise.

"Scream, Dani. Scream until my ears ring," he says, and without warning, he flips me so that my knees are on the mattress. He's mindful to keep my stomach off the bed, placing a pillow between my body and the soft sheets.

I hear a noise and then feel cool liquid rolling down from the top of my ass until it rolls onto the mattress. His fingers move from where he was holding my hips in place, and I feel him rub the lube until his fingers and my crack are slippery.

His fingers dip slowly and deep into my ass, scissoring and stretching my hole to take his cock. The feeling burns in pleasure and makes me feel a delicious fullness. His other hand squirts some more lube, this time gathering some on his fingers. I lean up on my hands and look over my shoulder to see his head thrown back, his teeth digging into his bottom lip, and his other arm—the one not thrusting two fingers into my ass—stroking his cock.

He looks down, locks eyes with me, and pulls his fingers from my dark hole. When I feel the steel of his piercing against my body, I tense and his eyes flash.

"Don't do that. Fucking beg me, Dani," he commands.

I take a deep breath, and before I can get the words out, I feel his palm against my ass, the feeling startling but not unpleasant. I moan and do as he said, begging him to take me.

"Yeah. That's what I want to hear. Louder, Dani." His words slur, and I feel him press harder against my body. "Make me believe you."

I do as he said, my body once again feeling like a coil that is being pulled too tight.

"Just. Like. That!" he roars before slowly pushing himself into my body. "Push out, baby. Push against me and take my cock."

The burn is almost too much. I can feel each of the piercings that line his cock until he's settled in as deep as he can go, and the one piercing that's left is pressed against my stretched hole. It hurts in a way that is so all consuming, and I scream out with the pleasure that his pain brings me.

"So fucking good," he pants, pulling out just an inch before rocking into my body again. "Made for my cock."

I cry out, scream just as he predicted, and hold on for dear life as he builds up his speed until he's pushing into my body in a pace that has me feeling like I can't breathe.

"So full of my cock, Dani-girl. Your ass is begging for it."

Thrust out and push in. Each time, gaining speed until I'm not sure if I'm even breathing anymore.

"God. Damn." His fingers dig into my hips before I feel his fingers circling my clit, and just like that—with that one simple touch—I explode in the most powerful orgasm my body has ever felt. My head is thrown back and his name is the last thing on my lips as my body milks his cock of every ounce of come he has left.

Chapter 33

Cohen

I'M NOT SURE WHAT'S GOTTEN into me.

One second, I was begging for my girl to forgive me. The next, I was demanding that she beg me for my cock.

I took my pregnant woman rough and hard. And I didn't just fuck her. No, I took one look at her body, ripe with the pregnancy of my child, and lost my fucking mind.

I move from behind her, careful that her spent body doesn't fall onto her stomach, and lay her on her side. After jumping off the bed, I walk to the bathroom to clean myself off. As I wash my cock with a warm washcloth, I look in the mirror at my flushed skin. Sweat is beading down my chest, and my cock is still impossibly hard even after having just come twice.

After making sure I cleaned myself off, I run a new washcloth under the warm water and walk back over to the bed. Her eyes are closed, and her chest is moving up and down in a slow rhythm. My eyes trail down her flushed neck, and when I see my come dry on her skin—all over her long neck and tits—my cock jumps. Fuck, that's hot.

I bring the washcloth to her skin and almost hate that I have to wipe myself off her body. She doesn't even flinch as I clean her chin, neck, and tits. Not even a twitch when I rub the warm cotton over the ass I just fucked hard. She does hum in her sleep, but other than that, nothing.

I use this time to take in her body. Her belly looks so large now that I'm getting a good look. Her slim body makes her look like she swallowed a ball. When I think again about our child growing inside her, I want to fuck her all over again. It's as if it wakes some primal desire to claim her that was dormant until now.

After tossing the dirty washcloth towards my hamper, I climb into the bed and pull the sheets over her body. My hand goes straight to her belly, and when I feel little bumps against my palm, my eyes go wide.

That. That right there is my child. A child I made with Dani.

That primal urge hits me again, reminding me that now she is connected to me forever. I know she loves me. There is no denying that. But this child? This child connects us in a way that will never change.

Our baby continues to make its presence known, and I close my eyes and let the peace that washes over me settle my heart.

"I'm going to marry you, Dani-girl," I vow to the silence around me.

"Okay, baby," she mumbles.

I thought she was asleep, so when I hear her sleepy voice answer me back, my eyes shoot to hers, and when I see her beautiful smile and bright-green eyes swimming with tears, I shake my head and move to kiss her deep.

"Why the tears?"

"I love you," she says, not answering me.

"Dani. The tears."

"I love you. That's why the tears. But if you plan on marrying me, you better ask me when you haven't just fucked me raw."

I laugh, kissing her again, "Noted."

"I missed you," she sighs.

"I know, Dani-girl. Never again. I won't leave you again, baby."

She shifts so that her eyes come to mine. "You can't promise that, Cohen. You don't know when they'll call you back." She doesn't say it, but I hear the fear in her voice, and I hate that it's there.

"Actually, I can promise that. I'm out, baby. I let them know that I was leaving the program two days ago. I still have some shit I need to tie up with them, but I won't be leaving."

Her eyes go wide, and she looks at me in shock before—much to my surprise—she lets out a pitiful noise and drops her head, wrapping her arms around my body and holding me as tight as she can while she loses her shit.

"Dani-girl, you need to calm yourself."

She doesn't stop, just sobs harder.

Helpless and unable to stop her from drowning us both with tears, I bring her body close and wait for her cries to end.

"You're not going to leave us?" she questions after a few minutes.

Us.

Her and our child.

"Never."

"My God," she cries. She looks up at me in awe, those eyes I love so much taking in every inch of my face. "You have no idea how happy that makes me."

"Yeah, the tears were a little questionable," I joke.

"You're going to be here . . . every day?"

"Every day from here on out."

She smiles and cuddles her body close, relaxing instantly in my arms.

"We need to talk about what happened today, Dani."

I probably could have timed it better, but the calm that was rolling down her body like a blanket evaporates the second I open my mouth.

"You don't have to repeat that shit, baby. I know everything, but we do need to talk about what you think. What you think and what your gut is telling you about these things happening. I don't fucking like it one bit, and until we figure out who's behind these threats, I don't want you leaving my sight."

She opens her mouth to complain—I'm sure—but I stop her before she has a chance.

"I won't waver on this, Dani. I just won't. Not when it comes to you and our child's safety. You can just think of it as us making up for lost time. Like it our not, I'm your new shadow, baby."

Her face scrunches up, and I wait for her to speak, my fingers trailing over the soft skin of her back.

"I hate this. I hate feeling powerless and terrified to even look out the window, Cohen."

"I know you do. But this shit will end. I won't stop until I find out who has been making you feel like you aren't safe. I won't let anyone take you from me."

We lie there in silence until she speaks again.

"Who do you think is doing this?" she whispers into the darkness.

"I'm not sure, but rest easy that I'll find out."

She nods her head against my shoulder and settles in deeper as if her body needs to get as close as possible to feel safe. I feel her stomach press against my side and smile into the darkness.

"A baby, huh?"

"Yeah," she breathes. "I know we didn't plan this, but I couldn't be happier. Knowing that a part of us is cooking away in there gives me the biggest sense of completion I've ever felt. It helped me fill the void that your being gone had left, but it wasn't until I had your arms around me again that I realized how right this feels."

"My Dani-girl is having my baby." I let that settle around us before another thought quickly takes its place. "Your father really is going to kick my ass."

Her giggles float around us, and with a smile, I fall asleep. And for the first time in almost seven long months, I sleep peacefully.

Chapter 34

Dani

COHEN DIDN'T LET ME OUT of his bed for two days. Of course, he kept me well fed and hydrated, but other than that, we spent the two days that followed his homecoming locked in his room with our bodies connected in every way possible.

The phone had long stopped ringing and it seemed that our family and friends were content to wait us out and give us the time we needed to become us after too long apart.

I asked him once between one of our long lovemaking sessions if he felt like it was weird that we came together so quickly. He laughed and told me that if we hadn't been dancing around it for so long, I would have been his years ago. There was no doubt in my mind that I was right where I was meant to be.

"Dani," I hear him call from the other side of his shower curtain. "I think they've given us as much space as we're going to get. Your brother called to give me a heads-up that our parents should be here in about twenty minutes."

Ugh. So much for staying wrapped up in each other.

"I'm surprised they lasted this long," I mumble and rinse the shampoo from my hair.

"Me too," he says, and I jump when I realize that he's stepped into the shower with me.

"You just took a shower," I say lamely.

"Yup," he responds and takes my conditioner from my hand. "Turn."

I do what he says and spin, giving him my back. I hear him groan as his free hand palms my cheek. "I love this ass," he says and gives it a light slap.

"So I noticed."

"We have twenty minutes, baby."

I look over my shoulder at him and raise my brow in question, wondering where he's going with this.

"I wonder how many times I can make you scream my name in that time." He drops the conditioner, forgotten on the bottom of the tub, and pulls me against his hard, naked body.

Thirty minutes later, he has made me scream his name four times, and even while the front door is being pounded on by our expected visitors, he takes my body until I give him one more.

I glare at my father and continue to attempt to brush the tangles out of my wet hair. Since I didn't use conditioner, the long locks have become almost unmanageable. My father, having noticed that we were both wet when we opened the door, hasn't taken his eyes off Cohen.

Cohen, who I'll press, hasn't let me away from his side. When our parents filed in his doorway, I gave each of them a hug, and then he had his arm around my shoulders and my body pressed against his. I offered to get everyone something to drink and he just said no and pulled me onto his lap when he dropped down on the oversized chair in this living room.

Where I'm currently sitting, glaring at my father.

"Dani has agreed that it's best if she took some time off work," Cohen says to the room, and I snap my head to his.

"I did?"

"Sure you did," he says, looking at me like I've lost my mind.

"I don't remember that."

"That's because you've been busy," he says with a wink.

I snap my eyes over to the corner where my father is standing with his arms crossed over his chest when I hear him growl. "Did you really just do that?" I snap at him.

"Axel," Mom warns him.

Cohen brings his arm around my waist and rests his palm on my stomach, and I can't even enjoy *that,* because once again, my father is acting like a dog, growling and all but frothing at the mouth.

"Seriously, Daddy!" I exclaim. "That's a bit much."

"Axel," Mom tries again, walking over, placing her hands on either side of his face, and attempting to bring his gaze to hers.

He doesn't budge though; his eyes stay locked on Cohen.

"Seriously?" she huffs. "You're acting like a caveman, Axel Reid. Time to stop."

Cohen seems to have a death wish, because his other hand moves from where it was lying against the armrest and his long fingers curl around one of my jean-clad thighs.

Daddy moves like he's about to push off the wall only to stop when my mom pushes against his chest. I look over at Cohen's parents, and my eyes widen when I see his mom wink at me and giggle softly, which earns her a squeeze by Greg.

"As I was saying," Cohen continues. "Dani is going to be taking some time off work. I've already talked to Sway, and in light of the other day's events, he agrees that is the best move. I've already talked to Chance and let him know that, as soon as Dani finds a house she feels works for the baby and us, we'll be moving out. I say we because I don't plan on her going anywhere until said house is found. He also sees the wisdom in this plan."

"The fuck you say," Daddy says, finally having enough and snapping. He pushes past my mother so swiftly that she almost tumbles. His arm shoots out and he helps her steady her footing, never once removing his heated gaze off Cohen. "The fuck. You say!"

He prowls forward, and when he gets about halfway to us, Cohen pats my thigh and indicates that he wants me to shift so he can stand. I do so, mutely, and wait to see how this plays out, knowing that it has to play out for us to be able to move forward.

"You knock up *my* girl. Demand that she move in. And not even plan on making an honest woman out of her?" he fumes.

Cohen stands toe-to-toe with him, their eyes almost level, but even with Daddy having a few inches on Cohen, he doesn't back down. His chest heaves, but for the most part, he remains calm.

"I didn't say that, Axel. I plan on marrying your daughter the first chance I get, but *that* is something that is between the two of us. I respect you enough that I *had* planned on coming to you privately to ask for your blessing, but I have to be honest with you—I will be marrying *my girl* whether you give that to me or not. With all due respect, I love your daughter and I couldn't really give two shits if you want to bless that or not."

"What did you just say?" Daddy turns and looks over at my mom. "What did he just say to me?"

"You heard him, honey," she says with a smile. "I think it's time you took that alpha male down a few notches, big boy."

My gaze shoots from my mom to my dad to see his reaction, and then it lands on Melissa when she throws her head back and laughs loudly.

"Hush, beauty," Greg tells his wife. "Son, I think you need to tread carefully here. I like your head right where it is."

Melissa snickers even louder at that.

"You don't care for my blessing?" Daddy tosses back at Cohen, and there's no mistaking his body language—he's ready to kill. His hands are flexing and his face is beet red.

"Ax—" Mom tries.

"Don't you dare 'Axel' me, Izzy. Don't you dare. Did you hear him? He just said he didn't give *two shits!*" he roars. "You're walking a tight line here, Cohen."

This is getting out of hand. I know there won't be a good outcome if I let the two men I love the most fight over this. Standing carefully from my seat, I give Melissa a wobbly smile when she nods her head in encouragement before I go to stand in front of Cohen and face my father.

I feel Cohen move, and before I can speak, I'm behind him and he's once again between my father and me. My eyes go from his solid back to the only two people I can see—his parents. Cohen's move of dominance and protection is one I know didn't go unnoticed by my father because I see Greg nod and Melissa smile so huge that it looks unnatural. I grasp his shirt in my hand and try to get his attention.

"Cohen," I start.

"Not now, Dani. I get you think you need to protect me from your father, but this needs to happen and it needs to happen now."

I sigh, drop my hands from his shirt, and do the only thing left I can. I wrap my hands around his stomach and spread my palms wide against his abs. It's another move I know doesn't go unnoticed because Melissa's smile gets even larger, and when I move my eyes to Greg's, I see that his are shining bright and his smile matches Melissa's in size and happiness.

"Are you going to do anything?" I ask him.

"Nope. My boy knows what he's doing." He leans back and pulls his wife to his chest, and they just watch with those big, loopy-loo smiles as Cohen stands his ground with my father.

The father who I know could kill him with his bare hands.

I gulp.

"I'm going to tell you this once, Axel. I love your daughter. I've loved her before it was right to feel that way. I fought those feelings until she was ready for me, because I'll tell you this. It was never a question that I was ready for her. What we have is something I will never feel worthy of. Not of her love. Something she gives me without hesitation. I know she deserves the best that life can hand her. You do *not* have to remind me of that. But even though I don't think *I'm* good enough for *her,* I'll spend my life making sure that she knows she's the best thing I will ever have. Do you understand that? I will make sure there isn't a day that passes that she doesn't know how much I love her. I'll spend every second I have left on this Earth giving her every-thing I possibly can. I waited, out of respect for you and for her, until I couldn't wait a second longer, and I will not—not for you—give up even a sliver of time with her now that she is mine."

I hold my breath and wait. I keep my eyes on Cohen's parents for some sort of clue of what's happening beyond the wall of Cohen's body.

It feels like a lifetime passes before I hear my father's laughter boom through the room.

What in the hell?

"Well. Why didn't you just say that to begin with?"

I repeat; What in the hell?

"You didn't really give me a chance, Axel," Cohen says.

"Right. Well, now that that is out of the way, let's talk."

Jesus Christ. I've entered the Twilight Zone.

It doesn't take long for us to settle back down. Cohen turns and gives me a kiss, and when I hear my father's growl again, I pull back and look over at him. He throws his arms up and gives me a tired look back.

"What? You don't expect me to just flip a switch and turn it off, do you?"

"Crazy old man," I mutter.

Cohen takes his seat again and pulls me back onto his lap. One hand goes to my belly and the other is resting back on my thigh. Without a thought, I wrap my arms around his shoulders and settle in for what promises to be a long chat.

"My dad filled me in on everything that's happened between the letter, flowers, and . . . yesterday." He pauses to look down at me. "I want to be fully briefed so that I'm able to understand this from every angle that I'm sure you have worked. My gut tells me that it's someone she knows. Someone she trusts. But until I have all the intel, I'm not comfortable making that call. I've been told that the police also have run into nothing but dead ends?" He looks between my father and his and they all nod. "This bastard is slick, I'll give him that," Cohen mutters.

"Slick, but he'll fuck up. I heard from my contact at the department that there was a print lifted from the bag. Dani's has been ruled out, so they're running it through their database to see if they get a match."

Cohen nods his head at my father's words but doesn't speak.

"I agree with you, son. This is too personal of an attack for it to be someone that she hasn't come in contact with."

I shiver when Greg's words hit me. Someone I know? I can't even think about who it might be.

"You think it could be a client?" I ask. "I have plenty of male clients, but until yesterday, no one really knew about the pregnancy. Until recently, I wasn't really showing much and I had been able to hide it well. I . . . well, yesterday, with the cameras back, I wanted to show my belly off."

"Client, or someone that you've been in contact with. However brief, it doesn't matter. They've latched on, and judging by everything that's been said with the two messages, they aren't happy that you're in a relationship with my son—well, anyone for that matter. You've always held back, Dani, and until Cohen, you didn't really date seriously. I don't think that this person saw a threat until Cohen."

I try to make sense of what Greg just said, but I just can't seem to wrap my mind around it.

"Little princess," my daddy says gruffly. "Think about this. The flowers started when Cohen left. I don't want to know details, but if this person has been watching you, it's reasonable to believe that he saw the connection between you, and when Cohen left, he pounced and attempted to make his feelings known with the flowers. When that didn't work, something triggered that first note. I've been over this with your mom, and she told me that you two had spent that afternoon discussing the seriousness of your relationship with Cohen. I have no doubt that, if he's that close, he didn't handle overhearing that very well."

I nod, following so far. Cohen's breathing has gone wild, and I look up into his eyes to see that he's having a hard time holding on to his cool after hearing all of this.

"After that, things calmed down, but the flowers continued," Greg adds.

"Right," Daddy starts and looks between Greg and Cohen. "Dani, you don't know this because, between all of us, your brother, and Liam, we were able to grab most of the deliveries before you even knew they had come . . . but they never stopped. I think they would have probably continued until Cohen came home and, once again, that threat against whatever he sees in his sick mind of you having with him is back. That is until you went out with your belly the focus and he realized that something he considered his had been touched by another."

"Oh my God," I gasp.

"I tell you, sweetheart, this motherfucker will pay. Not only has he threatened you, but as of yesterday, he's now threatening my grandbaby."

"Agreed," Greg says forcefully.

"I agree with what Cohen's said. You need to stop working for a little while. Stay home and enjoy the rest of your pregnancy. After the baby is born, then you can decide what to do about work, but until this fucker is caught, it would make everyone feel a lot better if we could limit the people you're around. Being at Sway's with everything going on with clients in and out as well as that show being filmed, just isn't safe."

I nod, seeing the reason in this.

"I'm not going to say that I agree with you two moving in together, but I know Cohen is trained well to take care of you and he's proven that he's willing to do whatever it takes to keep you safe in my eyes. Kills me, baby, to admit this, but you're better off staying put right here."

Oh wow. "That must have been hard to say," I say, trying to make light of how big this moment is.

"You have no idea." He smiles.

I look up at Cohen and give him a smile before I move to climb off his lap. He lets me go without argument, and I walk over, bend, and wrap my arms around my daddy's neck.

"You'll always be the first man I loved, Daddy."

"I know, little princess. I know."

I swallow the lump in my throat, kiss his tan cheek, and walk back over to Cohen. When I feel his arms wrap around my body again, I let their strength soak in, and I listen as the men in the room go about what the best course of action from here on out is.

I don't think I'll feel settled until the invisible threat around me is gone, but right here, in this moment, I feel as safe as I've ever felt in my life because I'm wrapped up in the arms of the man I love.

Chapter 35

Cohen

"DO YOU WANT MY COCK or my mouth, Dani?" I ask and trail my fingers down the center of her collarbone and between the valley of her tits.

"Your cock, baby," she pleads.

"Do you want my cock in your pussy or your ass?" I question, continuing my path down her body until my fingers dance over the smooth skin on her mound.

"My pussy?"

"You don't sound so sure about that, baby," I murmur and dip my finger into her body. "Although your cunt is begging for it. Is your ass going to milk my fingers if I dip them in deep?" I ask, pumping my fingers into her wet center.

"Ye-yes," she stutters.

"I'm sure it would, but right now, I want my cock right here," I say and curl my fingers until I hit that spot that has her juices running down my fingers and down her crack. "So responsive."

I pull my fingers out of her body, and she watches with heated eyes as I pop them in my mouth and hum.

"Fucking taste so good."

I push my fingers back in and give her a few hard pumps before I take them and offer them to her mouth, wiping her juices along the seam of her lips before she opens and sucks them clean.

"Fuck," I groan and move so that my cock is rubbing against her.

Her legs drop open and she starts to rock with my hips. My cock ring and other piercings make her cry out each time they roll over her clit.

"Do you want me hard or do you want me soft?" I ask, rocking even harder when those hot fucking mewling sounds start climbing up her throat.

"Soft . . . and hard," she pants.

"Yeah," I say and pull my hips back, and when I line up, I push home in one slow thrust. Her eyes go glossy and her moan is long. "Yeah, baby. Soft and hard."

I give her what she wants. Soft thrusts until my balls can't take it any longer. The second I feel her walls start to flutter and I know she's seconds away from coming apart in my arms, I start to slam into her hard enough that the headboard bangs against the wall. She takes every thrust I have, and right before I feel my balls tighten, she throws her head back and screams my name loud enough that the sound pierces my ears painfully. My climax tears through my body, and my cock is milked dry by her tight walls.

After a few more thrusts to feel her walls quivering against my sensitive cock, I pull out and lean back on my knees to watch our combined come drip out of her body.

"Fuck that's hot. I wish you could fucking see us falling out of your body," I tell her.

I bring my hand to her pussy and thrust my finger deep into her still-shuddering cunt. When I pull my finger out, it's gleaming with our joined come, and I look past her rapidly falling chest to meet her wide, turned-on eyes.

"You see how fucking hot we are together?"

She nods, and her eyes darken to the hunter-green color they always take when she's turned on.

"My girl likes that?" I ask and move my hand back down to her pussy. I rub my hand through her slit and rub our come into her skin. "Open," I demand and wait for her to understand my meaning.

My fingers, wet and dripping with *us,* start moving towards her head, and without question, she opens her mouth wide and waits for my fingers.

When her warm lips close around two of my wet fingers and suck me hard, I almost come again.

"Fucking hell," I groan.

"Mmmm," she moans in return, and I look down to see her rubbing her legs together.

"Already?" I question.

"Always," she retorts.

Fucking hell, indeed.

Hours later, with Dani passed out in my bed, I throw on some sweats and walk into the living room.

Chance sees me coming from his spot in the chair by the window and pulls off his Beats. "I take it I can remove these now?" he asks with a raised brow.

"She's asleep if that's what you're asking."

"She isn't screaming, so that's my answer."

"Did you find out anything?" I question, ignoring his comment.

"Nothing you're going to like."

"Well, fucking give it to me." I spit in his direction.

"Questioned each person who was in the salon when that package came. So far, I've been able to sit down with everyone except two people. Don W. Johnson—one personal assistant to Devon Westerfield— and one of their cameramen. That's as far as I've gotten. I looked into the background checks Axel had run when they first started coming around, but so far, nothing is sticking out. Devon, the producer, is being as helpful as he can. My gut tells me that he is no threat. His other assistant, Mark Seymour, has also been very forthcoming. He and Dani had struck up a friendship and he was very concerned about how she is fairing in light of all of this. He did mention that Don wasn't too happy about Dani being pregnant. Something about it putting a wrench into their filming."

"I see," I tell him, careful to calm myself before I snap about some douchebag being close with Dani.

"I'll keep digging."

"You do that," I tell him. "I'm taking Dani to look at houses next week. Are you sure you're cool with this?" I ask, knowing that, even though he's a loner as of late, that isn't something he deals with well. Chance has his own issues, but I know that the front he puts on for the world to see isn't the man I know.

"I'm not going to swallow a bottle of pills or cut my wrist because my buddy is moving out, Cohen. I'll be fine. Plus, I won't be around much anyway. We've picked up some big clients lately at CS and I'll be doing some bodyguard work until we can train more men."

"You'll let me know if the nightmares come back?" I ask.

"Fuck," he sighs and rubs the back of his neck. "Yeah, all right, I'll fucking let you know." He stands from his chair and walks over to the desk in the corner of the room, grabbing some papers and tossing them to me. "Printed the ones I felt would fit what you two need. Some I grabbed are a little more than you'll be needing right away, but with the way you two go at it, you'll need the space."

I look down, confused, and laugh when I see the handful of printouts of houses for sale he gave me. "Thanks, brother."

"Yeah," he mumbles and walks down the hall.

I wait until I hear his door click shut before I laugh to myself and toss them down on the coffee table before I pad back down the hall and climb back in bed with Dani in my arms.

Chapter 36

Dani

"**I**'M NOT SEEING HOW A house *this* big is something we need, Cohen." I look up at the large colonial house and my eyes hit every window—and there are many—and I look over to my left at the four-car garage that sits at an angle to the house. "Four cars seems like overkill."

"Nah," Cohen says and grabs my hand before pulling me up the front steps.

We've been house-hunting for the last three weeks and I'm over it. True to his word, he hasn't left me for a second. He came with me a few days after it was decided for me that I would move in with him and helped my brother and Lee move all of my stuff back out of the townhome I shared with the girls and into his apartment. Lee thought it was hilarious, and after Nate got over trying to act like our dad when it came to Cohen and me, he joined in and thought that my being basically kidnapped was the funniest thing he had ever seen.

Of course, that was after I kneed him in the balls.

Lyn and Lila were over the freaking moon about the new status in Cohen's and my relationship. Maddi was just happy I was happy. They thought that it was the best thing in the world.

Megan was the only voice of reason I had, but even that was short-lived when she witnessed firsthand how Cohen was around me. Her eyes got wet, and after I fussed, she told me that we reminded her of how her husband had been towards her when they'd first gotten together. Of course, that concerned me, but she was able to settle her emotions and, after that, was another cheerleader Cohen had in his corner.

After that, I just decided to say the hell with it and roll with what came.

We're about to be parents, so it makes sense.

Plus, there's that whole thing with my heart feeling like it's breaking in two when he isn't near.

All things considered, living with the man of my dreams and the love of my life isn't exactly a hardship.

Between looking for our future home, we've spent the last three weeks becoming closer than ever before. In between family dinners at either my parents' house or his, we've spent the majority of the time in bed either making love or talking about everything we can think of.

It's been some of the best times of my life.

"Come on, Dani-girl. There's something I want you to see," he says and gives my arm another tug.

"Okay, okay . . . Jeez," I laugh and follow him through the front door.

He leads me past the smiling real estate agent and up the huge staircase that dominates the front entry. He doesn't stop until we're both facing one of the many closed doors in the upstairs.

"Go ahead," he urges and nods to the door.

I give him a look but reach out and turn the nob. When my eyes settle around the room he's found, my lip quivers. "Oh, Cohen."

"It's perfect, hmm?" he says, coming up behind me and wrapping his arms around my body until he has his hands against my belly. His lips press against my temple. "I figured, with us deciding not to find out the gender, that this color would be perfect. You can match anything you want with a green like this. It reminded me of your eyes, and that made me think about our little one having the same green eyes as you, and it just seemed like a sign."

"It's perfect." And it is.

The large room has light-green walls and a dark hardwood finish. The back wall has a huge floor-to-ceiling window that overlooks the wooded backyard. I walk deeper into the room and notice the huge walk-in closet through one doorway. The other doorway leads into a connecting bathroom. I imagine where each item I have carefully planned on buying for our child would go, seeing the room come together instantly.

"This is it, Cohen," I tell him and watch his handsome face brighten with happiness.

"I hoped you would say that since I put an offer on this one last week."

"You did what?" I laugh. "Then why have we been looking at house after house since then?"

"Even on paper, it was perfect, Dani. There's more than enough room for us and our family to grow. I had no problem putting our future in writing. I wanted you to see your choices before I showed you mine. Had you liked something better, I would have pulled my offer and gotten you that one." He walks over and rubs my belly. "You, me, and baby against the world."

I nod my head and lean up on my tippy-toes to give him a kiss. "That's right, Superman." I giggle.

I'm not sure what kind of strings Cohen pulled to have us in our home so quickly, but not even a week after he showed me the beautiful home with our child's perfect nursery, we are moving our stuff in.

Against his better judgment and a lot of convincing from me that I would be perfectly fine at the apartment with Chance, Liam, and my brother—not to mention that my girls were all on their way to help—he left to meet with the realtor and the contractor we had hired to finish our basement and to wait for the furniture company to deliver ninety percent of our stuff. He had a busy day at the new house, and with all of us busy boxing up the rest of Cohen's and my stuff, it was best for him to leave me here to make sure it gets done.

"Chance!" I yell out Cohen's bedroom door. "Where is the packaging tape?"

When no one answers, I heave my almost eight-month-pregnant body off the floor and walk into the living room, where I left them arguing over which PlayStation games belong to Cohen and which ones he had stolen from them. Sometimes, I wonder if they're really grown children.

"Hey, where are you guys?" I ask, looking around.

"Danielle."

I jump and spin towards the familiar voice.

"I've been waiting for you."

My eyes widen when I see the blood staining the knife in his hands, and when I move my eyes back to his, I notice that they're wild.

Oh. My. God. This isn't happening. I quickly look around and search for the guys. The blood on his knife could only mean one thing, and my stomach drops when I realize what that is.

"Where are my friends?" I question. *Keep him talking . . .* I think that's what Dad said to do in a situation like this. Keep him talking until you can figure out a way to get help.

"Your *friends*," he says as if the words taste bad against his lips. "Those men that you've been whoring yourself to aren't going to be a problem. The big one and your brother left a second ago, and I took care of that other motherfucker just like I took care of Don and Clint."

"Don and Clint? Clint the cameraman? What are you talking about, Mark?"

"I saw the way they looked at you. Always looking at you. And you let them. You shouldn't have done that, Danielle." He laughs, the sound making my skin crawl. "You shouldn't encourage that they had a chance with you. *YOU* are mine and I'm tired of watching you act like a slut when you know, YOU KNOW, what we have."

I gape at him, dumbfounded. "I have no idea what you're talking about, Mark." A sense of dread starts to take hold of my body, and I try to think of a way out of this mess.

Until he speaks again and I'm shocked to my core.

"I saw the way that you would look at me. I know you felt it. All of our dates we would have. When you would tell me what you loved about me as a boyfriend. I remember it all, Danielle. But you've been a naughty girl. It's time to take care of all of these . . . complications." He waves the knife around until the tip is pointing down. At my swollen belly.

"No," I gasp and clutch my stomach. "No!" My scream goes unnoticed by him as he takes a step forward. "Mark, those weren't dates. We had lunch—with about five other people—in the breakroom at Sway's. That was it. You were asking my advice for the girl you were dating. Mark, we aren't anything." My attempt at reasoning with him only angers him further.

"No!" he bellows, repeatedly jabbing the knife in my direction. "We're EVERYTHING!" his voice takes on a manic level of insanity, and he starts to advance on me.

"Please . . . I'm begging you. Don't hurt my baby. I'll do whatever you want, but please!"

"That," he says harshly. "That is an abomination and it must be removed from you. I won't stand for it."

I grip my stomach tighter and sob. The tears mix with the snot as they roll down my face. The hope I was holding on to that I would be able to talk him off the ledge starts to dwindle. I look around again, praying that I'll find something that will give me the answer on how to escape this impending doom.

This is it. I'm going to die right here where my future started. Right where it started, we're going to die, and I know there is no way Cohen will survive this kind of loss. That knowledge and my love for him are the only hope I have left. I spot the lamp just an inch away from my fist right when Mark makes his move and lunges forward. Given the fact that my belly has gotten huge in the last seven weeks since Cohen returned home, my movements are slower than normal, and right when I feel his knife pierce my left side, I heave the lamp with everything I have and clip him right on his temple.

Mark goes down hard, dazed but not out, so I bring my arm back—weakly now that my side is killing me—and swing at him again. His lifts and his knife digs into the top of my hip. Desperate to do what I can to protect my stomach, I twist and fight with everything I have in me. If this is the last moment I have on this Earth, I'm not going to be taken out easily.

"Stop fucking moving so I can get that thing out of you!" he bellows, and it isn't lost on me just how far gone he is on the sanity scale.

"You won't get my baby, you sick fuck!" I scream, and with a renewed strength, I start to kick my legs between driving the heavy lamp down onto his face. "You can't have my baby," I sob, my body growing weaker. "Never!" I scream out and never stop, my throat burning with the raw sounds coming out.

I feel it before my mind registers that there is nothing else I can do, and as my body is pulled down with nothing left to give, I use the last bit of my strength to twist so that, when I fall, my baby is protected.

Chapter 37

Liam

"**H**OW HARD WOULD IT HAVE been to carry this shit down when Cohen got here and could help us?" I ask Nate after dusting my hands off on my jeans.

We've just spent the better part of thirty minutes trying to get Cohen's big-ass seventy-inch television down three flights of stairs and attempted to get the damn thing loaded into the back of my truck without breaking it.

"It seemed easier than it was when I planned it out in my head. It's not my fault it's heavier than it looks. Damn thing looked like it would be easy."

Yeah. Famous last words of Nate Reid.

"Plus, if Chance wouldn't have been so fucking lazy, he could have helped out too."

"Chance"—I reach over and shove Nate as we start to walk back up the stairs—"is up there keeping an eye on Dani. Something that, I'll remind you, *we* should be doing as well."

"Seriously, Lee? She's right up there! What the hell is going to happen in the two seconds we took to take care of that shit?" He pulls his UGA ball cap off and scratches his thick, black hair before jamming it back down. "Fuck, it's hot out here."

Right when my booted foot touches the bottom step, I hear a sound that stops my heart. I look over at Nate to see if he heard it and see all the color drain from his face.

"Fuck!" I yell and start to bound up the steps in threes. "Call Cohen, Nate. Call Cohen and then call your dad." I keep running, letting my training take over and my instincts kick in.

For the last two months, I've been in training with the local police department, and for the first time, I'm thankful for every second of that training. I don't look behind me to see if Nate's coming. I grab my cell and dial 911 as I continue up the stairs. As I reach their landing, the operator picks up and I give her the short version of what I know. Which is nothing. After rattling off Cohen's address and telling her to send an ambulance as well as the police, I stop talking and ease up on the cracked door.

"Sir, is the intruder still on the scene?" the female voice says through the line.

I feel Nate coming up behind me and hand him the phone. I hardly register his response to the operator. When I don't hear anything from inside the apartment, I slowly toe open the door and ease inside.

What I see is a scene I will never forget. If I should live to be one hundred, this image will still be branded in my mind. The walls, floor, and tan couches are all stained red.

Blood red.

I can't see over the loveseat that blocks the view from the doorway into the living room, but I see Chance's crumpled form behind it, and I slowly move towards him and check for a pulse.

Strong and steady, thank Christ.

He has one hell of a bump forming on his forehead, and I check the knife wound he has to his left shoulder, but it's a clean cut that isn't bleeding heavily anymore.

I stand, move around the chair, and feel a sob bubble up my throat.

"Dani!" I yell and rush towards her. I step over the unrecognizable man that is lying—unmoving—in front of her.

"He has the knife," I hear Nate say weakly behind me. He rushes forward and kicks it away before checking the douchebag for a pulse. "Fuck! She fought, Lee. She fought while we were down there dicking around with a goddamn TV!" He stands and kicks the body behind me. "She fought hard enough that she killed a man threatening her with a knife with a damn lamp."

I don't move my eyes from Dani as I check for her pulse and find it weakly beating against my fingertips. "Help me stop the bleeding until the ambulance gets here, Nate!"

We both rush, careful of her pregnant stomach, and hold down the wounds we can, and I look into Nate's eyes and see the same panic I feel.

That panic never leaves. Not while we soak through the towels we have held against her body and not when I notice that the pulse I keep checking is slowing down.

Not once—even when the paramedics rush through the door and take over care.

It doesn't stop as we rush behind them as they carry an unmoving Dani on a stretcher.

And not when we're speeding down the highway behind them on the way to the hospital.

That panic never leaves, and I know that, if Dani doesn't make it, it's a feeling I'll never get over.

"Did you get Cohen?" I whisper towards Nate.

He's rubbing his bloodstained hands together and doesn't move his eyes from the back of the ambulance holding his sister.

"No."

I look away from the road, shocked. "No?"

"He didn't answer and I rushed after you before I called back. I'll do that now," he says with a monotone voice. His movements are robotic as he grabs my cell from the cupholder between us and presses the screen until I hear the ringing echoing throughout the cab.

"What's up, Lee?" Cohen asks when the call connects. He sounds happy, I notice. "I should be back soon. I've—"

"Coh," I say, my voice cracking.

He doesn't say anything until I hear him roar through the phone. "Where is she?" he screams. "Where the fuck is she?!" I can hear the strain in his voice, and I imagine that he's running towards his truck.

"We're headed to Grady Memorial, Cohen. She's in the ambulance in front of us."

"Is she—"

"I don't know, brother. I honestly just don't know."

Cohen disconnects the call, but not before I hear the sob that tears out of his throat.

Another thing I'll never forget.

Never.

Chapter 38

Cohen

MY MIND GETS ME TO Grady on autopilot.

Every second it takes to get me there feels like eternity. Not knowing how she is, the status of her injuries, is like fuel to the fire of my misery.

After slamming the truck in park, I jump out and run towards the emergency entrance.

Fifteen minutes *after* the call from Lee.

Fifteen unknown minutes filled with thoughts of Dani and our child.

"Coh."

I look over when I hear Lee croak out my name, and when I take in his appearance, I drop to my knees and feel every second of those fifteen minutes weighing me down as I cry out for my family.

It isn't until I feel two strong hands press down on my shoulders that I look up and see both my father and Dani's standing on either side of my fallen body.

"Get up, son. Get up and pull yourself together and be there for Dani and the baby. Until you hear otherwise, you don't ever fucking give up hope," my dad says and holds his hand out to help me stand.

I nod and accept his hand, standing and turning towards Axel. His eyes are red and bright with emotion. He doesn't even try to stop the tears that are falling.

"Her mother will be here soon. She was at the salon when we got word. Melissa went to get her. Let's go get word on our girl so that I can give my wife something good to focus on, yeah?" He doesn't stick around to see if I follow.

I push down my despair and follow behind my girl's father, praying with every fiber in my being that we get that good news.

When Izzy came crashing through the emergency room doors with Melissa, Dee, and Sway hot on her heels, we were still waiting for word from the doctor. Shortly after they arrived, my sisters and brothers rushed in. Lyn and Lila rushed to my side and wrapped their arms around me. My brothers, never the ones to wear their emotions on their sleeves, went to Mom's side but looked at me with unmasked sympathy.

It didn't take long before we had overtaken the emergency room and were taken to a private room. Maddox and Asher showed up with their families in tow. Beck came in next, and after checking on Lee, he grabbed his wife and has held them both in his arms since. Megan was the last one to show, explaining that she got here as quickly as she could find a sitter for Molly.

Chance walked into the room last, and there wasn't an eye that didn't land on him. I untangled my body from the girls and walked over to him, grabbing his shoulder and pulling his body in toward mine, hugging him tight.

"I'm sorry," he rasps. "I'm so fucking sorry. I didn't even see him," His voice breaks, and I hold him as he loses it.

"Don't. He got the jump on you, Chance. You can't blame yourself for a crazy fuck getting the jump on you."

"It was my job to keep her safe, Cohen. My fucking job."

"No, it was my job. A job that, when she pulls through from this, I will never, not once, take a break from," I vow.

I can tell he doesn't believe me. His guilt and worry are getting the best of him. I shake my head, and after watching him walk over to the chairs on the other side of the room—away from everyone else, who's huddled together—I walk back over to where Lyn and Lila are sobbing softly to each other and take them in my arms.

And wait.

"Reid family?"

My eyes snap up from the floor, and I rush from my post against the wall.

"Yeah. That's me. Well, us. That's us."

"And you are?" the doctor asks.

"Her husband," I hear and look over my shoulder to see Axel stand next to me. "And I'm her father. How is my daughter?"

The doctor looks between Axel and me before he moves his eyes to the clipboard in his hands.

"Sir, your wife lost a good bit of blood, but we were able to re-plenish that quickly and she was very lucky that her wounds weren't deeper than they were. The blade missed two major arteries by a hair. She went into labor in transit, and after delivery, our major concern was blood loss and the wound that she had gotten to her side. I can't stress enough just how lucky your wife is."

"She's okay?" I question.

The doctor looks between us again, and for the first time, I notice the noise around us as the family realizes that she's alive and going to be fine.

"The baby?" Axel asks.

And just like that, the room is silenced.

"Ah . . ." He looks down at his notes. "You'll have to excuse me. I was in charge of your wife, and after delivery, she became my sole patient." He moves a few things before pausing to read some notes. "It says here that the baby is in the NICU at the moment being monitored, but for a thirty-two-week baby, his vitals are strong."

"His?" I choke out.

"Yes, his. Congratulations. You have a son."

And then I pass out.

Chapter 39

Dani

I OPEN MY EYES AND jerk when my last memories hit my like a tsunami.

Mark. The knife. The lamp. And my will to live—to fight.

"She's waking up, honey."

I move my head and look at my mom, who is standing on the left side of my bed. My daddy is standing right behind her with his arms wrapped tight around her, their eyes red and swollen. I move my eyes around the room and see Nate, his eyes dripping with tears. I give him a weak smile, and he turns his face from mine as he struggles to take control of his emotions.

I continue my rotation until I look down at the weight pressing against my hip. The dark-brown hair buzzed on the side and overgrown on the top. The strong shoulders heaving with emotion. And I feel his tears wetting my hand he's holding against his parted lips.

My heart breaks for the pain he's in, and I know there isn't anything I can do to ease it until he works out on his own whatever is running through his mind. I squeeze him, anxious to see those dark-brown eyes. I need him to see that I'm okay—I need to see that *he's* okay.

"Cohen—" I rasp and clear my throat. "Baby," I beg, feeling my own tears roll down my cheeks.

His shoulders start to heave when my voice hits his ears. I watch helplessly as the man I love falls apart. I look over to my parents and pray for answers, but I watch as my mom's own tears cascade down her porcelain skin. My dad has his head bowed and his forehead resting against her shoulder, his body hunched in a way I know can't be comfortable. I hear the door click and look over to see that Nate has left the room.

Without getting any help, I move my attention back to Cohen and try again. "Baby, please look at me. I need your eyes."

He struggles to control his emotions, and I watch with my eyes filling with tears as he lifts his head and I get a good look at my handsome man.

His chocolate eyes are filled with pain, and through the red-rimmed swelling around them, his tears continue to fall. His lips are dry from what I'm guessing is the sobbing I felt against my skin.

I reach up and run my fingers across his cheek. "It's you and me against the world, Cohen. Never goodbye, remember?"

He closes his eyes at my words and gives me a nod. I watch as he struggles again, but he wins against his pain, and when he opens his eyes again, I see *my* Cohen looking back at me.

"Just see you soon," he sighs.

"Every time I close my eyes."

He smiles. It's slightly wobbly, but it's a smile nonetheless, and I return it.

"We have a son," he says in reverence.

"He's okay?" I study his face for clues, and when the little sadness that was left in his eyes vanishes and he hits me with the full force of his smile, my heart bursts.

"He's perfect."

"Perfect," I cry. "Tell me more," I beg.

"He's big considering he was preterm. Just under five pounds, but he's a fighter, Dani-girl. They have him in NICU being monitored, but when I spoke to the nurse, she said she could see him coming home in a month at the most. He looks like me," he adds with his smile growing. "With your lips."

I soak it in, the fact that we have a son. Cohen and my baby together. Our little fighter.

Seems fitting that a love we've both been fighting to withstand, overcome, and, in the end, fight for would produce a little miracle that was a fighter in his own right.

"Our little fighter," I say, repeating the words I just thought.

He nods, and I swallow the lump in my throat.

"I thought I lost you," he says after studying my face for the longest time.

"Never, baby. Never."

"I thought I lost you, and that was one of the most terrifying experiences I have ever felt. I won't spend another second without you being mine. I mean it, Dani. When we get you and our boy home, I'll drag you right to the courthouse, but you will be mine."

I reach out, wrap my hand around the back of his neck, and pull him towards me. "When you learn how to ask me, then we'll talk."

His eyes flash, and his leans down to give me a deep kiss. I hear a growl from my side and smile against his lips.

"Hush, Axel."

I feel Cohen laughing softly against my mouth, and I join him only seconds after.

Four Weeks Later

"Cohen!" I yell up the stairs. "We don't need the diaper bag. Come on please. I need to get him home."

I smile when he comes bounding down the stairs and scoops me up in his arms, twirling me in a circle before placing me back on my feet.

"Our boy is coming home today!" he bellows through the room, the sound bouncing off each wall and echoing through our house.

"Stop acting crazy and take me to our son," I beg with a smile on my face.

For four long weeks—a solid month of going back and forth—we've been spending every second we had between the house and the hospital. With the help of our mothers, his sisters, and Megan, our house was fully decorated and the baby's nursery fully stocked before I even left the hospital. They kept me for four days to monitor my injuries as well as my recovery from my C-section, and since my emotions were so crazy when I got home, I cried for hours as I walked from room to room before finally settling in the nursery glider.

It was hard to come home without our baby, and I suffered from a bit of postpartum depression, so things amplified after that. I needed my son home and there just wasn't anything that would make that feeling better.

Cohen was my rock through it all. He held me when I needed to cry and then again when I needed to scream. He talked me through every second of pain I felt over the events that had happened and taught me that it wasn't right to feel guilt over a second of it.

Easier said than done. Because some crazy man had fixated on me, and I'd entertained that by thinking he was a friend. We'd almost lost our son—and Cohen had almost lost us both.

I know it's irrational, that guilt, but it's part of the healing process. Or so I'm told by my therapist. But it's a feeling I'm not alone in carrying. Nate had a hard time coping after the attack. He felt guilt worse than mine because he hadn't been in the room. Lee was dealing with similar issues, but he was able to rationalize his pain and focus on the positive—that he was able to save me. They have both joined me for more than a few of my therapy sessions, and I know they've been helping us all heal. Cohen is there for everyone. We've talked about how he felt and how he's coping with it all. I wasn't surprised in the least that he was still feeling a deep fear about losing me.

He's been working on his issues with letting me out of his sight. It took my father's sitting him down for him to finally come to terms with the fact that what had happened was a horrible, traumatic experience, and that, if we can't focus on moving forward and healing, then it will just drag us down until we're smothered in memories.

In the end, we were helpless and in a situation beyond our control. Had it not been for their swift response, I have no doubt that both the baby and I would have died in that apartment.

Chance is another part of the reason I've been struggling with so much pain. It kills me that he blamed himself—likely still does. But until he's ready to cope with that and work on healing, I'm afraid there isn't anything I can do.

It's been easier. He comes around, but I notice that his eyes never leave mine. Like he's afraid to look away for fear that someone might attack. He threw himself into the investigation of Mark Seymour like a man possessed.

We found out about two weeks after I was released from the hospital that Mark had been staying in the apartment directly under Cohen's. Not only had he been watching me for over a year, but he had also had a sick collection of photos of him and me that were horribly Photoshopped. He had created a whole fantasy life—albums after albums of us.

If that weren't bad enough, he had set up the apartment with items of mine that he had stolen throughout the year. Things I hadn't even known were missing. He had a whole life made up for us, and the only thing that was missing was . . . me.

After his death, the police were able to locate the bodies of the two men he had slain before he'd stormed us that day. He had left detailed notes about where he'd tossed their bodies. At least, with that, their families would get some closure.

It's been hard for everyone. We are struggling with just how insane the man who almost stole my life before it could truly begin was, but we're all slowly healing. Today will be a big step in that process.

"I can't wait to get him home, Cohen. To show him the house and have him under our roof."

Cohen reaches over and grabs my hand, the one he placed a ridiculously huge diamond on three weeks ago—without proposing. "Same here, Dani-girl. It's going to feel damn good to have my family together in our home." He kisses my knuckles, flicks my ring with his thumb, and looks out the windshield with a huge grin.

We make it to the hospital in record time and have our son discharged and strapped to his car seat as soon as the last form is signed. I hug all the nurses we had gotten to know over the last month, and we make quick work of leaving the hospital behind on our way back to our house.

It is past time to get our family home.

Owen—meaning little fighter—James Cage. Our gorgeous son. I smile to myself and look over at his sleeping face from my spot in the back seat.

Just like Cohen said, Owen looks just like him. His dark hair, tan skin, and perfectly handsome face.

But those lips are all mine.

Chapter 40

Dani

*I*T'S BEEN TWO WEEKS SINCE we brought Owen home from the hospital, and leaving him today for my six-week checkup was harder than I ever imagined. Cohen and I had agreed that, since the visit would be a short one and I could pump any milk Cohen would need to feed him while I was gone, I would use this as a dry run to leave the baby.

In the last two weeks, I've struggled to do something as mundane as take a shower. The fear I've had over letting him out of my sight is unexplainable. I know Cohen is worried about me, so I agreed with him more or less to placate his concerns.

But sitting here, with the paper sheet over my naked bottom half while my ass sits on the cold chair, isn't making me feel like I've hit some big milestone. It makes me feel like I need to have my baby in my arms.

"I think it's time to stop freaking out, Dani."

I look up, meet my mom's eyes, and give her a small smile. I don't even try to hide my mild embarrassment.

"I understand how you feel, my darling girl, but leaving your son for a few hours isn't the end of the world. It's good for him to bond with his father alone—or his grandparents. I'm not saying you should start planning vacations, but sitting at home day in and day out while never letting him out of your sight isn't healthy."

I sigh. "I know." And I do. I know it isn't normal, but I can't seem to get my body to get with the program and physically leave him.

"If it would make you feel better, we can call Cohen. He can give you the reassurance that you need."

I shake my head, knowing that, if I call home thirty minutes after leaving to check on Owen, all it will do is make Cohen worry about me more. "No. I trust Cohen, and I know he won't let anything happen to Owen. I just need to get over my issues that something bad is going to happen. Ever since the whole . . . Mark thing, I keep thinking that something else is going to come and take away my happiness."

Mom sighs and walks over to me, grabbing my hand and looking me in the eyes. "There isn't one thing in this life that's a guarantee, Dani. Nothing. I've lived a life that I can say that with clarity. But if you continue to have yourself stuck in the past of worry and fear, there is no way you're going to be able to enjoy the life and future you hold in your hands."

I study her face, finding love in her eyes and the hope that I understand what she's saying.

"I need to get out of my head," I respond.

"Yeah, sweetheart. You need to get out of your head," she says with another big smile.

I felt a little better after my doctor's visit. The two hours I had been gone from the house didn't feel as stifling by the time Mom pulled us back up to the house and I rushed through the door, eager to see my boys.

I smile when I hear Cohen muttering to the television at whatever sports show he's watching. When I round the corner and see him sitting in our big, overstuffed chair with Owen laying on his naked chest, my heart swells. He has his thick hand resting under the baby's diaper-padded bum, and I smile when I see Owen's big, round—blue for the moment—eyes looking off at nothing. His fist is pulled up to his thick, Cupid-bowed lips, and he's sucking away while his father explains to him the finer points of football.

"You look cozy," I hum. Walking around the couch, I slide onto Cohen's lap and run my fingers over Owen's silky-smooth skin. "How was he?"

"Fine, Dani-girl. Just like I told you he would be. You're looking at the extent of our day of fun."

"Oh, a little party animal, huh?" I joke.

"What did the doctor say?" Cohen asks, shifting his weight so that I can crawl into the chair next to him.

I place my head against his shoulder and look into Owen's eyes. I lay my hand against his back, and Cohen's rests over mine.

"Everything looks good on the healing end. He still wants me to wait a few more weeks before we resume any sexual activities or exercising. I think that, with everything that happened, he just wants to make sure my body has time to heal. Especially since I explained that our workouts tend to be a little . . . vigorous."

"Vigorous, huh?" Cohen laughs. "Everything else looked okay though?"

"Yeah." I pause and look up at him. "I talked to him about my separation anxiety, and he's given me some antidepressant medication to take for a while. Given everything we've been through, I think it's a good call. But I feel a lot better abut not being around Owen all of the time. Leaving today helped a lot."

"I'm glad, baby. I was worried."

"I know you were and I'm sorry."

"Don't be sorry. I love that you love our boy so much that you don't want to be without him, but you have to make sure that you're taking care of yourself too. I can't stand the thought of something happening to you, Dani-girl."

"I'm not going anywhere," I tell him—not for the first time.

"Yeah, baby, and neither is our boy."

I look up at him, and I think for the first time that I really get what he's trying to tell me and has been trying to impress upon me since we got home with Owen.

I nod my head and give him a smile before returning my head to his shoulder so that I can look into our boy's eyes. I let the love I feel for both of these people wrap around me, and I fall asleep while Cohen holds us both safe within his arms.

Chapter 41

Cohen

OWEN'S TAKEN TO THE CHANGE from hospital to home like a champ. Though I'm not shocked that my son is perfect. He's a calm baby who only fusses when he wants to eat. Or when he wants his mother's attention, but I can't fault him there. When I want his mother's attention, I get fussy too. The first month home was a slight challenge. Between Dani's not wanting and not feeling like she couldn't leave our son and our getting used to having a little human to care for, we were slow in adjusting to our new life. Now, though? Now, we're freaking pros.

Dani has gotten so much better about leaving Owen. It started small. The doctor visit, then a quick run to the store, and eventually, she was able to leave without thought. Of course, I think a lot of that had to do with her finally realizing that, by letting her fear consume her, she wasn't able to enjoy the life we had.

I walk down the hall in search of my woman. She took Owen to his room to get him dressed for the day out, and I haven't seen her in almost thirty minutes. Which usually means she's breastfeeding.

Not shockingly, the sight of her breastfeeding my son has been a major turn-on for me. Since she isn't clear for sex yet, the fact that I almost come in my pants when she pulls her swollen tits out and I see them leaking with milk . . . Yeah, she started leaving the room when Owen needed to eat after that. I have no clue why I find it so fucking hot, but when I see her tits leak, all I can think about is pushing them together and fucking her tits while her milk works as lube.

Goddamn, I need to go jerk off again. I press my hand against my cock—which is now standing at full attention—and continue my search for her. It's been eight weeks; if I don't have my wife soon, I might die. Literally die. From blue balls.

"Our mothers are on the way, Dani," I say when I find her rocking in the glider in Owen's nursery. I bend to kiss her before placing a kiss on Owen's soft head. "And from what my dad said, they have every bridal magazine known to man. I told you—the court house is just a second away, baby."

"I didn't get my proposal. I'm getting my wedding," she smarts.

"So I've been told. How much longer until you're done planning this damn thing, Dani? I need you to be mine."

She smiles but doesn't answer. I give her another kiss before standing and walking out of Owen's nursery. I've been summoned to the CS offices today, and it's been a request I've put off for the month since we brought home Owen. Time to suck it up and leave my house—even if the thought of leaving Dani and Owen has my stomach in knots.

Yeah. Hey, pot. Meet kettle. I harp on Dani about getting over her fears, but I'm just as bad.

I run down the stairs and into the kitchen to get breakfast ready for Dani. She's been running on fumes lately since Owen has been going through some growth spurt and feeding more than usual. Even though it isn't much, at least it's something I can do to help.

"Hey, baby?" Dani says, walking into the kitchen a short while later. "Mmm, that smells good." She walks by, Owen in her arms, and snags a piece of bacon off the plate. "My mom texted and asked if you could bring me over to her place on your way to the office. It would be easier since all of the wedding planning stuff they've been collecting is over there anyway."

I wave her off when she goes to nab another piece. "Yeah, baby."

"I can drive us over if you need to get down to CS," she offers, her head tilting slightly.

"No, Dani-girl. It's never a problem if I'm a little late because I'm taking care of my family." And it isn't. They are and forever will be my number-one priority.

"So," she starts, and something in her tone has me looking away from the eggs and waiting for her to finish. "My mom mentioned keeping Owen tonight. I think we should take advantage, baby. I can pump enough so that she has all the milk she needs and we can celebrate my eight-week mark."

I feel my brows pull in as I try to understand what she's saying. "I'm a little lost here?" I try to play it off, but the fact that she's talking about leaving him overnight is a huge milestone here.

"I noticed. Had you realized what I was talking about, I'm pretty sure breakfast would be forgotten and we would have Owen dropped off already. It's been two weeks since my appointment with the doctor, baby. He said eight weeks until all activities could return as normal. It's time to make love to your woman."

And then I switch off the burner, eggs forgotten, and rush up the stairs to pack Owen's bag.

Tonight, I fuck my woman.

Dani

"I thought you wouldn't ever get over here," Lyn complains and reaches out to take Owen from my arms. She doesn't even pay me any attention as she walks over to the couch and starts to make baby sounds in Owen's face.

Lila rolls her eyes and takes Owen's bag from me. "Come on. The makeup guru is waiting for you."

Following her lead, I walk into a kitchen full of insanity. My mom is running around with her hair in rollers, Melissa is barking at a Mexican man who looks terrified, and Maddi is standing with her hands on her hips, clearly not happy that I'm late.

"Sorry," I grumble and sit in the chair she's pointing to.

"How hard was it to stay on track, Dani? How hard, huh?" she snaps and starts to apply my makeup. I wisely decide to keep my mouth shut and let her do what she does best.

I feel my hair move, and I open my eyes.

Sway pops his head around and gives me a big smile. "Almost show time, little mama." He reaches over my shoulder, and I slap his hand away when I feel him trying to pop my top button.

"You crazy man!"

He laughs, straightens, and starts to work on my hair.

Almost an hour later, my hair is pulled back in a loose chignon and my makeup is done flawlessly in a natural way that highlights all of my features. My eyes are lined heavily to showcase my eyes, and Maddi decided to paint my lips a bright red.

I walk into my parents' bedroom, and with the help of Melissa, I step into my dress. She gives me a huge hug and quickly walks from the room, but not before I see the first tear fall from her eyes.

"Mom!" I call as I walk through the insanity.

Lyn is trying to step into her dress without letting her sister hold Owen. Maddi is finishing up Stella's makeup while doing hers as well. Sway's decided that Owen's little baby hair needs to be styled into some type of baby mohawk. Megan and Molly are laughing from the sidelines as Sway starts to make blowfish faces at the baby.

"Out here, baby."

I follow the sound of her voice out the back door and onto the back deck.

When my eyes take in the transformation their backyard has taken, I take a deep breath and will myself to believe that this moment is happening.

Today, I'm surprising the man of my dreams with the wedding he's been begging for. He's waited this long, and I know he would have waited longer, but I'm ready to be Dani Cage. For our family to become whole.

With our fathers' help, I had them enlist him in some case they needed help with at CS, and I got a promise from both of them that they wouldn't return him home until later that evening.

They have one job: get my man to the end of the dock before the sun sets on the lake. Well, I should say that Greg has one job since, as I look down at the backyard, I meet the very emotional eyes of Axel Reid, and I smile as my daddy visibly struggles to get a hold of his emotions.

"You look like a little princess," his awestruck voice whispers hoarsely. "I can't believe this day has come. My baby is getting married."

"Do you need a tissue, Daddy?" I joke.

"Very funny." He reaches over and carefully pulls me against his body.

I dust a piece of lint off of his tux-covered chest.

"No matter where you are in the world, you will always be *my* little princess, Dani. Married or not, you were my girl first. I love you, baby. I know I don't say it often, because we wouldn't want him to get a big head, but I'm thrilled with the man who won your heart."

I struggle with the lump in my throat and, in the end, settle for a nod of my head.

"I knew you would grow into a beautiful woman, and I'm damn proud of who you've become. I know, with Cohen by your side and Owen in your arms, that beauty is just going to blossom even further." He leans down and kisses my head before walking away.

I let him go, knowing that he needs the same moment with his thoughts that I do.

I keep my eyes on the family as they move around the tables set up on the back lawn and smile when I see the lights strung out along the railing on the deck. They light the way that will bring Cohen to me in just one short hour.

Cohen

Fucking pointless afternoon. My dad and Maddox kept me up to my elbows in old case files. Anything from the last ten years that had gone cold was suddenly something I needed to help them with right that second.

I finally had enough when I realized it was getting closer to dinnertime and the only thing I had on my mind was getting to my girl and getting her back home.

"I'm done. We can pick this up another day? Right now, I'm going to Axel's house and I'm taking my girl home for our first night alone."

"Alone?" Dad questions.

"Her parents offered to keep Owen tonight so we can have some alone time."

He gives me a knowing look. "Ah. It's all-clear time." He throws his head back and gives a booming laugh. "I completely understand, son."

"I hear you," Maddox adds in. "One of the best nights with Emmy was when the doctor finally cleared her after having our girls. I swear she turned into an animal."

My dad goes to open his mouth, but I stop him with my hand. "Don't even think about adding to that. I don't want to know about it and I damn sure don't want to think about it."

They laugh, and I narrow my eyes.

When I stand from the conference room table, Dad reaches his hand out and grabs my arm. "Go into the back bathroom There's something in there for you."

"What the hell?" I ask his back, and he and Maddox walk out of the room. "Crazy old man."

I walk toward the back bathroom, and when I walk in to see a perfectly pressed tux, I feel my eyes narrow in confusion. Seeing the note that's attached to the hanger, I snatch it off and read the words that bring a rush of overwhelming love through my body.

Today, I marry my best friend. I marry my lover. I marry my heart. I love you. I'll see you where it all began.

I turn the paper over and feel the lump in my throat grow when I look at the picture Dani wrote her message on. The picture she'd had blown up and placed over her bed when I was overseas.

The one of her in my arms at the end of her parents' dock when we were just children.

It takes me no time to shed my clothes and don the tux. The promise of marrying my girl is all I need to get to the Reids' house as quickly as possible.

Today, I'm marrying my girl.

Chapter 42

Cohen

I'M NOT SURE WHAT I expected to happen when I got to Axel and Izzy's house. I was prepared for anything. I think one part of me expected Axel to jump my ass the second I stepped foot on his property.

However, what I am met with almost brings me to my knees. My mom opens their door with tears streaming down her smiling face, and without a word, she hands me my son. I watch her walk away, her light-blue dress flowing behind her, before I look down at my wiggling boy.

Owen is dressed similarly to me, a little tux looking as out of place on my little baby's body as I feel like it does on mine.

"Hey, little man," I say softly and notice the piece of paper sticking out of his mini jacket. "What do you have for Daddy, baby boy?"

He looks me in the eye, his mouth puckering up with the cutest little pout. He's content to be held in his father's arms. He's filled out so much in the last two months that he's started to get the most adorable chubby cheeks.

God, my son is perfect.

Carefully, I adjust Owen in my arms and unfold the paper I pulled from his little jacket.

I smile when I read the words and feel my heart beat wildly in my chest. With my son in my arms and a smile on my face, I take off in the direction my mom went—through their large living room, then through their kitchen, and out on the back deck. I still don't see anyone, so I keep walking until Owen and I are standing against the railing, looking down at every family member and friend we love.

My dad is standing with my mom, my sisters and brothers at his side, all of them beaming. Axel is next to him with Izzy between his arms and Nate at his side. Again, not one of them is missing a huge grin. I follow the lines of Maddox's family, Beck's, Asher's, and Sway's. I see Megan and Molly and Chance before my eyes follow the white flower trail that leads me to the end of the dock.

Where I see a vision in white that has my eyes stinging. There, waiting with a smile on her face and tears in her eyes, is *my* Dani-girl.

"Let's go get the girl, son." I whisper to Owen.

I walk down the stairs that bring me to the backyard and walk through the lines of our loved ones until I reach our parents. I look to my left and smile at my parents and siblings, handing Owen to Lyn when her arms come up.

"I love you, son." My dad says gruffly.

"We're so happy for you and Dani," Mom says. "I love you, handsome boy."

I give them each a kiss before facing Dani's parents.

Her mom wraps her arms around me, giving my cheek a quick kiss. Her eyes are wet and shining with happiness. I give Nate a slap on the back and laugh when he puckers up. Then I look at Axel.

I am prepared for battle, but when I see his eyes—bright with happiness and not anger—I am momentarily struck dumb.

"You didn't think I would be able to do it, did you?" he asks me.

"Not for a second," I laugh.

"If you make her cry one tear that isn't out of happiness, I'll cut your balls off," he warns.

"Noted."

"I'm proud of you, Cohen. Of the man you've grown to be and for the love you have for my girl. I mean it when I say that I couldn't have picked a better man for her myself."

"Thank you for that," I tell him honestly. No matter what I said in the past, having his blessing was something I desired when it came to Dani becoming my wife. "She's my life," I remind him.

"I know the feeling," he says and looks down the dock. "Go on and stop keeping my daughter waiting."

I nod, taking a few measured breaths before I turn and let my eyes take her in.

She's wearing a simple, long, and flowing, white dress. It fits tight to her body while still rippling in the slight breeze around us. Her shoulders are bare, and with her hair swept away from her face, she looks so angelic with the sun setting behind her and casting a soft glow around her body.

I take the last remaining steps that take me to where she is standing with the man I assume is the minister.

"Surprised?" she asks.

"Yeah, baby."

"Are you ready to be my husband?"

I smile. "I was born ready, my Dani-girl."

And with the sun setting around us, our family surrounding us, I marry my unexpected fate.

By the time we were able to get away from the family and I was able to pull Dani away from Owen without having her melt down, the sun had long since set and my girl had become my wife. We danced and ate. Laughed and smiled. It was a magical night full of love. We danced our first dance together as man and wife to Brett Young's "Kiss by Kiss," and I held her in my arms while she softly cried. When my lips dropped to hers and I heard the all-familiar growl at my side, she threw her head back and her laughter rained down on me.

It was equal parts joyful and torture because all I could think about was getting her home. Since the second my lips touched hers after the minister pronounced us man and wife, I've been rock hard to take my wife and make her mine in every way that counts.

"Slow down, husband," she snickers when I pull her from the truck and up to our porch. Her squeal when I pull her up into my arms is like music to my ears.

"Are you ready for me to carry you over the threshold, wife?"

She smiles her radiant smile and nods her head.

I don't waste a second. The key hits the lock, and in a flash, I have her rushed through, slamming the door behind us. She reaches out and keys in the code to our alarm, and the second I hear her reactivate it, I bound up the stairs. Her pearls of laughter trail behind us and don't stop until I prowl into our bedroom and toss her in the air and onto the middle of our mattress.

She pushes up on her elbows and looks at me with heated eyes.

I watch her move until she's up on her knees and groan when she pulls her dress over her head and tosses it carelessly to the floor.

"If I had known you were naked under there, I wouldn't have made it as long as I did today," I tell her.

"I know." Her hands come up and cup her breasts.

I smile when her eyes follow my hands when I place them on my belt. It's a smile that doesn't last long because her next words have me fighting not come in my pants.

"I want your cock, husband. First, I want to lick you from your neck to your balls, and then I'm going to suck them deep until you're begging me to take your cock in my mouth." She pauses in her speech to lick one of her fingers before tracing her puckered nipple with it. "Then I'm going to fuck myself with your fingers. If you're a good boy, I'll let you lick them clean. And when your balls feel like they're about to bust from the power that your orgasm promises, I'm going to ride you until you come deep inside me."

"Fuck yeah, you are," I growl and pounce.

She jumps back, laughing, and I swallow her happiness when I take her mouth in a bruising kiss.

"Fuck me, wife," I command and lie back in the bed.

Dani

"Fuck me, wife," he orders in a tone that is wild with desire.

"I'm going to lick and suck you first," I promise, climbing up until my legs are straddling his hips and my mouth is trailing kisses along his neck and collarbone.

I feel my pussy lips spread wide to accommodate the side of his hips, and his hard cock settles right between them. The second I feel his hot, velvet skin against my wet lips, I moan and start to rub myself against him. His hands go to my hips, and I feel him thrusting to meet each rotation of my hips.

I trace my mouth down his chest, and when I hit one of his nipples, I lightly bite it between my teeth. His hips jump off the bed, and I squeal when I feel the tip of his erection jab against my swollen clit.

"Do that again and you're going to get my cock in your pussy or your ass and you can forget your mouth having a turn."

I smile against his skin and keep moving my lips down his body. He moans and twitches every time I hit a sensitive spot—which, I'm learning, my husband has a lot of.

"I'm going to take your cock into my mouth until I choke on it," I huskily whisper.

"Fuck," he splutters when I wrap my lips around his swollen cock head.

I move slowly until I have the tip of his cock touching the back of my throat. Relaxing my throat, I breathe through my nose and take him into my throat.

"Fucking hell!" he exclaims and shoots off the bed.

His fingers go into my hair, his hips thrusting his cock into my mouth on their own accord. My eyes water with the force of his thrusting, but I take everything he has to give to me and love every second.

When his movements start to stall, I lean back on my knees and lick my lips. "Why did you make me stop, baby? Was that not good?"

"Any better and you would have killed me, but when I come for the first time as your husband, it's going to be while my cock is pounding that sweet, fucking tight pussy. Climb up here and ride me . . . hard." He adds the last as an afterthought, and I don't even hesitate.

I'm up, straddling his hips and resting my weight on his chest with one hand as I use the other to guide his thick cock into my wet core.

"Fuck yourself on my cock, Dani-girl," he moans when I start moving. "Fuck your husband," he continues.

I bounce as quickly as I can, and when my movements start to falter, he grabs my hips and starts thrusting like a piston into my body from his position on his back.

"That's right, baby. Fuck me hard."

"I can't. My legs," I whine, feeling my climax slipping away.

He flips me before I can even think and pushes my legs over his shoulders.

"I'm going to fill you with my come, Dani. Fill you with my come and fucking pray that another child takes root. I'm going to come so hard that it will leak from your pussy while my cock is still buried deep. You want to taste us when I finish, baby?"

When he stops talking, I swallow thickly, already craving the taste of *us*.

"My girl—my wife—wants my come?"

I nod.

"Fuck, I love you," he says through clenched teeth.

His hips start to power against my body, and it only takes a few more thrusts until I'm screaming out his name, following it with a bunch of gibberish.

"Love this cunt. Fuck me, Dani. I love it when you come all over my cock. Hold on, baby. Going to take you harder."

My eyes widen because I never imagined that he could take me harder than he already was. His balls slap so loudly against my ass that it sounds like hands clapping. He curls my body so that my knees are pressing into my tits, and the first mighty thrust he takes into my body has me screaming. The second has me coming. And every one that follows after has me sobbing and coming and coming and sobbing. And a weird mix of the two.

"Fucking love this pussy."

"Fucking love this cock."

He looks down at me, his eyes ablaze before he throws his head back and rumbles out his release in one loud thundering roar.

After he pulls his spent cock from my pussy, he makes true on his promise to give me a taste of *us*.

When it's all said and done, we don't make it four hours—another long session of him taking his wife—before we're throwing our clothes on and driving to my parents to get our boy.

Epilogue

Dani

Five years later

"DO YOU KNOW WHERE YOUR brother is?" I ask Lyn.

"He said he was running to the grocery store," she says over her shoulder and turns her attention back to her computer.

"What? I just went the other day."

"Yeah—well, in case you didn't notice the last time you were pregnant, you tend to eat a lot when you're knocked up." She laughs and goes back to her computer browsing.

"Well, where is your sister?" I ask.

"She has Evan with her at my parents.' Something about giving you some time to rest before your husband got home and kept you up all night. I think she's still scared from the last time she spent the night and you two kept her up all night moaning."

I throw my head back and laugh because she isn't wrong.

In the five years Cohen and I have been married, the desire we crave for each other hasn't changed one bit. Which explains why I'm pregnant again. I swear he's made it his life's mission to see me pregnant forever. I got pregnant with Evan almost right after our wedding. Cohen was pretty proud of himself and convinced that it was our wedding night that did the deed.

I managed to keep him away from me long enough to not get pregnant for six months after I had Evan. Unfortunately, that pregnancy ended in a miscarriage that we both took hard. We waited a while before we tried again, and now here I am, pregnant again.

Cohen took a job at Corps Security shortly after Owen was born. He said that his dad was thinking about retiring soon and it was time that he learned the business. This was something I supported one hundred percent. I loved knowing that he was going to never leave us for any more deployments.

"What do you think about this one?" Lyn asks and spins her computer. I laugh when I see the tiny newborn dress she has pulled up on Baby Gap.

"You do realize that it's probably going to be another boy, right?"

"No way, Dani! I'm going to get my girl, dammit. You hear that, baby? You better be a girl."

"I'm pretty sure it doesn't work that way, Lyn," I laugh.

She gives me a hard look and turns back to her computer. I roll my eyes and stand up, walking around until I find my phone and dial Cohen's number.

He picks up almost immediately. "Hey, Dani-girl."

"Where are you?"

"Owen wanted to go find ninjas, so we're in the back lot—looking for ninjas." He explains it like that should make all the sense in the world.

"And why are you looking for ninjas?"

"Because he wanted to fight them," Cohen says.

"Is that supposed to make any sense to me, baby?"

"Nope, probably not. But it makes sense to us and that's all that matters. Plus, he started asking about the earring in my cock again today and there is only so much I can take, Dani-girl. It was mission 'divert and distract' this morning."

The second he stops talking, I throw my head back and laugh.

Since the day Owen walked in on a naked Cohen and got a good look at his hardware, he hasn't stopped for a second. All he talks about is those damn earrings in his daddy's cock. Which is something Cohen's parents think is hilarious. Cohen, not so much.

"Hurry home, baby. I miss you."

"You just saw me an hour ago." He laughs.

"So? I miss you."

"See you soon, my heart."

"Every time I close my eyes." I smile.

An hour later, I'm sitting on the back deck with Lyn, who is still looking up baby clothes, when I hear a rustling in the leaves. I stand and move to the railing, and when I see my two big boys walking towards the house, my smile goes from normal to wonky.

Cohen has Owen on his shoulder, Owen's little fist holding tight to his father's hair, and behind both of them flaps their matching capes.

My heroes.

My unexpected beautiful fate.

Cohen looks up, gives me a wink, and taps Owen's knee with the hand that's resting there. Owen looks up and gives me the biggest toothy grin.

"Mama! We faught awel does bad guys!"

"All of the bad guys? I'm so proud of you, my handsome man."

"I wuv you!" he yells.

I look down at his face and smile. "And I you, son."

They climb the stairs, and Owen drops from his father's shoulders and rushes to his aunt's side. I walk over to my husband, wrap my arms around him, and give him a deep kiss.

"I love you," I tell him.

"And I you, my Dani-girl."

The End

Keep reading for a preview of *Jaded Hearts,*
book 1 in the Loaded Replay series.

PROLOGUE

Signing with the record company of our dreams should have been the best thing that ever happened to us. And it was . . . for a short while. While the glitz and glamour of the fame's promise was shining as bright as our stage lights we could forget where we came from and live in the glory. The money bought us every happiness we ever craved. Those false securities that you think will make your life better. The instant friends, lovers—you name it-would do whatever we asked just to spend a second in our presence.

We had it all.

The only problem was when we had those quiet moments in between the insanity. When we were slapped in the face with the reality that all we really had—all we could count on—was each other.

My brother, Weston, is the only constant I've ever had in my life. He's the person that I know will never let me down and will always be my biggest support. We grew up with parents that hated us. Really . . . it sounds ridiculous, the notion that parents could hate their children, but ours do. They made no secret of it when we were younger. And continue to attempt to pick at our very souls like the vultures that they are.

My earliest memory of them is somewhere around third or fourth grade when they would scream at us about how we ruined it all for them. How *they* were on the edge of fame and then we came along and it all went down hill. We were essentially their bad luck.

When we hit middle school it got worse, but only because they knew that they could leave us for long periods and we wouldn't die.

Our parents, like us, were born to be stars . . . or at least they assumed they were and they had no qualms about reminding us that fact daily. Unfortunately for them, they lacked the drive and ambition to never back down until they had everything they ever wanted. The first challenge that was thrown in their path they decided to take the low road full of scavengers and sinners.

Like I said, vultures through and through.

Our dad knocked up mom in the early eighties, when big hair rock bands were all the rage and *theirs* was seconds away from signing the record deal that would make their careers.

Then they found out about us.

The twins that ruined it all.

And all those long nights performing in whatever local hole they could find, bouncing from town to town just waiting for their big break was washed away.

Mom was no longer the singer that men would lust over. Not when we ruined her body. And our dad was so deep in the bottle I'm not sure he realized he was swimming in it.

And when the band fell apart, they decided hating us was almost easier than hating each other. They had a common goal in their blame and right or wrong, to them we would never be anything other than a reminder of why they aren't living their dream.

Their band mates obviously didn't share the same bond that Weston and I have with Jamison and Luke. God forbid I ever found myself in a position like that they would band together and the show would go on. Because for us, this is it. This is our future's promise of a better life and even if for me it's starting to look like more of a curse than a promise, it's something that we would die before we gave up.

Unfortunately for me, I'm pretty sure that there are a few people that would love to make that happen.

Who am I?

I'm Wrenlee Davenport, lead singer of Loaded Replay, and I've learned the hard way that there is plenty of people in the world that would love to have a piece of me, but they don't give one shit about the person behind the voice.

They see the persona. The *fake* me that the record label loves to market as the sexy singer with the voice of a saint, but for me—I'm probably always going to be that stupid little girl that believes that my prince charming will come riding in on his black horse—because really, black horses are so much more badass than white ones—and prove to me that every little jaded piece of my heart is worth loving.

And *he* will love me for me. For *Wren*. And not the *Wrenlee* that has more times than I care to admit has to drink herself stupid just to face this fucking life I'm living.

Yeah . . . fame and fortune is far from everything I ever dreamed it was.

It's my own personal hell and I pray that there's something or someone out there that can prove to me that the world isn't screwed because the majority of humanity is too busy licking the windows on the outside to see the beauty behind it. All they care about is what's at face value when what matters is skin deep.

I should feel bad for prince charming. My knight in tarnished armor. Because he'll have one giant battle on his hands to make me believe that there might be someone left out there that doesn't just want a piece of me.

Release date for *Jaded Hearts* is tentatively set for early Spring.

Acknowledgments

TO MY FAMILY—for putting up with me when I get insane and jump into my head for weeks at a time. For putting up with me leaving for Starbucks for HOURS and then not going to bed at night. And to my husband for making sure the kids are still alive when I come out of my head and rejoin you guys. ☺

To my amazing readers.
For your endless support and love for the worlds I bring you.
And the men that dominate them.
For loving my females just as much as you love those sexy alpha males.
And of course, for just being you and putting a smile on my face.
Love that can last a lifetime on carefully placed building blocks.

To my amazing support system, friends, daily motivators . . . you get the point. Ella, Rochelle, Crystal, and Tessa. I would probably die without you ladies. Well, I might not die—but I would be lonely as hell. A HUGE thank you to Ro and Ella for reading UF while I was writing and for all the feedback.

Kelly, Andee, and Felicia. You ladies have become three of my bestestestest friends in the world. I am so blessed for everything you guys do and continue to do.

Ellie—YOU, my dear, rock my world. Not only did you bring me the beautifully perfect models that are 100% Cohen and Dani, but you are an editing queen and I'm so thankful that you took on my world. I can't wait for many more books to come with you!

Sommer—I'm really not sure what I can say here that means more than thank you. You gave me Cohen and Dani in a way that made me think you were in my head. I adore you.

Stacey—My books would be terribly plain without you. Every little detail and touch that you put into them to makes them shine is phenomenal. I'm so thankful to you and all that you do for me (and my books.)

Made in the USA
San Bernardino, CA
19 July 2016